# DEEP BLUE

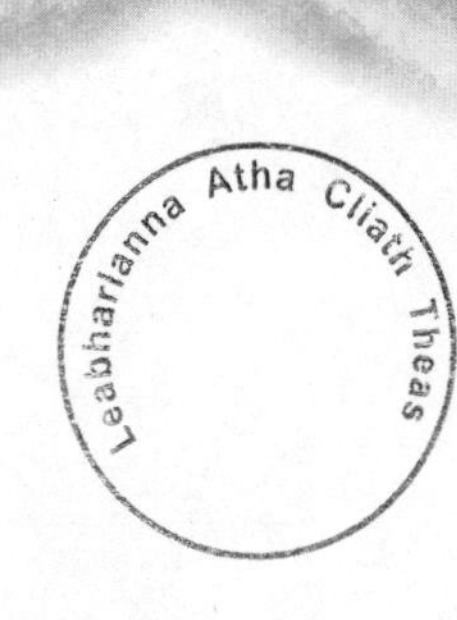

*The Waterfire Saga*

Deep Blue

Rogue Wave

Dark Tide

# DEEP BLUE

JENNIFER DONNELLY

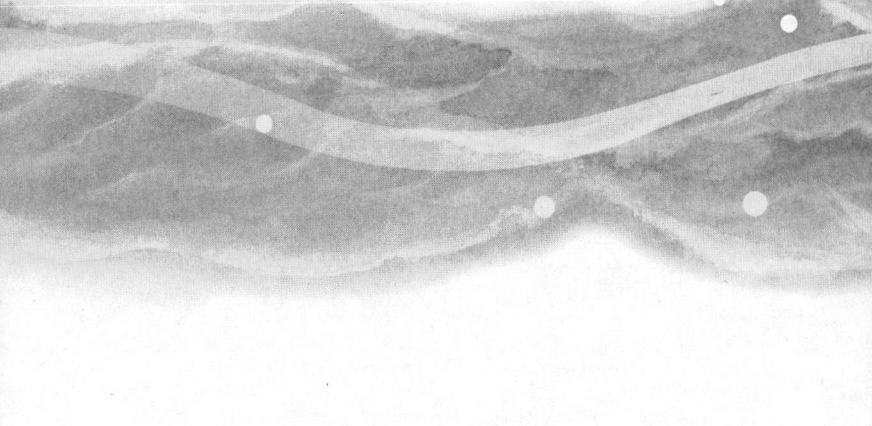

a division of Hachette Children's Books

First published in the US in 2014

First published in Great Britain in 2014 by Hodder Children's Books

This edition published in 2015



1



A Catalogue record for this book is available from the British Library

ISBN 978 1 444 92120 5

Printed and bound in Great Britain by Clays Ltd, St Ives plc

The paper and board used in this paperback by Hodder Children's Books are natural recyclable products made from wood grown in sustainable forests. The manufacturing processes conform to the environmental regulations of the country of origin.

Hodder Children's Books
a division of Hachette Children's Books
338 Euston Road, London NW1 3BH
An Hachette UK company

www.hodderchildrens.co.uk

*For Daisy,*
*with all my love*

VENICE
Lagoon
CERULEA
TSARNO
MIROMARA
MIROMARA
MIROM

REALM of MIROMARA
River Olt
River Dunarea
MIROMARA
AQUABA
RADNEVA
MIROMARA
RUINS OF ATLANTIS
BARRENS OF THIRA

*For more than once dimly down to the beach gliding,*
*Silent, avoiding the moonbeams, blending myself with the*
*shadows,*
*Recalling now the obscure shapes, the echoes, the sounds and*
*sights after their sorts,*
*The white arms out in the breakers tirelessly tossing,*
*I, with bare feet, a child, the wind wafting my hair,*
*Listen'd long and long.*

—From 'Out of the Cradle Endlessly Rocking,'
by Walt Whitman

# PROLOGUE

DEEP IN THE black mountains, deep in the Romanian night, deep beneath the cold, dark waters of the ancient Olt, the river witches sang.

*Daughter of Merrow, leave your sleep,*
*The ways of childhood no more to keep.*
*The dream will die, a nightmare rise,*
*Sleep no more, child, open your eyes.*

From her place in the shadows, the elder, Baba Vrăja, watched the blue waterfire, her bright eyes restive and alert.

'*Vino, un rău. Arată-te,*' she muttered in her age-old tongue. *Come, evil one. Show yourself.*

Around the waterfire, eight river witches continued their song. Hands clasped, they swam counterclockwise in a circle, their powerful tails pushing them through the water.

*Daughter of Merrow, chosen one,*
*The end begins, your time has come.*
*The sands run out, our spell unwinds,*
*Inch by inch, our chant unbinds.*

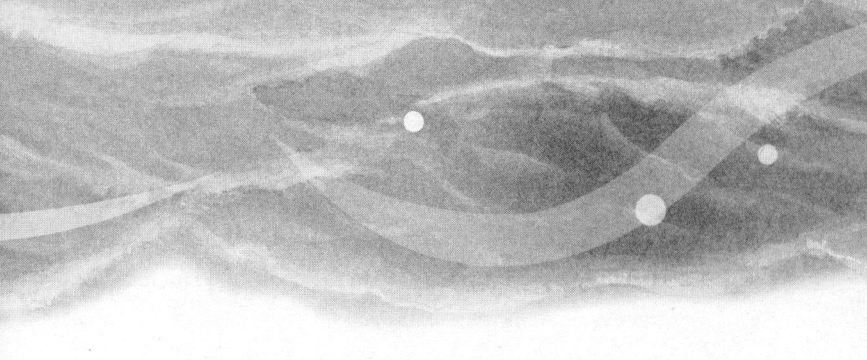

'Vin, diavolul, vin,' Vrăja growled, drawing closer to the circle. *'Tu esti lângă . . . te simt . . .' Come, devil, come . . . you're near . . . I feel you . . .*

Without warning, the waterfire rose, its flames licking out like serpents' tongues. The witches bowed their heads and tightened their grip on one another's hands. Suddenly one of them, the youngest, cried out. She doubled over as if in great pain.

Vrăja knew that pain. It tore inside like a sharp silver hook. She swam to the young witch. 'Fight it, dragă,' she told her. 'Be strong!'

'I . . . I can't. It's too much! Gods help me!' the witch cried.

Her skin – the mottled grey of river stones – paled. Her tail thrashed wildly.

'Fight it! The circle must not break! The Iele must not falter!' Vrăja shouted.

With a wrenching cry, the young witch raised her head and wove her voice once more into the chant. As she did, colours appeared inside the waterfire. They swirled together, coalescing into an image – a bronze gate, sunk deep underwater and crusted with ice. A sound was heard – the sound of a thousand voices, all whispering.

*Shokoreth . . . Amăgitor . . . Apateón. . . .*

Behind the gate, something stirred, as if waking from a long sleep. It turned its eyeless face to the north and laughed.

*Shokoreth . . . Amăgitor . . . Apateón. . . .*

Vrăja swam close to the waterfire. She shut her eyes against the image. Against the evil and the fear. Against the coming blood-red tide. She dug deep inside herself and gave all she had, and all she was, to the magic. Her voice strengthened and rose above the others, drowning out the whispering, the cracking of the ice, the low, gurgling laughter.

*Daughter of Merrow, find the five*
*Brave enough to keep hope alive.*
*One whose heart will hold the light,*
*One possessed of a prophet's sight.*

*One who does not yet believe,*
*Thus has no choice but to deceive.*
*One with spirit sure and strong,*
*One who sings all creatures' songs.*

*Together find the talismans*
*Belonging to the six who ruled,*
*Hidden under treacherous waters*
*After light and darkness duelled.*

*These pieces must not be united,*
*Not in anger, greed, or rage.*

*They were scattered by brave Merrow,*
*Lest they unlock destruction's cage.*

*Come to us from seas and rivers,*
*Become one mind, one heart, one bond.*
*Before the waters, and all creatures in them,*
*Are laid to waste by Abbadon!*

The thing behind the bars screamed with rage. It hurled itself against the gate. The impact sent shockwaves through the waterfire into the witches. The force tore at them viciously, threatening to break their circle, but they held fast. The thing thrust a hand through the bars, as if it wanted to reach inside Vrăja and tear out her heart. The waterfire blazed higher, and then all at once it went out. The thing was gone, the river was silent.

One by one, the witches sank to the riverbed. They lay on the soft mud, gasping, eyes closed, fins crumpled beneath them.

Only Vrăja remained, floating where the circle had been. Her wrinkled face was weary, her old body bent. Strands of grey hair loosed from a long braid twined like eels around her head.

She continued the chant alone, her voice rising through the dark water, ragged but defiant.

*Daughter of Merrow, leave your sleep,*
*The ways of childhood no more to keep.*

*Wake now, child, find the five*
*While there's time, keep hope alive.*
*Wake now, child, find the five*
*While there's time, keep hope alive.*
*Wake now, child . . .*

# ONE

'WAKE *UP*, CHILD! Suffering Circe, I've called you five times! Have you sand in your ears this morning?'

Serafina woke with a gasp. Her long, copper-brown hair floated wildly around her face. Her eyes, darkly green, were fearful. That thing in the cage – she could still hear its gurgling laughter, its horrible screams. She could feel its cunning and its rage. She looked around, her heart pounding, certain it was here with her, but she soon saw that there was no monster in her room.

Only her mother. Who was every bit as terrifying.

'Lolling in bed today of all days. The blood ceremony, the Dokimí, is tonight and you've so much to do!'

La Serenissima Regina Isabella, ruler of Miromara, was swimming from window to window, throwing open the draperies.

Sunlight filtered through the glass panes from the waters above, waking the feathery tube worms clustered around the room. They burst into bloom, daubing the walls yellow, cobalt blue, and magenta. The golden rays warmed fronds of seaweed anchored to the floor. They shimmered in the glass of a tall gilt mirror and glinted off the polished coral walls. A small green octopus that had been curled up at the foot of the bed – Serafina's pet, Sylvestre – darted away, disturbed by the light.

'Can't you cast a songspell for that, Mum?' Serafina asked, her voice raspy with sleep. 'Or ask Tavia to do it?'

'I sent Tavia to fetch your breakfast,' Isabella said. 'And *no*, I can't cast a songspell to open draperies. As I've told you a million times—'

'Never waste magic on the mundane,' Serafina said.

'*Exactly*. Do get up, Serafina. The emperor and empress have arrived. Your ladies are waiting for you in your antechamber, the canta magus is coming to rehearse your songspell, and here you lie, as idle as a sponge,' Isabella said. She batted a school of purple wrasses away from a window and looked out of it. 'The sea is so calm today, I can see the sky. Let's hope no storm blows in to churn up the waters.'

'Mum, what are you doing here? Don't you have a realm to rule?' Serafina asked, certain her mother had not come here to comment on the weather.

'Yes, I *do*, thank you,' Isabella said tartly, 'but I've left Miromara in your uncle Vallerio's capable hands for an hour.'

She crossed the room to Serafina's bedside, her grey sea-silk gown swirling behind her, her silver scales gleaming, her thick black hair piled high on her head.

'Just *look* at all these conches!' she exclaimed, frowning at the pile of white shells on the floor by Serafina's bed. 'You stayed up late last night listening, didn't you?'

'I had to!' Serafina said defensively. 'My term conch on Merrow's Progress is due next week.'

'No wonder I can't get you out of bed,' Isabella said. She picked up one of the shells and held it to her ear. '*The Merrovingian Conquest of the Barrens of Thira* by Professore Giovanni Bolla,' she said, then tossed it aside. 'I hope you didn't waste too much time on *that* one. Bolla's a fool. An armchair commander. He claims the Opafago have been controlled. Total bilge. The Opafago are cannibals, and cannibals care nothing for decrees. Merrow once sent a messenger to tell them they were being sanctioned, and they ate him.'

Serafina groaned. 'Is *that* why you're here? It's a little early in the day for a lecture on politics.'

'It's *never* too early for politics,' Isabella said. 'It was encirclement by Miromaran soldiers, the acqua guerrieri, that bested the Opafago. Force, not diplomacy. Remember that, Sera. Never sit down at the negotiating table with cannibals, lest you find *yourself* on the menu.'

'I'll keep that in mind, Mum,' Serafina said, rolling her eyes.

She sat up in her bed – an enormous ivory scallop shell – and stretched. One half of the shell, thickly lined with plump pink anemones, was where she slept. The other half, a canopy, was suspended on the points of four tall turritella snail shells. The canopy's edges were intricately carved and inlaid with sea glass and amber. Lush curtains of japweed hung down from it. Tiny orange gobies and blue-striped dragonets darted in and out of them.

The anemones' fleshy fingers clutched at Serafina as she rose. She pulled on a white sea-silk robe embroidered with gold thread, capiz shells, and seed pearls. Her scales, which were the bright, winking colour of new copper, gleamed in the underwater light. They covered her tail and her torso, and complemented the darker copper shade of her hair. Her colouring was from her father, Principe Consorte Bastiaan, a son of the noble House of Kaden in the Sea of Marmara. Her fins, a soft coral pink with green glints, were supple and strong. She had the lithe body, and graceful movements, of a fast deep-sea swimmer. Her complexion was olive-hued, and usually flawless, but this morning her face was wan and there were dark smudges under her eyes.

'What's the matter?' Isabella asked, noticing her pallor. 'You're as white as a shark's belly. Are you ill?'

'I didn't sleep well. I had a bad dream,' Serafina said as she belted her robe. 'There was something horrible in a cage. A monster. It wanted to get out and I had to stop it, but I didn't know how.' The images came back to her as she spoke, vivid and frightening.

'Night terrors, that's all. Bad dreams come from bad nerves,' Isabella said dismissively.

'The Iele were in it. The river witches. They wanted me to come to them,' Serafina said. 'You used to tell me stories about the Iele. You said they were the most powerful of our kind, and if they ever summon us, we have to go. Do you remember?'

Isabella smiled – a rare occurrence. 'Yes, but I can't believe *you* do,' she said. 'I told you those stories when you were a tiny merl. To make you behave. I said the Iele would call you to them and box your ears if you didn't sit still, as a well-mannered principessa of the House of Merrow should. It was all froth and seafoam.'

Serafina knew the river witches were only make-believe, yet they'd seemed so real in her dream. 'They were *there*. Right in front of me. So close, I could have reached out and touched them,' she said. Then she shook her head at her foolishness. 'But they *weren't* there, of course. And I have more important things to think about today.'

'Indeed you do. Is your songspell ready?' Isabella asked.

'So *that's* why you're here,' Serafina said archly. 'Not to wish me well, or to talk about hairstyles, or the crown prince, or anything *normal* mothers would talk about with their daughters. You came to make sure I don't mess up my songspell.'

Isabella fixed Serafina with her fierce blue eyes. 'Good wishes are irrelevant. So are hairstyles. What *is* relevant, is your songspell. It has to be perfect, Sera.'

*It has to be perfect*. Serafina worked so hard at everything she did – her studies, her songcasting, her horse-riding competitions – but no matter how high she aimed, her mother's expectations were always higher.

'I don't need to tell you that the courts of both Miromara and Matali will be watching,' Isabella said. 'You can't afford to put a fin wrong. And you won't as long as you don't give in to your nerves. Nerves are the foe. Conquer them or they'll conquer you. Remember, it's not a battle, or a deadlock in Parliament; it's only a Dokimí.'

'Right, Mum. *Only* a Dokimí,' said Serafina, her fins flaring. '*Only* the ceremony in which Alítheia, the sea-spider, declares me of the blood – or kills me. Only the one where I have to songcast as well as a canta magus, the keeper of magic, does. Only the one where I take my betrothal vows and swear to give the realm a daughter someday. It's nothing to get worked up about. Nothing at all.'

An uncomfortable silence descended. Isabella was the first one to break it. 'One time,' she said, 'I had a terrible case of nerves myself. It was when my senior ministers were aligned against me on an important trade initiative, and—'

Serafina cut her off angrily. 'Mum, can you just be a *Mum* for once? And forget you're the regina?' she asked.

Isabella smiled sadly. 'No, Sera,' she said. 'I can't.'

Her voice, usually brisk, had taken on a sorrowful note.

'Is something wrong?' Serafina asked, suddenly worried. 'What is it? Did the Matalis arrive safely?'

She knew that outlaw bands often preyed upon travellers in lonely stretches of water. The worst of them, the Praedatori, was known to steal everything of value: currensea, jewellery, weapons, even the hippokamps the travellers rode.

'The Matalis are perfectly fine,' Isabella said. 'They arrived last night. Tavia saw them. She says they're well, but weary. Who wouldn't be? It's a long trip from the Indian Ocean to the Adriatic Sea.'

Serafina was relieved. It wasn't only the crown prince and his parents, the emperor and empress, who were in the Matalin travelling party, but also Neela, the crown prince's cousin. Neela was Serafina's very best friend, and she was longing to see her. Serafina spent her day surrounded by people, yet she was always lonely. She could never let her guard down around her court or her servants. Neela was the only one with whom she could really be herself.

'Did Desiderio ride out to welcome them?' she asked.

Isabella hesitated. 'Actually, your father went to meet them,' she finally said.

'Why? I thought Des was supposed to go,' said Serafina, confused. She knew her brother had been looking forward to greeting the Matalis. He and Mahdi, the crown prince, were old friends.

'Desiderio has been deployed to the western borders. With four regiments of acqua guerrieri,' Isabella said bluntly.

Serafina was stunned. And frightened for her brother. 'What?' she said. 'When?'

'Late last night. At your uncle's command.'

Vallerio, Isabella's brother, was Miromara's high commander. His authority was second only to her own.

'*Why?*' Sera asked, alarmed. A regiment contained three thousand guerrieri. The threat at the western borders must be serious for her uncle to have sent so many soldiers.

'We received word of another raid. On Acqua Bella, a village off the coast of Sardinia,' Isabella said.

'How many were taken?' Serafina asked, afraid of

the answer.

'More than two thousand.' Isabella turned away, but not before Serafina saw the unshed tears shimmering in her eyes.

The raids had started a year ago. Six Miromaran villages had been hit so far. No one knew why the villagers were being taken, or where, or who was behind the raids. It was as if they'd simply vanished.

'Were there any witnesses this time?' Serafina asked. 'Do you know who did it?'

Isabella, composed now, turned back to her. 'We don't. I wish to the gods we did. Your brother thinks it's the terragoggs.'

'The *humans*? It can't be. We have protective songspells against them. We've had them since the mer were created, four thousand years ago. They can't touch us. They've never been able to touch us,' Serafina said.

She shuddered to think of the consequences if humans ever learned how to break songspells. The mer would be hauled out of the oceans by the thousands in brutal nets. They'd be bought and sold. Confined in small tanks for the goggs' amusement. Their numbers would be decimated like the tunas' and the cods'. No creature, from land or sea, was greedier than the treacherous terragoggs. Even the vicious Opafago only took what they could eat. The goggs took everything.

'I don't think it's the humans,' Isabella said. 'I told your brother so. But a large trawler was spotted in waters close to Acqua Bella, and he's convinced it's involved. Your uncle believes Ondalina's behind the raids, and that they're planning to attack Cerulea, our Royal city, as well. So he sent the regiments as a show of strength on our western border.'

This was sobering news. Ondalina, the realm of the arctic mer, was an old enemy. It had waged war against Miromara – and lost – a century ago, and had simmered under the terms of the peace agreement ever since.

'As you know, the Ondalinians broke the permutavi (the peace agreement) three months ago,' Isabella said. 'Your uncle thinks Admiral Kolfinn did it because he wished to derail your betrothal to the Matalin crown prince and offer his daughter, Astrid, to the Matalis instead. An alliance with Matali is every bit as valuable to them as it is to us.'

Serafina was worried to hear of Ondalina's scheming, and she was surprised – and flattered – that her mother was discussing it with her.

'Maybe we should postpone the Dokimí,' she said. 'You could call a Council of the Six Waters instead, to caution Ondalina. Emperor Bilaal is already here. You'd only have to summon the president of Atlantica, the elder of Qin, and the queen of the Freshwaters.'

Isabella's troubled expression changed to one of impatience, and Serafina knew she'd said the wrong thing.

'The Dokimí can't be postponed. The stability of our realm depends upon it. The moon is full and the tides are high. All preparations have been made. A delay could play right into Kolfinn's hands,' Isabella said.

Serafina, desperate to see approval in her mother's eyes,

tried again. 'What if we sent another regiment to the western border?' she asked. 'I listened to this conch last night . . .' She quickly sorted through the shells on her floor. 'Here it is – *Discourses on Defence*. It says that a show of force alone can be enough to deter an enemy, and that—'

Isabella cut her off. 'You can't learn to rule a realm by listening to conches!'

'But, Mum, a show of force worked with the Opafago in the Barrens. You said so yourself five minutes ago!'

'Yes, it did, but that was an entirely different situation. Cerulea was not under the threat of raids then, so Merrow could afford to move her guerrieri out of the city to the Barrens. As I *hope* you know by now, Sera, six regiments are currently garrisoned here in the capital. We've already sent four to the western border with Desiderio. If we send another, we leave ourselves with only one.'

'Yes, but—'

'What if the raiders who've been attacking our villages attack Cerulea instead and we have only one regiment of guerrieri left here to defend ourselves and the Matalis?'

'But we have your personal guard, too – the Janiçari,' Serafina said, her voice – like her hopes of impressing her mother – growing fainter.

Isabella flapped a hand at her. 'Another thousand soldiers at most. Not enough to mount an effective defence. Think, Serafina, think. Ruling is like playing chess. Danger comes from many directions, from a pawn as well as a queen. You must play the board, not the piece. You're only hours away from being declared heiress to the Miromaran throne. You *must* learn to think!'

'I *am* thinking! Gods, Mum! Why are you *always* so hard on me?' Serafina shouted.

'Because your enemies will be a thousand times harder!' Isabella shouted back.

Another painful silence fell between mother and daughter. It was broken by a frantic pounding.

'Enter!' Isabella barked.

The doors to Serafina's room swung open. A page, one of Vallerio's, swam inside. He bowed to both mermaids, then addressed Isabella. 'My lord Vallerio sent me to fetch you to your staterooms, Your Grace.'

'Why?'

'There are reports of a another raid.'

Isabella's hands clenched into fists. 'Tell your lord I'll be there momentarily.'

The page bowed and left the room.

Serafina started towards her mother. 'I'll go with you,' she said.

Isabella shook her head. 'Ready yourself for tonight,' she said tersely. 'It must go well. We desperately need this alliance with Matali. Now more than ever.'

'Mum, please. . . .'

But it was too late. Isabella had already swum out of Sera's bedchamber.

She was gone.

# TWO

TEARS THREATENED as the doors closed behind Isabella, but Serafina held them back.

Nearly every conversation with her mother ended in an awkward silence or heated words. She was used to it. But still, it hurt.

A slender tentacle brushed Serafina's shoulder. Another curled around her neck. A third wound around her arm. Sylvestre, finely tuned to his mistress's every mood, had turned blue with worry. She leaned her head against his.

'I'm so nervous about tonight, Sylvestre,' she said. 'My mother doesn't want to hear about it, but maybe Neela will. I've got to talk to *somebody*. What if Alítheia tears my head off? What if I mess up my songspell? What if Mahdi doesn't . . .'

Serafina couldn't bear to voice that last thought. It scared her even more than the ordeal that lay ahead.

'Serafina! Child, where *are* you? Your hairdresser is here!'

It was Tavia, her nurse, calling from her antechamber. Sylvestre shot off at the sound of her voice. There was no more time to fret. Sera had to go. She was expected – by

Tavia, by the canta magus, by her entire court.

'Coming!' she called back.

She started towards the doors, then halted. As soon as she opened them, she was no longer Serafina. She was *Your Grace*, or *Your Majesty*, or Most Serene Principessa. She was *theirs*.

She hated the hot-spring atmosphere of her court. She hated the whispers, the glances, the toadying smiles. At court, she must dress just so. Always swim gracefully. Never raise her voice. Smile and nod and talk about the tides, when she'd much rather be riding Clio or exploring the ruins of the reggia, Merrow's ancient palace. She hated the suffocating weight of expectation, the constant pressure to be perfect – and the pointed looks and barbed comments when she was not.

'Two minutes,' she whispered.

With a flick of her tail, she rushed to the opposite end of her bedroom. She pushed open a pair of glass doors and swam onto her balcony, startling two small sea robins resting on its rail. Beyond the balcony was the royal city.

Cerulea, broad and sprawling, had grown through the centuries from the first mer settlement into the centre of mer culture that it was today. Ancient and magnificent, it had been built from blue quartz mined deep under the seabed. At this time of day, the sun's rays penetrated the Devil's Tail, a protective thorn thicket that floated above it, and struck the rooftops, making them sparkle.

The original palace had been built in the centre of Cerulea. Its roof had collapsed several centuries ago and a new palace had been built high on a seamount – a baroque construction of coral, quartz, and mother-of-pearl – for the royal family and its court. The ruins of the reggia still lay preserved within the city, a reminder of the past.

Serafina's eyes travelled over Cerulea's winding streets to the spires of the Kolegio – with its black-robed professors and enormous library (the Ostrokon), to the Golden Fathom – where tall town houses, fashionable restaurants, and expensive shops were located. And then farther still, out past the city walls to the Kolisseo, where the royal flag of Miromara – a branch of red coral against a white background, and that of Matali – a dragon rampant holding a silver-blue egg – were flying. The Kolisseo was where, in just a few hours, Serafina would undergo her Dokimí in front of the court, the Matali royals, the mer of Miromara . . .

. . . and Mahdi.

Two years had passed since she'd last seen him. She closed her eyes now and pictured his face: his dark eyes, his shy smile, his serious expression. When they were older, they would marry each other. Tonight, they would be betrothed. It was a ridiculous custom, but Serafina was glad he'd be the one. She could still hear the last words he'd spoken to her, right before he'd returned to Matali.

'My choice,' he'd whispered, taking her hand. '*Mine*. Not theirs.'

Serafina opened her eyes. Their green depths were clouded with worry. She'd had private conches from him when he'd first returned home, carried by a trusted messenger.

Every time one arrived, she would rush to her room and hold the shell to her ear, hungry for the sound of his voice. But after a year had passed, the private conches had stopped coming and official ones arrived instead. In them, Mahdi's voice sounded stilted and formal.

At about the same time, Serafina started to hear things about him. He'd become a party boy, some said. He stayed out shoaling until all hours. Swam with a fast crowd. Spent a fortune on mounts for caballabong, a game much like the goggs' polo. She wasn't sure she should believe the stories, but what if they were true? What if he'd changed?

'Serafina, you *must* come out now! Thalassa, the canta magus, is due at any moment and you know she doesn't like to be kept waiting!' Tavia shouted.

'Coming, Tavia!' Serafina called, swimming back into her bedroom.

*Serafina. . . .*

'Great Goddess Neria, I *said* I'm coming!'

*Daughter of Merrow, chosen one . . .*

Serafina stopped dead. That wasn't Tavia's voice. It wasn't coming from the other side of the doors.

It was right behind her.

'Who's there?' she cried, whirling around.

*The end begins, your time has come. . . .*

'Giovanna, is that you? Donatella?'

But no one answered her. Because no one was there.

A sudden, darting movement to her left caught her eye. She gasped, then laughed with relief. It was only her looking glass. A vitrina was walking around inside it.

Her mirror was tall and very old. Worms had eaten holes into its gilt frame and its glass was pocked with black spots. It had been salvaged from a terragogg shipwreck. Ghosts lived inside it – vitrina – souls of the beautiful, vain humans who'd spent too much time gazing into it. The mirror had captured them. Their bodies had withered and died, but their spirits lived on, trapped behind the glass forever.

A countess lived inside Serafina's mirror, as did a handsome young duke, three courtesans, an actor, and an archbishop. They often spoke to her. It was the countess whom she'd just seen moving about.

Serafina rapped on the frame. The countess lifted her voluminous skirts and ran to her, stopping only inches from the glass. She wore a tall, elaborately styled white wig. Her face was powdered, her lips rouged. She looked frightened.

'Someone is in here with us, Principessa,' she whispered, looking over her shoulder. 'Someone who doesn't belong.'

They saw it at the same time – a figure in the distance, still and dark. Serafina had heard that mirrors were doorways in the water and that one could open them if one knew how. Only the most powerful mages could move through their liquid-silver world, though. Serafina didn't know anyone who ever had. Not even Thalassa. As she and the countess watched, the figure started moving towards them.

'That is no vitrina,' the countess hissed. 'If it got in, it can get out. Get away from the glass! *Hurry!*'

As the figure drew closer, Serafina saw that it was a river

mermaid, her tail mottled in shades of brown and grey. She wore a cloak of black osprey feathers. Its collar, made of twining deer antlers, rose high at the back of her head. Her hair was grey, her eyes piercing. She was chanting.

*The sands run out, our spell unwinds,*

*Inch by inch, our chant unbinds. . . .*

Serafina knew the voice. She'd heard it in her nightmare. It belonged to the river witch, Baba Vrăja.

The countess had warned Serafina to move away, but she couldn't. It was as if she was frozen in place, her face only inches from the glass.

Vrăja beckoned to her. 'Come, child,' she said.

Serafina raised her hand slowly, as if in a trance. She was about to touch the mirror when Vrăja suddenly stopped chanting. She turned to look at something – something Serafina couldn't see. Her eyes filled with fear. 'No!' she cried. Her body twisted, then shattered. A hundred eels writhed where she had been, then they dived into the liquid silver.

Seconds later, a terragogg walked into the frame, sending ripples through the silver. He was dressed in a black suit. His hair, so blond it was almost white, was cut close to his head. He stood sideways, gazing at the last of the eels as they disappeared. One was slower than the rest. The man snatched it up and bit into it. The creature writhed in agony. Its blood dripped down his chin. He swallowed the eel, then turned to face the glass.

Serafina's hands came to her mouth. The man's eyes were completely black. There was no iris, no white, just darkness.

He walked up to the glass and thrust a hand through it. Serafina screamed. She swam backwards, crashed into a chair, and fell to the floor. The man's arm emerged, then his shoulder. His head was pushing through when her nurse, Tavia, piped up.

'Serafina! What's wrong?' she called through the doors. 'I'm coming in!'

The man glared hatefully in her direction. A second later, he was gone.

'What happened, child? Are you all right?' Tavia asked.

Serafina, shaking, got up off the floor. 'I – I saw something in the mirror. It frightened me and I fell,' she said.

Tavia, who had the legs and torso of a blue crab, scuttled over to the mirror. Serafina could see that it was empty now. There was no river witch inside it. No terragogg in black. All she saw was her nurse's reflection.

'Pesky vitrina. You probably haven't been paying them enough attention. They get peevish if you don't fawn over them enough,' Tavia said.

'But these were different. They were . . .'

Tavia turned to her. 'Yes, child?'

*A scary witch from a nightmare and a terragogg with freaky black eyes*, she was about to say. Until she realized it sounded insane.

'. . . um, *different*. I've never seen them before.'

'That happens sometimes. Most vitrina are right in your face, but occasionally you come across a shy one,' Tavia said. She rapped loudly on the glass. 'You quiet down in there, you hear? Or I'll put this glass in a closet!' She pulled a sea-silk throw off a chair and draped it over the mirror. 'That will scare them. Vitrina hate closets. There's no one in there to tell them how pretty they are.'

Tavia righted the chair Serafina had knocked over, then chided her for taking so long to join her court.

'Your breakfast is here. So is the dressmaker. You *must* come along now!' she said.

Serafina cast a last glance at her mirror, questioning herself already. Vrăja wasn't real. She was of the Iele, and the Iele lived only in stories. And that hand coming through the glass? That was simply a trick of the light, a hallucination caused by lack of sleep and nerves over her Dokimí. Hadn't her mother said that nerves were her foe?

'Serafina, I am *not* calling you again!' Tavia scolded.

The princess lifted her head, swam through the doors to her antechamber, and joined her court.

# THREE

'NO, NO, NO! Not the *ruby* hair combs, you tube worm, the *emerald* combs! Go get the right ones!' the hairdresser scolded. Her assistant scuttled off.

'I'm sorry, but you're *quite* mistaken. Etiquette demands that the Duchessa di Tsarno *precede* the Contessa di Cerulea to the Kolisseo.' That was Lady Giovanna, chatelaine of the chamber, talking to Lady Ottavia, keeper of the wardrobe.

'These sea roses just arrived for the principessa from Principe Bastiaan. Where should I put them?' a maid asked.

A dozen voices could be heard, all talking at once. They spoke Mermish, the common language of the sea people.

Serafina tried to ignore the voices and concentrate on her songspell. 'All those octave leaps,' she whispered to herself. 'Five high Cs, the trills and arpeggios. . . . Why did Merrow make it so *hard*?'

The songspell for the Dokimí had been composed specifically to test a future ruler's mastery of magic. It was cast entirely in canta mirus, or special song. Canta mirus was a demanding type of magic that called for a powerful voice and a great deal of ability. It required long hours of practice to master, and Serafina had worked tirelessly to excel at it. Mirus casters could bid light, wind, water, and sound. The best could embellish existing songspells or create new ones.

Most mermaids of Serafina's age could only cast canta prax – or plainsong – spells. Prax was a practical magic that helped the mer survive. There were camouflage spells to fool predators. Echolocation spells to navigate dark waters. Spells to improve speed or darken an ink cloud. Prax spells were the first kind taught to mer children, and even those with little magical ability could cast them.

Serafina took a deep breath now and started to sing. She sang softly, so no one could hear her, watching herself in a decorative mica panel. She couldn't rehearse the entire spell – she'd destroy the room – but she could work on bits of it.

'Alítheia? You've never seen her? I've seen her twice now, my dear, and let me tell you, she's absolutely terrifying!'

That was the elderly Baronessa Agneta talking to young Lady Cosima. They were sitting in a corner. The grey haired baronessa was wearing a gown in an alarming shade of purple. Cosima had on a blue tunic; a thick blonde braid trailed down her back. Serafina faltered, unnerved by their talk.

'You have no reason to fear her, so don't,' had always been Isabella's advice, but from what Sera had heard of Alítheia, that was easier said than done.

'The gods themselves made her. Bellogrim, the smith, forged her, and Neria breathed life into her,' Agneta continued. Loudly, for she was quite deaf.

'Is there kissing during the Dokimí? I heard there's kissing,' Cosima said, wrinkling her nose.

'A bit at the end. Close your eyes. That's what I do,' the baronessa said, sipping her sargassa tea. The hot liquid – thick and sweet, like most mer drinks – sat heavily in an exquisite teacup. The cup had been salvaged, as had all of the palace porcelain, from terragogg shipwrecks. 'The Dokimí has three parts, child – two tests and a vow.'

'Why?'

'Why? *Quia Merrow decrevit!* That's Latin. It means—'

'"Because Merrow decreed it,"' Cosima said.

'Very good. *Dokimí* is Greek for trial, and a trial it is. Alítheia appears in the first test – the blooding – to ensure each principessa is a true daughter of the blood.'

'Why?' Cosima asked.

'*Quia Merrow decrevit*,' the Baronessa replied. She paused to put her cup down. 'The second test is the casting. It consists of a diabolically difficult songspell. A strong ruler must have a strong voice, for, as you know, a mermaid's magic is *in* her voice.'

'Why is that?' Cosima asked. 'I've always wondered. Why can't we just wave a wand? It would be *sooo* much easier.'

'Because the goddess Neria, who gave us our magic, knew that songspells carry better in water than wandspells. Danger is everywhere in the sea, child. Death swims on a fast fin.'

'But why do we *sing* our spells, Baronessa? Why can't we just speak them?'

The baronessa sighed. 'Do they actually *teach* you anything in school nowadays?' she asked. 'We sing because song *enhances* magic. Why, song *is* magic! *Cantare*. More Latin. It means . . .'

'. . . to sing.'

'Yes. And from *cantare* come both *chant* and *enchantment*, *canto* and *incantation*, music and magic. Think of the sounds of the sea, child . . . whalesong, the cries of gulls, the whispering of the waves. They are so beautiful and so powerful that all the creatures in the world hear the magic in them, even the tone-deaf terragoggs.'

The baronessa picked up a sea urchin from a plate, cracked its shell with her teeth, and slurped it down. 'If, and only if, the principessa passes both tests,' she said, 'she will then undertake the last part of the Dokimí – the promising. This is where she makes her betrothal vows and promises her people that she will marry the merman chosen for her and give the realm a daughter of the blood, just as her mother did. And her grandmother. And so on, all the way back to Merrow.'

'But *why*, Baronessa?' Cosima asked.

'Good gods! *Another* why? *Quia Merrow decrevit!* That's why!' the baronessa said impatiently.

'But what if Serafina doesn't *want* to marry and rule Miromara and give the realm a daughter? What if she wants to, like, open a café and sell bubble tea?'

'Don't be ridiculous. Of *course* she wants to rule Miromara. The things you come up with!'

Agneta reached for another urchin. Cosima frowned. And Serafina smiled ruefully. For as long as she could remember, she'd been asking the same questions, and had been given the same answer: *Quia Merrow decrevit*. Like many rules of the adult world, a lot of Merrow's inscrutable decrees made no sense to her. They still had to be followed, though, whether she liked it or not.

*Of course she wants to rule Miromara!* the baronessa had said. But the truth was, sometimes she didn't. She wondered, for a few rebellious seconds, what would happen if she refused to sing her songspell tonight and swam off to sell bubble tea instead?

Then Tavia arrived with her breakfast and started to chatter, and all such foolish thoughts disappeared.

'Here you are, my darling,' she said, setting a silver tray down on a table. 'Water apples, eel berries, pickled sponge . . . your favourites.' She slapped a green tentacle away. 'Sylvestre, keep out of it!'

'Thank you, Tavia,' Serafina said, ignoring the tray. She wasn't hungry. She took a deep breath, preparing to practise her songspell again, but Tavia wasn't finished.

'I didn't get a chance to tell you this yet,' she said, pressing a blue pincer to her chest, 'but Empress Ahadi's personal maid was in the kitchens this morning, getting tea for her mistress. I happen to know that she's very fond of Corsican keel worms, so I made sure she got plenty. After her second bowl, she told me that the emperor is in good health and the empress is as bossy as ever.'

'Did she?' Serafina asked lightly. She knew she must not betray too much eagerness for news of the Matalis, especially the crown prince. Her slightest reaction to any news of him would be noted and commented upon. 'And the Princess Neela, how is she? When is she coming to my rooms? I'm dying to see her.'

'I don't know, child, but Ahadi's maid – the one in the kitchens – she told me more things . . . things about the crown prince,' Tavia said conspiratorially.

'Isn't that nice?' Serafina said. She knew that Tavia – a terrible gossip – desperately wanted her to ask what the *things about the crown prince* were, but she didn't. Instead, she practised a trill.

Tavia waited as long as she possibly could, then the words burst out of her. 'Oh, Serafina! Don't you want to know what *else* the maid said? She told me that the crown prince's scales are the *deepest* shade of blue, and he has an earring, and he wears his hair pulled back in a hippokamp's tail!'

'Mahdi has an *earring*?' Serafina exclaimed, forgetting for a moment that she wasn't supposed to be interested. 'That's ridiculous. Next you'll tell me he's dyed his hair pink and pierced his tail fin. The last time I saw him he was skinny and goofy. A total goby, just like my brother. All he and Desiderio wanted to do was play Galleons and Gorgons.'

'Principessa!' Tavia scolded. 'Crown Prince Mahdi is heir to the Matali kingdom, and Principe Desiderio is a commander of this one, and neither would appreciate being called a *goby*! I should think you would at least be relieved to know that your future husband has grown into a handsome merman!'

Serafina shrugged. 'I suppose so,' she said.

'You *suppose* so?'

'It makes no difference if he's handsome or not,' Serafina said. 'The crown prince will be my husband even if he looks like a sea slug.'

'Yes, but it's easier to fall in love with a good-looking merman than a sea slug!'

'Love has nothing to do with it, Tavia, and you know it. My marriage is a matter of state, not a matter of the heart. Royal alliances are made to strengthen bonds between realms and advance common interests.'

'Fine words coming from one who's never actually *been* in love,' Tavia sniffed. 'You're your mother's daughter, that's for certain. Duty above all.' She scuttled off to chide a chambermaid. Serafina smiled, pleased she'd thrown Tavia off the scent. If she only knew.

But she didn't. And she wouldn't. Serafina had kept her secret, and she wasn't about to reveal it now.

She took a deep breath again and tried once more to practise her songspell.

'Coco, *stop* pestering Baronessa Agneta, and try on your gown!' a voice scolded. This time it was Lady Elettra, Cosima's older sister, who interrupted her.

'Gowns are *boring*,' Cosima said, darting off.

Then Serafina heard another voice, secretive and hushed. 'Is that what you're wearing to the procession? You shouldn't try so hard to outshine the princess.'

There was laughter, throaty and low, and then a second voice, beautiful and beguiling: 'I don't *have* to try. It's no contest. He's only going through with the betrothal because he has to. Everyone knows that. He couldn't care less about it. Or her.'

The words cut like shark's teeth. Serafina dropped a note and bungled the measure. She looked straight ahead, into the mica panel. In it she saw Lucia Volnero and Bianca di Remora, two of her ladies-in-waiting. They were at the far end of the chamber, holding up a spectacular gown and whispering. They didn't know it, but the room's vaulted ceiling channelled sound. Words spoken on one side of the chamber could be heard on the other, just as the ones speaking them could be seen in the mica panels.

Bianca, the second lady, continued the conversation. 'What everyone knows, *mia amica*, is that you want him for yourself,' she said. 'Better give up *that* idea!'

'Why should I?' the first, Lucia, said. 'A duchessa's daughter is a catch, too, don't you think? Especially *this* duchessa's daughter. *He* certainly seems to think so.'

'What do you mean?'

'A clutch of us snuck out last night. We went to the Lagoon.'

Serafina couldn't believe it. The Lagoon, the waters off the human city of Venice, was not far from Miromara, but it was forbidden to merfolk. It was a treacherous place – labyrinthine, dark, and full of dangerous creatures.

It was also full of humans – the most dangerous creatures of all.

'You did *not*!' Bianca said.

'Oh, yes we did. It was totally awesome. We were shoaling all night. The Matalis, me, and a few other merls. It was *wild*,' Lucia said.

'Did anything happen? With you and the prince?'

Lucia smiled wickedly. 'Well, he *really* knows how to shoal. He has some fierce moves and . . .'

Bianca giggled. 'And? And *what*?'

Lucia's reply was drowned out by a group of chattery maids bustling in with gowns.

Serafina's cheeks burned; she looked at the floor. She was hurt and furious. She wanted to tell Lucia that she'd heard every rotten word she'd said – but she didn't. She was royalty, and royalty did not shout. Royalty did not slap their tails. Royalty did not lose control. Ever. *Those who would command others must first command themselves*, her mother often told her. Usually when she complained about sitting next to a dull ambassador at a state dinner. Or got caught fencing in the Grand Hall with Desiderio.

She glanced at Lucia again. *She's always causing trouble. Why does she even have to be here?* she wondered, but she knew the answer: Lucia was a member of the Volnero – a noble family as old, and nearly as powerful, as her own. The Volnero duchessas had the right to be at court and their daughters had the hereditary privilege of waiting upon the realm's principessas.

Lucia, with her sapphire eyes, her silver scales, her nightblue hair swept up off her shoulders. You could bungle a hundred trills if you looked like that, and nobody would even notice, Serafina thought. Not that Lucia Volnero would bungle *anything*. Her voice was gorgeous. It was said the Volnero were descended from sirens.

Serafina didn't know if that was true, but she knew that Portia, Lucia's mother, had once enchanted Serafina's own uncle Vallerio. Portia and Vallerio had wished to marry, but Artemesia—the reigning regina and Vallerio and Isabella's mother—had forbidden the match. The Volnero had traitors in the branches of their family coral, and she hadn't wanted her son to marry into a tainted line.

Angry, Vallerio had left Cerulea and spent several years in Tsarno, a fortress town in western Miromara. Portia married someone else – Sejanus Adaro, Lucia's father. Some said she only married him because he looked like Vallerio with his handsome face, silver scales, and black hair. Sejanus died only a year after Lucia's birth. Vallerio never married, choosing to devote himself to the welfare of the realm instead.

Portia has taught Lucia her secrets, Serafina thought enviously. She sighed, thinking how *her* mother taught her the correct form of address for Atlantica's foreign secretary, or that Parliament must be convened only during a spring tide, never a neap tide. She wished that once, just *once*, her mother would teach her something merly – like which anemones to kiss to get those pouty, tentacle stung lips, or how to make her tail fin sparkle.

*Stop it, Serafina*, she told herself. *Don't let Lucia get to you. Neela will know if Mahdi went to the Lagoon or not. Just practise your songspell.* She comforted herself with the knowledge that her best friend would be here soon. Just seeing her face would make this whole ordeal easier.

Serafina straightened her back, squared her shoulders, and tried, yet again, to practise her songspell.

'Your Grace, may I compliment you on your dress?' a voice drawled from behind her. 'I hope you're wearing it tonight.'

Serafina glanced in the mica. It was Lucia. She was smiling. Like a barracuda.

'No, I'm not, but thank you,' she said warily. It wasn't like Lucia to be forthcoming with the compliments.

'What a pity. You should. It's so simple and fresh. Totally genius. Contrast is *absolutely* the way to go in a situation like this,' Lucia said.

'Contrast?' Serafina said, puzzled. She turned to Lucia.

'Your look. It's a fabulous contrast.'

Serafina looked down at her dress. It was a plain, light-blue sea-silk gown. Nothing special. She'd changed into it hastily, right after she'd swum into the antechamber.

'My look is all one colour – blue. And we're in the *sea*, Lucia. So, it really doesn't contrast with anything.'

'Ha! That is so funny, Your Grace! Good for you for joking about it. I'm glad it doesn't bother you. Don't let it. Merboys will be merboys and, anyway, I'm sure he's given her up by *now*.'

The whole room had gone quiet. Everyone had stopped what she was doing to listen. Blood sport was the court's favourite game.

'Lucia, who's he? Who's her? What are you talking about?' Serafina asked, confused.

Lucia's eyes widened. She pressed a hand to her chest. 'You don't *know*? I am *such* an idiot. I thought you knew. I mean, *everyone* knows. I – I'm sorry. It's nothing. I made a mistake.' She started to swim off.

Lucia *never* admitted to making a mistake. Serafina saw a chance to best her, to pay her back for the mean things she'd said. And though a voice inside her told her not to, she took that chance.

'What mistake, Lucia?' she asked.

Lucia stopped. 'Really, Your Grace,' she said, looking deeply embarrassed. 'I wouldn't like to say.'

'No, tell me.'

'If you insist,' Lucia replied.

'I do.'

As soon as the words left her lips, Serafina realized *she* was the one who'd made the mistake. Lucia turned around. Her barracuda smile was back. She'd only been pretending embarrassment.

'I was talking about the crown prince and his merlfriend,' she said. 'Well, his *latest* one.'

'His . . . his *merlfriend*?' Serafina said. She could barely breathe.

'That's *enough*, Lucia! You're going too far!' Bianca

hissed.

'But, Bianca, would you have me defy our principessa? She wishes me to speak,' Lucia said. She fixed her glittering eyes on Serafina. 'I'm *so* sorry to be the one to tell you. Especially on the day of your Dokimí. I was certain you knew, otherwise I would never have mentioned it. I only meant to compliment you by telling you that your look was a contrast to hers. All *she* has going for her is blonde hair, turquoise scales, and more curves than a whirlpool.'

Lucia, triumphant, dipped her head. Serafina felt humiliated, but was determined not to show it. This was her own fault. She'd stupidly fallen right into Lucia's trap and now she had to swim out.

'Lucia, thank you *so* much for telling me,' she said, smiling. 'It's *such* a relief to know. I hope she's taught him a few things.'

'I beg your pardon, Your Grace?'

'Look, we all know it – it's no secret – the last time the crown prince visited, he was a bit of a goby and pretty hopeless with merls,' Serafina said.

'You're not upset?'

'Not at all! Why would I be? I just hope she's done a good job with him. Taught him a few dance strokes or how to send a proper love conch. *Someone* has to. Merboys are like hippokamps, don't you think? No fun until they're broken in. Now, if you'll excuse me, I really do need to practise.'

Lucia, thwarted, turned on her tail and swam away, and Serafina, a fake smile still on her face, resumed her songspell.

The performance cost her dearly, but no one would have known. Used to the ways of her court, to its sharp teeth and claws, she was an expert at hiding her feelings.

Sylvestre, however, was not.

Crimson with anger, the octopus swam after Lucia. When he got close to her, he siphoned in as much water as he could hold, then shot a fat jet of it at her, hitting her squarely in the back of her head. Her updo collapsed.

Lucia stopped dead. Her hands went to her head. 'My hair!' she screeched, whirling around.

'Sylvestre!' Serafina exclaimed, horrified. 'Apologize!'

Sylvestre affected a contrite expression, then squirted Lucia again – in the face.

'You little sucker! I'll *gut* you!' she sputtered. 'Avarus! After him!'

Lucia's pet scorpion fish zipped after the octopus. Sylvestre darted under the table where Serafina's breakfast tray was resting. Avarus followed him. The table went over; the tray went flying. Sylvestre grabbed a water apple and fired it at Avarus. Avarus ducked it and charged. He swam up to Sylvestre and stung him. Sylvestre howled, and a few seconds later, Serafina's antechamber was engulfed by a roiling cloud of black ink.

Serafina could see nothing, but she could hear her ladies coughing and shrieking. They were crashing into tables, chairs, and one another. When the cloud finally cleared, she saw Lucia and Bianca wiping ink off their faces. Giovanna was shaking it out of her hair. Tavia was threatening to hang

Sylvestre up by his tentacles.

And then another voice, majestic and fearsome, was heard above the fray: 'In olden days, royals had their unruly nobles beheaded. What a pity that custom fell out of use.'

# FOUR

THALASSA, the canta magus, was not amused.

She floated in the doorway of the antechamber, arms crossed over her considerable bosom, tentacles twining beneath her. Her hair, the grey of a hurricane sky, was styled in an elegant twist. A cluster of red anemones bloomed like roses at the nape of her neck. She wore a gown of crimson, and a long cape of black mussel shells. At a snap of her fingers, two cuttlefish removed it.

The entire chamber had gone quiet. Thalassa, Miromara's keeper of magic, was the most powerful songcaster in the realm. No one misbehaved in her presence – *ever*. Even Isabella sat up straighter when Thalassa entered the room.

'Causing trouble again, Lucia?' she finally said. 'Nothing surprising from a Volnero. Do you remember what bad behaviour got your ancestor Kalumnus? No? Let me remind you. It got him his head in a basket. Likewise your great-aunt Livilla. I would watch myself if I were you.'

Lucia's eyes flashed menacingly at the unwelcome reminder of her ancestors' dark deeds. Kalumnus had tried to assassinate Merrow and rule in her stead. He'd been captured and beheaded, and his family banished. Two thousand years later, Livilla Volnero tried to raise an army against the Merrovingia. She, too, had been executed. Though these events had happened centuries ago, suspicion still shrouded the Volnero like sea mist.

'And *you*, Bianca,' Thalassa continued. 'A true di Remora. Always following the big fish. You might want to reassess your loyalties. The Merrovingia are Miromara and always will be. Alítheia ensures that.' She waved a heavily jewelled hand. 'Out. Now,' she ordered. 'All of you except the principessa.'

Serafina knew that Thalassa had come to drill her on her songspell. She was her teacher.

'Your Dokimí's only a few hours away. As of yesterday, that trill in the fifth measure wasn't where it should be. It should be quick and bright, like dolphins jumping, not lumbering like a whale shark. We have work to do,' Thalassa said.

'Yes, Magistra,' Serafina said.

'From the beginning, please.'

Serafina started to sing . . . and immediately stumbled.

'Again,' the canta magus demanded. 'No mistakes this time. The songspell is supposed to demonstrate excellence, and you are not even showing me competence!'

Serafina started over. This time, she got well into the songspell – and past the difficult trill – without a mistake. Her eyes darted from the wall ahead of her, where she'd focused her gaze, to Thalassa.

'Good, good, but stop biting off your words,' Thalassa chided. 'Legato, slowly, legato!'

Serafina nodded to show she understood and tried to soften her words, gliding smoothly from phrase to phrase. She was doing more than merely singing now; she was songcasting.

Merrow's songspell, if sung correctly, told listeners of the origins of the merfolk. Like all principessas before her, Serafina had to cast the original songspell, then compose several movements of her own that illustrated the progression of the merfolk after Merrow's rule. She had to sing of her place in that progression, and her betrothed's, and she had to use colour, light, and movement to do it. The greater her mastery of magic, the more dazzling her songspell.

She was just conjuring a likeness of Merrow when Thalassa started waving her hands.

'No, no, no! *Stop!*' she shouted.

'What is it? What's wrong?' Serafina asked.

'The images, they're far too pale. They have no life!'

'I – I don't understand, Magistra. I hit all the notes. I had that phrase totally under control.'

'That's the problem, Serafina – too much control! That's *always* your problem. I want emotion and passion. I want the tempest, not the calm. Again!'

Serafina took a deep breath, then picked up where Thalassa had stopped her. As she sang, the canta magus whirled around her, pushing her, challenging her, never letting up. As Serafina began a very tricky section of the songspell, a tribute to her future husband, Thalassa swam closer, propelled by her strong tentacles.

'Expression, Serafina, more expression!' she demanded.

Serafina had conjured a water vortex as part of an effect. She added two more.

'Good, good! Now use the magic to make me *feel* something! Amaze me!'

Raising the vortices with her voice, Serafina made them taller and spun them faster. She forgot she was inside the palace, forgot to keep the magic small. Her voice grew louder, stronger. She swept a graceful hand out in front of her, curving the vortices. She bent them once, twice, three times, folding the water in on itself, forcing it to refract light.

'Excellent!' Thalassa shouted.

Sera's voice was soaring. It swooped over arpeggios, ranged up and down octaves effortlessly. She bent the water again and again, and a dozen more times until it cracked and broke into shards and light shot from it in so many directions, it looked like a mountain of diamonds glittering in the chamber. She was now coming to the part where she had to conjure an image of the crown prince.

She tried to make the most beautiful image she could imagine, but as soon as she saw Mahdi's face shimmering before her, her voice broke. All she could think about was Lucia telling her that he had a merlfriend. What if she was right?

All at once, her emotion boiled over. She lost control of her songspell. The vortices spun apart violently and splashed to the floor, knocking over a table, smashing a chair, and cracking two windows.

'I can't do it!' she shouted angrily, slapping the water with her tail. 'It's an *impossible* songspell!' She turned to Thalassa, her composure entirely gone. 'Tell my mother the Dokimí's off. Tell her I'm not good enough! Not good enough for her! Not good enough to cast this rotten songspell! And not good enough for the crown prince!'

# FIVE

THALASSA PRESSED a hand to her chest. 'What *is* this outburst?' she asked. 'This isn't like you, child. You know the songspell inside and out. All you have to do is cast it!'

'Yes. Right. That's all,' Serafina said hotly. 'Just cast it. In front of the entire court. And the Matalis. And oh, I don't know, ten thousand Miromarans! It's too hard. I won't be able to pull it off. I'll bungle that trill. My voice isn't strong enough. It's not as *beautiful* as other voices are. It's not as beautiful as . . . as . . .'

Thalassa raised an eyebrow. 'As Lucia's?'

Serafina nodded unhappily. To her surprise, Thalassa didn't lecture or scold. Instead, she laughed.

'Tell me, where does the voice come from?' she asked.

Serafina rolled her eyes. 'From the throat. Obviously,' she said.

'That's true for many,' Thalassa said. 'And it's certainly true for Lucia. But it's *not* true for you. Your voice comes from here.' She touched the place over Serafina's heart. 'It's a beautiful voice. I know. I've heard it. All you have to do is let it out. Show me your heart, Serafina. That's where the truest magic comes from.'

Serafina laughed bitterly. 'Show my heart? Here at court? Why? So Lucia Volnero can stick a knife in it?'

'I heard what Lucia said. Ignore her. She wishes she were principessa. She wants the power, the palace, and the handsome crown prince,' Thalassa said.

Worry darkened Serafina's eyes at the words *crown prince*. She blinked it away so quickly that anyone else would have missed it. But Thalassa was not anyone else.

'Ah,' she said sagely. 'So *that's* what's behind all this.' She sat down on a settee and patted the place next to her. 'Tell me, does he love you?'

'Yes. No. Oh, I don't *know*, Magistra!' Serafina said tearfully. 'I think so. I *thought* so. But now I'm not sure. Not after what Lucia said.' She sat down next to her teacher.

'Oh, Serafina,' Thalassa said, putting an arm around her. 'Have you told anyone how you feel? Your mother? Tavia? What do they say?'

Serafina shook her head. 'I haven't told them. I haven't told *anyone*. I *won't*.'

'Why not?'

'Because it'll get out somehow. The courtiers will find out and then it won't be mine any more. It'll be theirs. You don't *understand*, Magistra. My whole life is public. I can't go anywhere alone. I can't do anything by myself. Every movement, every word, every look is talked about and picked apart. I wanted this, this *one* thing, for myself alone.'

Thalassa took Serafina's hand. 'You're wrong, you know. I *do* understand. I know something of a life lived in public. I *am* the canta magus, after all.'

Serafina looked at her questioningly.

'My talent was recognized when I was a small child,' Thalassa said. 'A voice like mine, my teacher said, came along once in a millennia. I could fold water, throw light, and whirl wind by the time I was four. I was taken from my parents and given over to the Kolegio at six. By eight I was songcasting for your grandmother Artemesia and her court.'

'How did *you* cope with it all, Magistra?' Serafina asked.

Thalassa laughed. 'Poorly. When I was little, I took joy in my music. I cast my songspells simply because I loved to do so. But as I grew older and started songcasting for the court, I began to listen to what others said. I heard their remarks – some spiteful and cruel – and I believed them. I let their voices get inside of me, into my heart.'

Thalassa released Serafina's hand. She touched her fingers to her chest, to the place over her heart, then pulled them away, wincing as they drew fine skeins of blood. The crimson swirled through the water like smoke in the air, then coalesced into images. As it did, Serafina saw the bloodsong – the memories that lived in her teacher's heart. She saw nobles from her grandmother's court whispering to each other behind their hands.

*She'll never become a mage . . . Her voice isn't strong enough . . . It's too low . . . It's too high . . . Her trills are muddy . . . She's too fat . . . She's too thin . . . She's not pretty . . .*

Thalassa waved the memories away. 'I tried to please the voices. I started making music for them, not me, and my songspells suffered,' she said. 'Luckily, I saw what the voices were doing to me and I vowed never to let them in again. I guarded my heart fiercely. I closed it off. I allowed no one inside, nothing but my music.'

'I'll do the same,' Serafina said resolutely.

'No, child. I am telling you these things to convince you *not* to close your heart.'

'But you just said—'

'What I *didn't* say, yet, is this: if you let no one into your heart, you keep out pain, yes, but also love. When I was sixteen, I wanted to be a canta magus. Music and magic were all that mattered to me. *You*, however, will become a ruler, and a ruler's greatest power comes from her heart—from the love she bears her subjects, and the love they bear her.'

Serafina thought about Thalassa's words. She'd longed to share her feelings for Mahdi with someone. She'd longed to open her heart, but she'd been too afraid. Impulsively, she touched her fingers to her chest now and drew a bloodsong. She gasped as she did, for she was much younger than Thalassa and her memories were sharper. It hurt to pull them.

'I'm touched by your trust, child,' Thalassa said. 'Are you certain you wish to show this to me?'

Serafina nodded and Thalassa watched as the blood swirled through the water, taking on shape and colour, making memory visible. Serafina watched too. It had happened two years ago, but for her it felt like yesterday. It had happened before the raids and disappearances. Before the tensions with Ondalina. Before the waters had grown so treacherous.

It had happened in the ruins of Merrow's ancient palace. Two long years ago . . .

# SIX

SERAFINA HAD BEEN HIDING.

From her mother, ministers, minions, and Mahdi.

She had stolen away. It drove everyone wild with worry, but she needed a few minutes a day, every day, to be free from the eyes and ears of the court. And she especially needed it today. The match had been decided. The announcement had been made. Serafina had met her future husband—and she didn't want any part of him.

Mahdi had arrived in Miromara a week earlier, with his parents, the emperor and empress; his cousins, Neela and Yazeed; and their royal entourage, to meet his future wife as custom demanded. He was sixteen – serious, smart, and shy. He didn't ride. He didn't fence. He preferred the company of Desiderio – Serafina's brother, a merboy his own age – and Yazeed to anyone else's. He barely spoke to Serafina, who was two years younger. He was courteous to her, as he was to everyone, but that was all.

'He's a goby. I'd rather marry Palomon,' she told Tavia, referring to her mother's bad-tempered hippokamp.

Their first real conversation had come about only by

accident. Serafina had been sitting in the gardens of the South Court, listening to a conch shell, when Mahdi and his chaperone, Ambassador Akmal, happened to swim by. They didn't see her. She'd hidden herself on a coral shelf above them, behind a giant sea fan.

'What do you think of the princess, Your Grace?' she heard the ambassador ask. 'She is very lovely, no?'

Serafina knew she shouldn't be eavesdropping, but she couldn't help herself. Curious, she leaned against the sea fan.

'Does it matter what I think?' he'd said. 'She's *their* choice – my parents', their advisers' – not mine. I have no choice.'

At that very second, the sea fan – old and brittle – cracked under Serafina's weight. It fell from the coral shelf and toppled heavily to the seafloor, sending up a cloud of silt. When the cloud finally settled, Sera peered over the shelf. Mahdi looked up and saw her.

'Wow. This is awkward,' she said.

'You heard us,' he said.

'I didn't *mean* to,' said Serafina. 'I was sitting here listening to a conch and then you swam by and . . . well, I couldn't help it. Look, I'm sorry. I'll go.'

'No, don't go. Please,' Mahdi had said. He turned to his ambassador. 'Leave us,' he ordered.

'Your Grace, is that wise? There will be talk.'

'*Leave us*,' Mahdi repeated through gritted teeth.

The ambassador bowed and left. As soon as he was gone, Mahdi swam up to Sera and helped her over the jagged edges of the broken sea fan. They sat down together on a nearby rock.

'I'm the one who's sorry,' he said. 'I shouldn't have said that.'

'You don't need to apologize. I know how you feel.'

He turned to look at her. 'But I thought—'

Serafina laughed. 'You thought what? That because I'm a merl, it's all just fine with me? Getting betrothed at sixteen and married at twenty? To someone chosen for me, not by me? How very enlightened of you, Your Grace. It's the forty-first century, you know, not the tenth. And to be perfectly honest, I'd much rather pursue a doctorate in ancient Atlantean history than marry you.'

After that, she had often felt Mahdi's eyes on her. They were beautiful eyes – dark, expressive, and fringed with long black lashes. She would look up at a dinner or during a pageant and catch him watching her. He would always look away.

The next time they were alone together, it was because Serafina had found *him* hiding. She'd had another history conch to listen to and had managed to sneak away from her court to do it. The only problem was that someone had beaten her to her new hiding place. Mahdi was sitting there, in a copse of kelp, with a knife in one hand and a small, ivory-coloured object in the other. When he heard her approach, he tried to hide them.

'Can't you give me one moment's peace?' he'd asked wearily.

Serafina backed up. 'I'm sorry. I didn't mean to disturb you,' she said.

Mahdi's head snapped up at the sound of her voice. 'Oh, *no*,' he said. 'I'm sorry, Serafina. I thought you were Akmal. He never leaves me alone.'

'It's all right, Mahdi. I'll find somewhere else to—'

'No, wait, Serafina. *Please*.' He opened his hand, showing her the object he'd tried to hide. It was a tiny octopus, about three inches long, intricately carved from a piece of bone.

'It looks just like Sylvestre!' she exclaimed, delighted.

'That was the idea,' he said.

'It's *beautiful*, Mahdi!'

'Thank you,' he said, smiling shyly. 'Nobody knows I carve. I've managed to keep it a secret. I don't even know why I do it.' He looked away. 'It's just . . . sometimes you want one thing, just one thing—'

'—that's for yourself alone,' she finished.

It was as if they were seeing each other for the first time.

'I have that with Clio,' she said.

'Clio?'

'My hippokamp. I'm not allowed to ride by myself, being principessa and all. If I want to go out, I have to go with guards. But I always manage to get ahead of them and for a few moments, it's just Clio and me. All I hear is the sound of her fins beating the water. If a pod of dolphins swims by, I see it alone. If a whale passes by, I hear her song alone.' She smiled ruefully. 'Of course, if I fall off Clio and break my neck, I do that alone too.'

When she finished speaking, Mahdi took her hand and placed the little octopus in her palm. 'For you,' he said.

A few nights later, she had felt him take her hand again – this time in the dark, during a waterlights display in his honour. He'd looked at her, asking her with his dark eyes if it was all right. She'd answered him with hers that it was. And then, one evening while they were playing hide-and-seek with Desiderio, Neela, Yazeed, and the younger members of the court in the reggia, he'd suddenly pulled her deep into the tumbled ruins.

'I found you,' he said, as they floated close together in the water.

'No, Mahdi, that's *not* how the game works. Don't you have hide-and-seek in Matali? It's not your turn. Desiderio's it,' she'd said, keeping an eye out for her brother.

'I'm not talking about the game,' he said. 'I found *you*, Serafina. You're the one thing. The one thing for myself alone.' He'd pulled her to him then and kissed her.

It was so lovely, that kiss. Slow and sweet. Serafina sighed as she relived it – then turned bright red when she remembered Thalassa was watching the bloodsong too.

There were more kisses in the days that followed. Stolen behind pillars. Or in the stables. There were long talks when they could break away, smiles and glances when they couldn't. And then, as Mahdi was leaving Miromara to return home, he'd given Serafina a ring. It wasn't gold or some priceless crown jewel taken from the Matalin vaults. It was a simple band with a heart in the middle, carved from a white shell.

He'd made it for her, alone in his room at night. As he was saying his official goodbyes in front of the court, he'd bent to kiss her hand. While he was holding it, he'd slipped the ring on her finger.

'My choice,' he'd whispered to her. '*Mine*. Not theirs. I only hope that I'm yours, Serafina.'

At that, the bloodsong spiralled into the water and faded away, and with it went the past.

Thalassa looked at Serafina. 'And you *wonder* if he loves you, you silly merl?' she asked.

'I never used to, Magistra,' Serafina said. She told Thalassa about the private conches Mahdi had sent and how they'd suddenly stopped. 'I've had only a few official communications over the last year. Nothing else. And now . . .' Her voice trailed off.

Thalassa cocked her head. 'And now?' she prompted.

'And now he sounds like a very different merboy from the one I fell in love with. A merboy with long hair and an earring, according to Tavia. And a merlfriend, according to Lucia,' Serafina said unhappily.

'Lucia would say anything to upset you. You know that. She would love nothing more than to see you fail today, so you must triumph instead. Come, let's work on that trill again, and on the—'

They were interrupted by the sound of a door banging open.

'Serafeeeeeeeeeena!' a voice squealed.

Serafina spun around, startled. A mermaid floated in

the doorway to the antechamber. She was wearing a yellow sari. Her glossy jet-black hair hung down to her tail fin. Her skin was glowing a pretty pale blue. She was flanked by servants, who were buckling under the weight of the gilded boxes, beribboned clamshells, and gossamer sacks they were carrying.

'Great Neria, who on earth—' Thalassa started to say.

But Serafina recognized the mermaid instantly. 'Neeeeela!' she shouted, forgetting all her worries in the joy of seeing her best friend.

'Spongecake! There. You. *Are!*' Neela said. 'I brought you soooooo many presents!'

The two mermaids swam to each other and embraced, whirling around and around in the water, laughing. Neela was bright blue now. She was a bioluminescent, like a lantern fish or a bobtail squid. A bewitching light emanated from her skin when her emotions ran high, or when other bioluminescents were near.

'Princess Neela, you're *not* supposed to be here,' Thalassa scolded. 'We're right in the middle of songspell practice! How did you get in?'

'Tavia!' Neela said, grinning.

Thalassa frowned. 'How many bags of bingas did it take to bribe her *this* time?'

'Two,' Neela replied. 'Plus a box of zee zees.' She released Serafina, plucked a pretty pink box from a teetering pile, and swam to Thalassa. 'I'm so sorry to interrupt, Magistra, really. May I offer *you* a zee zee?' she asked, opening the box.

'You may not,' Thalassa said sternly. 'I know what you're up to. You can't bribe *me* with sweets.'

'A chilla, then? How about a shapta? You *can't* say no to a shapta. And these are the very best. They take the palace chefs three full days to make. They have eight layers and five different enchantments,' Neela said, popping one of the sweets into her mouth. 'Mmm! Krill with a caramalgae filling . . . *sooo* good! See?'

'What I see is that our minds are elsewhere at the moment.' Thalassa sniffed, taking a sweet from the box. 'You cannot stay long, you know, Princess Neela. Only a minute or two. We really *do* have to practise.'

'Of course, Magistra. Only a minute or two,' Neela said.

Thalassa, mollified, sampled the sweet. 'Oh. Oh, *my*. Is that curried kelp?'

Neela nodded. She handed her another. 'Beach plum with comb jellies and salted crab eggs. It's *invincible*.'

Thalassa bit into it. 'Oh, that *is* good,' she said. 'I suppose, perhaps half an hour's break might be in order,' she said, her fingers hovering over the box.

Neela gave it to her. As Thalassa called to her cuttlefish servants to bring her a pot of tea, Neela grabbed Serafina's hand, pulling her out of the antechamber and into a wide hallway with windows on both sides, all of which were open to let in fresh water.

'Tail slap, merl!' she whispered, closing the doors behind them. 'My evil plan succeeded. I thought you could use a break from practice.'

'You thought right,' Serafina said, grinning.

'Uh-oh. Opafago at twelve o'clock,' Neela said.

It was no Opafago, but a palace guard swimming towards them.

'Your Grace? Is there something wrong? You shouldn't be in the hallways unescorted,' the guard said.

Serafina groaned. Privacy, solitude, time alone with a friend. She dearly craved these things, but they were nearly impossible to find at the palace.

'Great whites at nine,' Neela whispered, nodding at the group of maids advancing with mops and buckets.

'Good morning, Your Graces, good morning,' the maids said, curtseying.

'A giant squid at six.'

That was Tavia. 'Serafina? Princess Neela? Why are you floating around in the hallway like common groupers?' She bustled towards them, glowering.

'We're surrounded, captain. I'm afraid there's only one way out of here,' Neela said under her breath.

Serafina giggled. 'You *cannot* be serious. We haven't done that since we were eight years old. And even then we got into trouble for it.'

'I call Jacquotte Delahaye,' Neela said.

'You *always* call Jacquotte!' Serafina protested. 'She's the *best* pirate!'

'Don't be such a baby. You can be Sayyida al Hurra.'

Neela swam to a window on the north side of the hallway. She narrowed her eyes at Serafina and said, 'Abandon ship!

Last one to the ruins is a landlubber!'

These were the exact words she'd said to Serafina when they were little, pretending to be pirate queens, and challenging each other to a race.

Serafina swam to a window on the south side. 'Eat my wake, bilge rat!'

'One . . . two . . . *three*!' the mermaids shouted together.

A split second later, Serafina and Neela dived out the palace windows and were gone.

# SEVEN

DETERMINED TO WIN THE RACE, Neela swooped around a spire, then dived. Hurtling down through the water, she shot under an archway, startling the Matali dignitaries coming the opposite way, and made for the ruins of Merrow's reggia. She was swimming way too fast, but she didn't care. It felt wonderful to slice through the water, to feel powerful and free.

Serafina had zipped around a turret and under a bridge and was now gaining on her. Neela put on a burst of speed, but Serafina caught up. They touched the front wall of the old palace – as much of it as was still standing – at the same time, then collapsed on a pile of red coral weed, laughing and out of breath.

'Beat you!' Neela shouted.

'You did *not*! It was a tie,' Serafina said.

'Yeah, except that I won.'

'I can't believe we dived out of windows. We're in so much trouble.'

Neela knew as well as Serafina did that swimming out of windows was bad form. Civilized mer came and went through doors. Aunt Ahadi would not be pleased.

'Yeah, we probably are, but it was worth it,' she said, pulling two sweets from her pocket. 'Here – purple sponge with pickled urchin. So good, you have no idea. Better than boys.'

'That good?' Serafina said, taking the sweet.

'Mmm-hmm,' Neela said, biting into hers. She was eating too many sweets. She did that when she was nervous. Like now. Sera was going to ask about him. That was a given. What on earth would she tell her?

Neela stretched out on the soft coral weed and stared up at the sun-dappled waters. 'It's so good to finally be here,' she said. 'The trip was totally nerve-racking. The dragons we rode spooked at every guppy. The sea elephants carrying our trunks bolted twice. I couldn't sleep, because I was having bad dreams the whole time.'

'Really? What kind of dreams?' Serafina asked.

'I can't even remember now,' Neela said. She *did* remember, but she didn't want to talk about them. They were silly. 'And Uncle Bilaal was *seriously* freaking out about Praedatori. He expected Kharkarias, their leader, to jump out at every turn. Even though he doesn't even know what Kharkarias looks like, since no one's ever seen him.'

'You weren't attacked, were you?' Serafina asked.

'No, we were fine. We had lots of guards with us. But I was so glad to see the spires of Cerulea last night, I can't even tell you.'

'I'm really happy you're here, Neela,' Serafina said. 'I can't imagine going through the Dokimí without you.'

Sera hadn't asked about him yet. Good. Maybe she could keep it that way. 'How's the songspell? Are you nervous? What are you wearing?' Neela asked.

'Not great. Very. I don't know,' Serafina said.

Neela sat up, startling some curious needlefish who'd come close. 'You don't *know* what you're wearing? How can you not know? Hasn't the Dokimí been planned for years?'

'My dress is a gift from Miromara. The best craftsmer in the realm work on it. Only my mother sees it in advance. And anyway, it's not *about* the dress,' Serafina said.

'It's *always* about the dress.'

'I'm casting a songspell, not competing in a beauty contest. This is serious, you know.'

'Merlfriend, *nothing* is more serious than a beauty contest. *Life* is beauty contest. At least that's what my mother always says,' Neela said. 'I can't wait for you to see what *I'm* wearing. It's totally invincible. It's a dark pink sari – the wrap is sea silk, but the top and skirt are made of thousands of tiny Anomia shells stitched onto tulle. I wanted it to be royal blue, but my aunt *insisted* on pink. I made it myself.'

'You did *not*.'

'I did. I swear it. But *shh*, don't tell anyone. You know how it is in Matali. Gods forbid a royal should actually *work* at anything,' Neela said unhappily.

'Trouble with your parents?' Serafina asked, her eyes full of concern.

'That's an understatement. We fought about it for weeks.

*Major* drama. I bet I ate twenty boxes of zee zees. In one day.'

Neela's dream was to become a designer, but her parents wouldn't allow that. Or anything else. She was a Matalin princess and Matalin princesses were to dress well, look decorative, and one day marry – and that was all. Neela wanted so much more, though. Colour made her heart beat faster. Fabric came alive in her hands. She had passion and talent and she wanted to use them.

Serafina took her hand. 'I'm sorry, Neels.'

'Oh, well. I can't ever be a designer, but I can pretend.'

'You *are* a designer,' Serafina said, suddenly fierce. 'Designers design. That's what you did. And it doesn't matter who likes it and who doesn't.'

Neela smiled. Sera was as loyal as a lionfish, quick to defend those she loved. It was one of the many reasons Neela adored her.

'I just hope Alítheia doesn't like pink. I don't want her thinking I look like a large and tasty zee zee,' said Neela. 'Is it true she's ten feet tall?'

'Yes.'

'Okay, like . . . *why*?'

'*Quia Merrow decrevit*. Because Merrow decreed it.'

'Why the long, tortuous songspell?'

'*Quia Merrow decrevit*.'

'Why a betrothal at sixteen? That's totally dark ages. Wait . . . don't tell me. Let me guess.'

'*Quia Merrow decrevit*.'

'But Merrow decreed it, like, *forty centuries ago*, Sera.

The tides have come in and gone out a few times since then, you know?'

'I do. Believe me, Neela, I've listened to so many conches on Atlantis and Merrow for various courses, and I still haven't figured out why she made all her weird decrees. The whole Dokimí thing is barbaric and backward. It's from a time when life expectancy was short and principessas had to be ready to rule at a young age,' Serafina said. 'The weirdest thing is, this ceremony declares me an adult, fit to rule, and yet I have no more idea about how to rule Miromara than I have about flying to the moon. I can't even rule my own court.' She sighed heavily.

'What? What's wrong?' Neela asked, her eyes searching Sera's.

'My court,' Serafina said, making a face. 'There's this one merl. . . . Her name's Lucia . . .'

'I remember her,' Neela said. 'The last time I was here, my skin had just started to glow. She told me I looked like fog light. In the nicest possible way, of course.'

'That sounds like Lucia,' Serafina said. 'Neela, she said some things, about Mahdi.'

*Oh, no*, Neela thought. *Time to change the subject*. 'Hey, you know what? Let's swim,' she said. 'Why don't we head into the ruins? Stretch our tails? We can talk as we go.'

Neela pulled Sera up from the coral weed and they set off, swimming, through what had once been a doorway. Time had crumbled its ancient arch. The walls of the old palace had tumbled down, and the roof along with them. Anemones, corals, and wrack had colonized the mosaic floors. In what had once been Merrow's Grand Hall, soaring blue quartz pillars still stood, hinting at lost glories.

'You should see the ruby necklace I'm wearing tonight. It's my mother's. It's completely invincible,' Neela said as they swam together. She was babbling, desperate to keep the conversation from veering back to Mahdi.

'How are your parents?' Serafina asked.

'Great! Fabulous! They send their best and wish they could be here. But somebody has to hold down the fort in Uncle Bilaal's absence.'

'And how are the emperor and empress? And your brother . . . and Mahdi?'

'Truly excellent. Although I haven't seen them yet today. We got in around eight last night. I was so tired, I went straight to my room and fell into bed. Everyone else did the same.'

'Neela . . .'

'Oh! Did I tell you about the *last* state visit we all made? Ha! It's *such* a funny story!' Neela said. She launched into all the details.

Serafina wasn't really listening, though. 'So, um, how's Mahdi?' she finally broke in.

Neela's heart sank. Her smile slipped.

Serafina stopped swimming. 'What is it?' she asked.

'Nothing,' Neela said brightly. 'Mahdi's fine.'

'He's *fine*? My great-aunt Berta is *fine*. What are you not telling me?'

Neela pulled another sweet from her pocket. 'Oh, *super* yum. Candied flatworm with eelgrass honey. Try it!' she said.

'*Neela!*'

'Well, he's probably a *little* bit different from what you remember,' she said. 'I mean, the last time you saw him was two years ago. We're *all* different than we were then.'

'Look, I know you're his cousin,' Serafina said. 'But you're also my friend. You *have* to tell me the truth.'

Neela sighed. 'All right, then – here it is: his royal Mahdiness seems to be going through a phase. At least, that's what Aunt Ahadi calls it. She blames it all on Yazeed.'

'Your brother? What does he have to do with it?'

'Yaz is a total party boy. Always the one with the lampfish on his head. My parents are at their wits' end and Aunt Ahadi is *furious*. She says he's led Mahdi astray. The two of them are out *all* the time. It started about a year ago. That's when they got their ears pierced. Aunt Ahadi went through the roof. She and my mother threatened to beach them for life.'

'That doesn't sound like the Mahdi I remember,' Serafina said, nervously fiddling with some trim on her dress. 'Neels, I have to ask you something else. Lucia said that—'

Neela unwrapped another sweet and bit into it. She made a face. 'Yuck. Fermented sea urchin.' She fed it to a passing damselfish.

'—she said that Mahdi has a merlfriend. She said he—' Serafina suddenly stopped speaking.

Neela, busy wiping her fingers on a frond of Caulerpa

weed, looked up. That's when she saw them. Bodies. Of two young mermen. They were stretched out under a huge coral at the back of the courtyard, motionless.

Serafina panicked. 'I – I can't tell if they're breathing or not. Neela, we have to get help. I think they're *dead*!' she said, swimming closer.

Neela panicked too, but for a totally different reason. 'No, they're not dead,' she said under her breath. 'But if Aunt Ahadi hears about this, they're going to *wish* they were.'

# EIGHT

NEELA CAUGHT UP to Serafina and grabbed her arm. 'Come on!' she said, trying to pull her away from the mermen. 'This is dangerous. We should get the palace guards.'

'But what if they're hurt or bleeding? We can't just leave them!'

'Yes, we can. We totally can.'

Serafina broke free of Neela's grip and swam back to the bodies. 'They're not dead! They're breathing and . . . *oh*. Wow. Didn't expect *that*.'

Neela closed her eyes. She pinched the bridge of her nose. *How could they be so stupid?* she wondered. *How?*

'Um, Neela? It's *Mahdi* . . .'

'. . . and Yazeed,' Neela said.

She looked down at them. The two merboys were lying on their backs. Mahdi had a purple scarf tied around his head and smudged lipstick kisses on his cheek. A gold hoop dangled from one ear. His black hair was pulled back in a hippokamp's tail. Yaz was wearing a pair of sparkly earrings. Someone had drawn a smiley face on his chest with lipstick.

He had a streak of pink in his cropped black hair, a heavy gold chain around his neck, and a tattoo on his arm. As she continued to stare at them, a large, homely humphead wrasse swam up to Yaz. It nudged his chin. Yaz flung an arm around it, pulled it close, and kissed it. As Mahdi snored on, Yazeed murmured compliments to the fish about her beautiful blonde hair.

Neela, livid, gave each boy a hard slap with her tail.

'Ow!' Mahdi cried.

'Dang, merl!' Yaz yelped, letting go of the fish. 'All I *said* was . . . *Neela*?' He blinked at his sister.

Mahdi, wincing at the light, said, 'Yaz, you squid! Where *were* you? I was waiting for you. I decided to hang here until you caught up. I must've fallen asleep. Why are you *always* the slowest common denominator?'

'Yazeed, take those stupid earrings off! And sit *up*, both of you!' Neela scolded. 'Serafina's here.'

Mahdi paled. 'What?' he said. 'Oh, *no*.' He sat up. 'Serafina? Is that you?'

'Nice to see you, too, Mahdi,' Serafina said.

Her voice was cool, but Neela could see the confusion in her eyes. She'd hoped to keep her cousin's foolishness a secret from Sera. She'd hoped he could behave during his stay. Apparently, that was too much to ask.

'Look, Serafina, I need to explain,' he started to say, getting up.

'Um, Mahdi? Are you *shimmering*?' Serafina asked.

'Hold on a minute . . . he's *shimmering*?' Neela said. She

swam up to Mahdi and looked him over, and then Yazeed. Parts of them were shimmering, other parts were completely see-through. She grabbed her brother's gold chain and pulled it over his head. A small whelk shell dangled from it. As she turned it over, two pink pearls fell out.

'Transparensea pearls,' she said. 'Let me guess . . . you two cast pearls last night, then snuck out of the palace. When you tried to sneak back in, all the doors were locked. The windows, too. So you spent the night here, passed out under a coral. The only question is: where did you go?'

'Nowhere,' Yazeed said innocently. 'Just out for a swim.'

'Oh, please. I bet you went to the Lagoon. You did, didn't you?' said Neela, crossing her arms over her chest.

Yazeed looked around, suddenly interested in the architecture.

Neela glanced at Sera again. Her friend's eyes were on the lipstick kisses on Mahdi's cheek. They travelled to the scarf on his head. It had an L embroidered on it. *L for Lucia*, Neela thought. Her heart clenched as she saw the hurt on Sera's face.

'You're really something, Mahdi,' she said angrily. 'We are guests of the Merrovingia – invited here for your betrothal, I might add – and you go shoaling?'

'We weren't *shoaling*. We were, um, attending a concert. Broadening our cultural horizons,' Yaz said.

Neela held up her hands. 'Just. Stop,' she said. She turned to her cousin, thumbed a smudge of lipstick off his cheek, and showed it to him. 'Broadening your horizons?'

Mahdi had the good grace to blush.

'Neela,' Serafina said in a small voice. 'I have to get back.'

But Neela didn't hear her. She was scolding her brother again.

As they continued to argue, Mahdi swam up to Serafina. 'Hey, Sera . . .' he said haltingly.

'Sorry, Mahdi. I have to go,' Serafina said.

'No, wait. Please. I'm sorry about this. Really. This is not how I thought we would meet again. I know how it looks, but things aren't what they seem,' he said.

Serafina smiled ruefully. 'I guess mermen aren't either.'

Mahdi flinched at that. 'Serafina,' he said, 'you don't know—'

'—*you*,' Serafina said. 'I don't know you, Mahdi. Not any more.'

'Serafina!' Yaz shouted. 'Help me *out*, merl! Tell Sue Nami here to cut me a break. All we did was hang out at the Corsair. The Dead Reckoners were playing. They're my favourite band. Mahdi's, too. We had to go. Otherwise, total FOMO.'

'FOMO?' Serafina echoed.

'Fear of Missing Out,' Yaz said.

'Don't encourage him, Sera. He thinks he's cool with his stupid gogg slang,' Neela said.

'We started dancing and some silly merls recognized Mahdi and went crazy and drew all over us with lipstick. Then some swashbucklers told us there was an all-night wave going on in Cerulea, so we swam back,' Yaz said. 'That's all that happened. I swear!'

'An all-night wave in the ruins of the reggia?' Neela said. 'Do you really expect us to believe that? It's a national monument!'

'Is *that* where we are? We're supposed to be in the Kolegio,' Yaz said. He gave Mahdi a look. 'Navigate much?'

Yaz was fibbing. Wildly. Neela was sure of it. He was trying to cover up whatever they'd really been doing.

'Look, I really do have to go,' Serafina said. She was good at hiding her feelings, but this time even she couldn't pretend.

'Wait, Sera,' Mahdi said, looking desperate. 'I'm *sorry*. You're hurt, I know you are—'

'Oh, no. I'm perfectly fine, Your Grace,' Serafina said, blinking back tears.

Mahdi shook his head. '*Your Grace?* Whoa, Sera, it's *me*.'

'Yes it is. I guess Lucia was right,' Sera said softly. She shook her head. 'Don't worry about it, Mahdi. I'm fine. I *would* be hurt . . . if I cared.'

# NINE

'GOOD MORNING, Your Grace!'

'Good morning, Principessa!'

'All good things to you on this happy day, Your Highness!'

In the Grand Hall, courtiers bowed and smiled. Serafina thanked them, accepting their good wishes graciously, but all the while, her tears were threatening to spill over. Her heart was broken. She'd given it to Mahdi, and he'd shattered it. He was not who she thought he was. He was careless and cruel and she never wanted to see him again.

Sera was swimming fast to her mother's stateroom, where the business of the realm was conducted, to tell her what had happened. She knew her betrothal was a matter of state, but surely, in this day and age, no one would expect her to pledge herself to someone like Mahdi.

As she arrived at the stateroom, her mother's guards bowed and pulled the huge doors open for her. Three of the room's four walls were covered floor to ceiling in shimmering mother-of-pearl. Adorning them were tall pietra dura panels – ornately pieced insets of amber, quartz, lapis, and malachite depicting the realm's reginas. Twenty massive blown-glass chandeliers hung from the ceiling. Each was eight feet in diameter and contained thousands of tiny lava globes. At the far end, a single throne, fashioned in the shape of a sea fan and made of gold, towered on an amethyst dais. The wall behind it was covered in costly mirror glass.

The stateroom was empty, which meant Isabella was probably in her presence chamber, working. Serafina was glad of that. She might actually be able to have her mother to herself for five minutes.

The presence chamber was a much smaller room. Spare and utilitarian, it was furnished with a large desk, several chairs, and had shelves stuffed with conches containing everything from petitions to minutes of Parliament. Only Isabella's family and her closest advisers were allowed inside it. As Serafina approached the door, she could see that it was slightly ajar. She was just about to rush in, sobs already rising in her throat, when the sound of voices stopped her.

Her mother *wasn't* alone. Sera peeked through the crack and saw her uncle Vallerio and a handful of high-ranking ministers. Conte Orsino, the minister of defence, was staring at a map on the wall. It showed Miromara, an empire that swept from the Straits of Gibraltar in the west, across the Mediterranean Sea, to the Black Sea in the east.

'I don't know if this has anything to do with the recent raids, Your Grace, but a trawler was sighted in the Venetian Gulf just this morning. One of Mfeme's,' said Orsino. He looked haggard and bleary-eyed, as if he hadn't slept.

Vallerio, who was staring out of a window, his hands clasped behind his back, swore at the mention of the name *Mfeme*.

Serafina knew it; everyone in Miromara did. Rafe Iaoro Mfeme was a terragogg. He ran a fleet of fishing boats. Some were bottom trawlers – vessels that dragged huge heavy nets over the seafloor. They caught great quantities of fish and destroyed everything in their paths, including coral reefs that were hundreds of years old. Others were long-line vessels. They cast out lines fitted with hooks that ran through the water for miles. The lines killed more than fish. They hooked thousands of turtles, albatrosses, and seals. Mfeme didn't care. His crew hauled the lines in and tossed the drowned creatures overboard like garbage.

'I don't think the trawler has anything to do with the raids,' Isabella said. 'The raiders took every single soul in the villages, but left the buildings undamaged. Mfeme's nets would have destroyed the buildings, too.' Her voice sounded strained. Her face looked troubled and tired.

'We've also had reports of Praedatori in the area of the raids,' Orsino said.

'The Praedatori take valuables, not people. They're a small band of robbers. They don't have the numbers to raid entire villages,' Isabella said dismissively.

Sera wondered how she knew that. The Praedatori were so shadowy, no one knew much about them.

'It's not Mfeme, either. He's a gogg. We have protective spells against his kind,' Vallerio said. He'd left his place by the window and was swimming to and fro, barely containing his anger. 'It's Ondalina. Kolfinn's the one behind the raids.'

'You don't know that, Vallerio,' Isabella said. 'You have no proof.'

Glances were traded between ministers. Serafina knew that her mother and uncle rarely agreed.

'Have you forgotten that Admiral Kolfinn has broken the permutavi?' Vallerio asked.

The permutavi was a pact between the two waters enacted after the War of Reykjanes Ridge. It decreed an exchange of the rulers' children. Isabella and Vallerio's younger brother, Ludovico, had been sent to Ondalina ten years ago in exchange for Kolfinn's sister, Sigurlin. Desiderio was supposed to have gone to Ondalina, and Astrid, Kolfinn's teenage daughter, was to have come to Miromara. Inexplicably, the admiral sent a messenger one week before the exchange was to have occurred to say that he was not sending her.

'In addition,' Vallerio continued, 'my informants tell me Kolfinn's spies have been spotted in the Lagoon.'

'Kolfinn has not yet informed us why he broke the permutavi. There may be an explanation,' Isabella said. 'And Ondalinian spies in the Lagoon are nothing new. Every realm sends spies to the Lagoon. *We* send spies to the—'

Vallerio cut her off. 'We must declare war and we must do it *now*. Before we are attacked. I've been saying this for weeks, Isabella.'

Serafina shivered at her uncle's words.

Isabella leaned forward in her chair. 'Desiderio sent a messenger with word that he's seen nothing – no armies, no artillery, not so much as a single Ondalinian soldier. I hesitate to declare war based on such flimsy accusations and without convening the Council of the Six.'

Vallerio snorted. 'You hesitate to declare war? You *hesitate*? Hesitate much longer, and the Council of Six will be a Council of Five!'

'I will *not* be pushed, Vallerio! *I* rule here. You would do well to remember that. I am not concerned with my life, but with the lives of my merfolk, many of which will be sacrificed if war breaks out!' Isabella shouted.

'*When* war breaks out!' Vallerio thundered back at her. He turned and smacked a large shell off a table in his anger. It shattered against a wall.

It was silent in the chamber. Isabella glared at Vallerio and Vallerio glared back.

Conte Bartolomeo, the oldest of Isabella's advisers, rose from his chair. He'd been refereeing these shouting matches since Isabella and Vallerio were children. 'If I may ask, Your Grace,' he said to Isabella, attempting to defuse the tension, 'how are the preparations for the Dokimí progressing?'

'Very well,' Isabella replied curtly.

'And the songspell? Has the principessa mastered it?'

'Serafina will not let Miromara down.'

Bartolomeo smiled. 'Is the principessa happy with the

match? Is she in love with the crown prince? From what I understand, every female in Miromara is.'

'Love comes in time,' Isabella replied.

'For some. For others, it does not come at all,' Vallerio said brusquely.

Isabella's face took on a rueful expression. 'You should have married, brother. Years ago. You should have found yourself a wife.'

'I would have, if the one I wanted hadn't been denied me. I hope Serafina finds happiness with the crown prince,' he said.

'I hope so too,' Isabella said. 'And, more importantly, as a leader of her people.'

'It's those very people you must think of *now*, Isabella. I beg you,' Vallerio said. The urgency had returned to his voice.

Serafina bit her lip. Though they fought constantly, her mother prized his advice above everyone else's.

'What if I'm right about Ondalina?' he asked. 'What if I'm right and you're wrong?'

'Then the gods have mercy on us,' Isabella said. 'Give me a few days, Vallerio. Please. We are a small realm, the smallest in all the waters. You know that. If we are to declare war, we must be sure of the Matalis.'

'Are we not sure of them? The Dokimí is tonight. When Serafina and Mahdi are united, their realms will be united. Their vows cannot be broken.'

'As I'm sure you recall, the betrothal negotiations with

Bilaal were long and hard. I suspect Kolfinn may have been negotiating with him at the same time on behalf of his daughter,' Isabella said. 'The Elder of Qin, too, for his granddaughter. Who knows what *they* offered him. Their ambassadors are here at court to witness the ceremony. For all I know, they're *still* making offers. Until a thing is done, it is not done. I won't rest easy until Sera and Mahdi have exchanged their vows.'

'And once they do, then you'll declare war?'

'Only if by so doing, I can avoid it. If we declare war on Ondalina by ourselves, Kolfinn won't so much as blink. If we do it with the Matalis' support, he'll turn tail.'

Serafina remembered her mother's visit to her room earlier. Now it took on new meaning. *That's* why she'd been so worried about her songspell, and why'd she'd said they desperately needed an alliance with Matali. They needed it to avoid a war with Ondalina. Or to win one.

Moments ago, Serafina had been desperate to see her mother. Now she was desperate to slip away without being seen.

Isabella worked tirelessly on behalf of her subjects, always putting their welfare ahead of her own, always stoically bearing the burdens and heartaches that came with wearing the crown. Sera could only imagine what her mother would have said if she'd barged into her chamber complaining that Mahdi had hurt her feelings.

She had to do it. She had to put her pain and loss aside and exchange vows with a merman she couldn't even bear to look at, in order to save her people from a war. That's what her mother would do, and that's what she would do, too.

*I always disappoint her*, Serafina thought, *but tonight I won't. Tonight, I'll make her proud*.

# TEN

'YOU'RE TUBE WORMS. Both of you. No, actually, *tube worms* doesn't do you justice. *Lumpsuckers* would be better,' Neela hissed. 'Mollusks. Total guppies.'

'*Shh!*' Empress Ahadi said. 'Sit still and be quiet!'

Neela was quiet for all of two seconds, then she poked Mahdi in the back.

'You don't deserve her. She's way too good for you. I wouldn't be surprised if she's a no-show. *I* wouldn't get betrothed to you.'

'I'll talk to her after the ceremony. I'll explain,' Mahdi said.

Neela rolled her eyes. '"Hey, Mahdi, good idea!" said no one ever.'

'Do I have to separate you like little children? The ceremony is about to start!' Empress Ahadi scolded.

Neela, Yazeed, Mahdi, and the rest of the Matalin royal party were seated in the royal enclosure inside the Kolisseo, a huge open-water stone theatre that dated back to Merrow's time.

Isabella and Bilaal sat together in the front of the enclosure on two silver thrones. The regina was spectacular in a jewelled golden crown, her long black hair coiled at the nape of her neck. A ceremonial breastplate made of blue abalone shells covered her torso and gossamer skirts of indigo sea silk billowed out below it. Emperor Bilaal was splendid in a yellow high-collared jacket and a fuchsia turban studded with pearls, emeralds, and – in the centre – a ruby as big as a caballabong ball.

Serafina's father, Principe Consorte Bastiaan, and her uncle, Principe del Sangue Vallerio, sat directly behind Isabella. There was no re, or king, in Miromara. The regina was the highest authority. Males could be princes of the blood if they were sons of a regina, or prince consorts if they married one.

And in front of them all, on a stone dais, was a circlet of hammered gold embedded with pearls, emeralds, and red coral – Merrow's crown. It was ancient and precious, a hallowed symbol of the unbroken rule of the Merrovingia.

The empress and crown prince sat directly behind Bilaal. Neela and Yazeed were behind them. Fanning out from the royal enclosure were the Miromaran magi – Thalassa, the canta magus, the keeper of magic; Fossegrim, the liber magus, the keeper of knowledge – and the realm's powerful duchessas. Neela recognized Portia Volnero. She knew Sera's uncle had been in love with her once. She could see why: Portia, dressed in regal purple, with her long auburn hair worn loose and flowing, was stunning. Lucia Volnero was there too, drawing every eye in a shimmering gown of silver.

Behind the duchessas sat the rest of the court – hundreds of nobles, ministers, and councillors, all in their costly robes of state. It was a sumptuous spectacle of power and wealth.

'Where's Sera?' Yazeed whispered.

'She's not in the Kolisseo yet. The Janiçari bring her here for the blooding, the first test,' Neela replied.

She looked out over the amphitheatre. Along its perimeter, the flags of Miromara and Matali fluttered in the night currents – Miromara's coral branch and Matali's dragon rampant, with its silver-blue egg. She knew the dragon depicted was a deadly razormouth, and that its egg was actually an ugly brown. The flag's designer, she guessed, had thought the egg too ugly and had changed it to silver-blue.

Every seat in the Kolisseo was taken and a tense, expectant energy filled the water. White lava illuminated the dark waters. It boiled and spat inside glass globes that had been set into large whelk shells and placed in wall mounts. To obtain the lava, magma was channelled from deep seams under the North Sea by goblin miners, the fractious Feuerkumpel, one of the Kobold tribes. It was refined and whitened, then poured into glass tough enough to withstand its lethal heat by goblin glassblowers, the equally unpleasant Höllebläser.

In the lava's glow, Neela could see the faces of the crowd. Many were excited. Others looked nervous, even fearful. *With good reason*, she thought. Generations of young mermaids had been crowned heiress to the Miromaran throne here, but others – impostors all – had died agonizing deaths. Her eyes flickered to the heavy iron grille that covered a cavernous opening in the floor of the Kolisseo. Twenty brawny mermen stood by it, wearing armour and holding shields. Fear's icy fingers squeezed her heart as she tried to imagine what lurked underneath it.

*Serafina must be terrified*, she thought. *She's right – this is a barbaric ceremony*. It was hard to reconcile the Miromarans, a people so cultured and refined, with such a gruesome ritual.

'It's about to start!' Yazeed exclaimed. 'I hear music! Look, Neela!'

He pointed to the archway on the opposite side of the Kolisseo. A hush fell over the crowd as a merman, grand and majestic, emerged from it. He moved at a stately pace, his red robes flowing behind him. A matching turban with a narwhal's tusk protruding from it graced his head. A scimitar, its gold hilt encrusted with jewels, hung from his belt.

Neela knew he was the Mehterbaşi, leader of the Janiçari, Isabella's personal guard. Fierce fighters from the waters off Turkey's southern coast, they wore breastplates made of blue crab shells and osprey-skull epaulets. A line of orca's teeth ran across the top of each of their bronze helmets.

The Janiçari followed their leader out of the archway, swimming in tight formation. Some played boru – long, thin trumpets. Others played the davul – bass drums made from giant clamshells. The rest sang of the bravery of their regina in deep, rumbling voices. It was an immense sound, intended to terrify Miromara's enemies. Neela thought it did the job well.

After twenty lines of Janiçari had marched into the

Kolisseo, another figure – one very different from the fearsome soldiers – appeared in the archway.

'Oh, doesn't Sera look gorgeous!' Neela whispered.

'Merl's so hot, she melts my face off,' Yazeed said.

'Wow. That's appropriate, Yaz,' said Neela.

Mahdi stared silently.

Serafina sat sidesaddle atop a graceful grey hippokamp. She wore a simple gown of pale green sea silk. The colour, worn by mer brides, symbolized her bond with her people, her future husband, and the sea. Over the gown, she wore an exquisite brocade mantle, the same deep green as her eyes. It was richly embroidered with copper thread and studded with red coral, pearls, and emeralds – the jewels of Merrow's crown. Her copper-brown hair floated around her shoulders. Her head was unadorned. Her face, with its high cheekbones, was elegant and fine. *But it's her eyes that make her truly beautiful*, Neela thought. They sparkled with intelligence and humour, darkened with doubt sometimes, and shone in their depths with love. No matter how hard she tried to hide it.

The second the Miromarans spotted her, they were out of their seats and cheering. The noise rolled over the amphitheatre like a storm. Serafina, solemn as the occasion demanded, kept her eyes straight ahead.

The Mehterbaşi reached the base of the royal enclosure and stopped. His troops – with Serafina in the midst of them – followed suit. He struck his chest with his fist, then saluted his regina. It was a gesture of both love and respect. In perfect unison, all five hundred Janiçari did the same. Isabella struck her chest and saluted back, and another cheer went up. The boru players blew loud blasts.

Serafina's hippokamp didn't like the noise. She pawed at the water with her front hooves and thrashed her serpentine tail. Her eyes, yellow and slitted like a snake's, shifted nervously.

As Serafina calmed her, the Mehterbaşi turned to his troops and raised his scimitar, then sliced it through the water. As he did, the Janiçari moved forward, splitting their formation in the middle, so that half marched to the right, and half to the left. When they had ringed the amphitheatre, the Mehterbaşi sheathed his scimitar, swam to Serafina, and helped her dismount. She removed her mantle and handed it to him. She would face Alítheia in only her dress. It would be her coronation gown or her shroud.

The Mehterbaşi handed her his scimitar, then led her hippokamp away. Serafina was alone in the centre of the amphitheatre. When the cheers died down she spoke, her voice ringing out over the ancient stones.

'Citizens of Miromara, esteemed guests, most gracious regina, I come before you tonight to declare myself of the blood, a daughter of Merrow, and heiress to the Miromaran throne.'

Isabella, regal atop her throne, spoke next. 'Beloved subjects, we the mer are a people born of destruction. In Atlantis's end was our beginning. For four thousand years we have endured. For four thousand years, the Merrovingia have ruled Miromara. We have kept you safe, worked tirelessly to see you prosper. Descended from the one who made us all, we are bound heart and soul, by oath and by blood, to carry on her rule. I give you my only daughter, this child of my body and of my heart, but I cannot give you your heiress. Only Alítheia can do this. What say you, good people?'

The Miromarans erupted into cheering again.

Isabella took a deep breath. Her back was straight. Her manner calm. But Neela could see her hands shaking. 'Release the anarachna!' she commanded.

'What's happening?' Yazeed whispered.

'This is the blooding, the first part of the Dokimí,' Neela explained. 'Where we find out if Serafina truly is a descendent of Merrow.'

'What if she's not?' Yazeed asked.

'Don't say that, Yaz,' Mahdi said. 'Don't even think it.'

Neela looked at him and saw that his hands were knotted into fists.

The armoured mermen posted around the iron grille in the centre of the amphitheatre worked together to raise it. Heavy chains were attached to thick iron loops on its front edge. The mermen heaved at the chains and, little by little, the grille lifted. Finally, it swung back on its hinges and clanged down loudly against the stone floor. A few seconds went by, then a few minutes. Nothing happened. The Miromarans, restless and tense, murmured among themselves. A few, very daring or very stupid, called the anarachna's name.

'Who are they calling?' Yazeed asked. 'What's in the hole?'

Neela had studied up on the Dokimí ceremony. She leaned in close to him to tell him what she'd learned. 'When Merrow was old and close to death,' she explained, 'she wanted to make sure only her descendants ruled Miromara. So she asked the goddess of the sea, Neria, and Bellogrim, the god of fire, to forge a creature of bronze.'

'Duh, Neels. I know that much. I'm not dumb.'

'That's highly debatable,' Neela said. 'When the Feuerkumpel were smelting the ore for the creature, Neria brought the dying Merrow to their blast furnace. As soon as the molten metal was ready, she slashed Merrow's palm and held it over the vat so the creature would have the blood of Merrow in her veins and know it from impostors' blood. Neria waited until the bronze was cast and had cooled, and then she herself breathed life into Alítheia.'

'Wow,' Yazeed said.

'Yeah,' Neela said. She looked at Mahdi. All the colour had drained from his face. He seemed positively ill.

Yazeed noticed too. He leaned forward. 'Mahdi, you squid! I *told* you to lay off the sand worms last night. They were way too spicy. Are you going to hurl? Want my turban?'

'I'm cool,' Mahdi said.

But he didn't look cool. Not at all, Neela thought. His eyes were rooted on Sera. His hand was on the scimitar at his side. He was tense, as if he was ready to spring out of his seat at any second.

A roar – high, thin, and metallic – suddenly shook the amphitheatre. It sounded like a ship's hull being torn apart on jagged rocks. An articulated leg, dagger-sharp at its tip, arched up out of the hole and pounded down against the stones. It was followed by another, and another. A head appeared. The creature hissed, baring curved, foot-long fangs. A gasp – part awe, part horror – rose from the crowd as it crawled all the way out of the hole.

'No. Possible. *Way*,' Yazeed said. 'M, are you seeing this? Because if you're not, then I'm, like, completely insane.'

'Sera, *no*,' Mahdi said.

Yazeed shook his head. 'I can't *believe* that thing's Ala . . . Alo . . .'

'A-LEE-thee-a,' Neela said. 'Greek for—'

'Big, ugly, scary monster sea spider,' Yaz said.

'—*truth*,' Neela said.

The creature reared, clawing at the water with her front legs. A drop of amber venom fell from her fangs. Eight black eyes looked around the amphitheatre – and came to rest upon her prey.

'Imposssstor,' she hissed.

At Serafina.

# ELEVEN

*QUIA MERROW DECRIVIT.*

*But how?* Serafina wondered desperately. How could she have done this? How could she have forced all those who came after her to endure this?

Looking up at the massive creature, its bronze body blackened by time, Serafina was certain she would collapse from terror.

'You fear me! As you ssssshould. I will have your blood, imposssstor. I will have your bonessss. . . .'

Alítheia scuttled towards her, her body low to the ground, her horrible black eyes glittering.

Serafina stifled a cry. In her head, she heard Tavia's voice, telling her the story of a treacherous contessa who'd lived hundreds of years ago. The contessa had stolen the real principessa when she was newly born, and put her own infant daughter – enchanted to look like the principessa – in her place. The young mermaid herself, the regina, and everyone else in Miromara believed she was the true principessa – everyone but Alítheia. She'd sunk her fangs into the mermaid's neck and dragged the poor impostor into her den. Her body was never recovered.

'We never know who we are, child, until we're tested,' Tavia had said.

*What if I'm not who I think I am?* Serafina asked herself. She imagined Alítheia's fangs sinking into her own neck, and being dragged off, half alive, to the creature's den.

The spider skittered over the stones. She was only yards away now.

'No heiresssss are you. . . . Ussssurper are you. . . . Death to all pretendersssss. . . .'

She circled, coming closer and closer, then lowered her head until her terrible fangs were only inches from Serafina's face. Another drop of venom fell on the stones.

'Who are you, imposssstor?'

Serafina felt her courage falter. She backed away from the creature, turning her eyes from its awful face. As she did, her gaze fell upon the mer seated in the amphitheatre – thousands and thousands of them. She was their principessa, her mother's only daughter. If she failed them, if she swam away like a coward, who would lead them when her mother's time was done? Who would protect them as fiercely as Isabella had?

And suddenly she knew the answer to the creature's question. And the knowledge filled her with new courage and with strength. Bravely, Serafina faced the spider. 'I am *theirs*, Alítheia,' she said. 'I am my people's. That's who I am.'

She raised the scimitar the Mehterbaşi had given her and

drew its blade across her palm. It bit into her flesh. Blood plumed from the wound. She raised her bleeding hand, palm up. The spider advanced.

'I am Serafina, daughter of Isabella, a princess of the blood. Declare me so.'

Alítheia hissed. She pressed her bristly palps against the wound and tasted Serafina's blood. And then she reared up, screaming in rage. She spun away from Serafina and slammed her legs down, cracking the stones beneath her. 'No flesshhhh for Alítheia! No bonesss for Alítheia!' she howled.

She scuttled around the amphitheatre, menacing her keepers, trying to crawl over them and get at the Miromarans. The merpeople screamed and rushed from their seats, but the keepers held her back by brandishing lava globes. The white, molten rock, hot enough to melt bronze, was the only thing in the world the spider feared.

'Alítheia!' a voice called out loudly. It was Isabella. 'Alítheia, hear me!'

The spider sullenly turned to her.

'What is your decree?'

Not a sound was heard. It was as if the sea itself was holding its breath. The spider crawled to the royal enclosure and took Merrow's crown in her fangs. She returned to Serafina and placed it upon her head. Then she bent her front legs in a bow, and said, 'Hail, Sssssserafina, daughter of Merrow, princesssss of the blood, rightful heiressssss to the throne of Miromara.'

Serafina made a deep curtsey to her mother. The cheer that went up was deafening. After a moment, she rose, carefully balancing Merrow's crown. It was heavier than she'd expected. Her heart was still hammering from her encounter with Alítheia, and her palm was throbbing, but she felt proud and exhilarated.

All around the amphitheatre, the merfolk rose, still cheering. In the royal enclosure, Isabella and Bilaal rose, and the rest of the royal party followed their example. A bright flash of blue caught Serafina's eye.

It was Mahdi. He was wearing a turquoise silk jacket and a red turban. It killed her to admit it, but he was so handsome. She'd seen his face in her dreams for the last two years. It was different from what she'd remembered. Older. More angular. He caught her eye and smiled. It was beautiful, his smile. But it was a little bit awkward, too. A little bit goby. In that smile, Serafina saw the Mahdi she'd once known.

It made her heart ache to see that Mahdi. Where had he gone?

She didn't have long to dwell on that question, or the sadness it made her feel. The boru players blew a fanfare. The Mehterbaşi swam to her with her mantle and helped her back into it. Then he wrapped a bandage around her wounded hand.

The blooding was over. She knew what came next – the second of her tests, the casting. Her stomach squeezed with apprehension. This was the moment she'd worked so hard for, the moment when talent, study, and practice came together.

Or didn't.

# TWELVE

NOW SERAFINA cleared her mind, of everyone and everything except for music and magic.

Magic depended on so many things – the depth of one's gift, experience, dedication, the position of the moon, the rhythm of the tides, the proximity of whales. It didn't settle until one was fully grown; Serafina knew that. But she needed it to be with her now, and she prayed to the gods that it would be.

Taking a deep breath, she pulled on everything strong and sure inside of her, and started to sing. Her voice was high and clear and carried beautifully through the water. She sang a simple, charming welcome to the Matalis, telling them how happy Miromara was to receive them. When she finished, she bent to the ground, scooped up a handful of silt, and threw it above her head. *Nihil ex nihil.* That was the first rule of sea magic: *Nothing comes from nothing*. Magic needed matter.

Serafina's voice caught the silt as it rose in the water, moulded it, and then embellished it with colour and light, until it took on the appearance of a lush island with bustling ports, palaces, and temples. She enlarged the image until it filled the amphitheatre. Next, she summoned a shoal of small, silver fish. These she transformed into the island's inhabitants and as she did, her image became a living tableau.

The island, she told her listeners, was the ancient empire of Atlantis, nestled in the Aegean Sea. Its people were the ancestors of the mer. It was their story she sang now. Her voice was not the most beautiful in the realm, nor the most polished, but it was pure and true, and it held her listeners spellbound.

Using her magic, she showed how humans from all over the world: artists, scholars, doctors, scientists – the best and brightest of their day – had come to Atlantis. She showed farmers in their fields, sailors on their ships, merchants in their storehouses – all prosperous and peaceful. She sang of the island's powerful mages – the Six Who Ruled: Orfeo, Merrow, Navi, Pyrra, Sycorax, and Nyx. She sang of its glory and its might.

And then she sang of the catastrophe.

Heavy with emotion, her voice swooped into a minor key, telling how Atlantis was destroyed by a violent earthquake. Pulling light from above, pushing and bending water, conjuring images, she portrayed the island's destruction – the earth cracking apart, the lava pouring from its wounds, the shrieks of its people.

She sang of Merrow, and how she saved the Atlanteans by calling them into the water and beseeching Neria to help them. As the dying island sank beneath the waves, the goddess transformed its terrified people and gave them sea magic.

They fought her at first, struggling to keep their heads above water, to breathe air, screaming as their legs knit together and their flesh sprouted fins. As the sea pulled them under, they tried to breathe water. It was agony. Some could do it. Others could not, and the waves carried their bodies away.

Serafina let the images of a ruined Atlantis fall through the water and fade. Then she tossed another handful of silt up, and conjured a new image – of Miromara.

*Show them your heart*, Thalassa had told her. She would. Miromara *was* her heart.

With joy, she sang of those who survived and how they made Merrow their ruler. She sang of Miromara and how it became the first realm of the merfolk. Her voice soared, gliding up octaves, hitting each note perfectly. She was conjuring images of the mer, showing them in all their beauty – some with the sleek, silver scales of a mackerel, some with the legs of crabs or the armoured bodies of lobsters, others with the tails of sea horses or the tentacles of squids. She sang of Neria's gifts: canta mirus and canta prax.

She showed how the merfolk of Miromara spread out into all the waters of the world, salt and fresh. Some – longing for the places they'd left when still human to journey to Atlantis – returned to the shores of their native lands and founded new realms: Atlantica; Qin in the Pacific Ocean; the rivers, lakes, and ponds of the Freshwaters; Ondalina in the Arctic waters; and the Indian Ocean empire of Matali.

Then Serafina pulled rays of sun through the water, rolled them into a sphere, and tossed it onto the seafloor. When the sunsphere landed, it exploded upward into a golden blaze of light. As the glittering pieces of light descended, she depicted Matali, and told its history, showing it from its beginnings as a small outpost off the Seychelle Islands to an empire that encompassed the Indian Ocean, the Arabian Sea, and the Bay of Bengal.

She sang of the friendship between Miromara and Matali and conjured dazzling images of the emperor and empress, praising them for their just and enlightened rule. Then, though it pained her deeply, she showed herself and Mahdi, floating together in ceremonial robes, as they would be shortly to exchange their betrothal vows, and expressed her hope that they would rule both realms as wisely as their parents had, putting the happiness and well-being of their people above all else.

The images faded and fell, like the embers of fireworks in a night sky. Serafina remained still as they did, her chest rising and falling, and then she finished her songspell as she had begun it – with no images, no effects, just her voice asking the gods to ensure that the friendship between the two waters endured forever. Finally, she bent her head, as a sign of respect to all assembled, to the memory of Merrow, and to the sea itself – the endless, eternal deep blue.

It was so quiet as Serafina bowed that one could've heard a barnacle cough.

*Too quiet*, she thought, her heart sinking. *Oh, no. They hated it!*

She lifted her head, and as she did, a great, roiling sound

rose. A joyous noise. Her people were cheering her, even more loudly than they had after the blooding. They'd abandoned all decorum and were tossing up their hats and helmets. Serafina looked for her mother. Isabella was applauding too. She was smiling. Her eyes were shining. There was no disappointment on her face, only pride.

She remembered her mother's words to her uncle in the presence chamber. *Serafina won't let Miromara down. . . .*

As the mer continued to cheer for her, Serafina's heart felt so full she thought it would burst. She felt as if she could float along, buoyed up by the love of her people, forever.

She would remember that moment for a long time, that golden, shining, moment. The moment before everything changed.

Before the arrow, sleek and black, came hurtling through the water and lodged in her mother's chest.

# THIRTEEN

SERAFINA WAS FROZEN IN PLACE.

Her mother's chest was heaving; the arrow was moving with every breath she took. It had shattered her breastplate and pierced her left side. Isabella touched her fingers to the wound. They came away crimson. The sight of blood – on her mother's hand, dripping down her skirt – broke Serafina's trance.

'*Mum!*' she screamed, lurching towards her, but it was too late. Janiçari had already encircled her. They were shielding Serafina from harm, but also preventing her from getting to her mother. 'Let me go!' she cried, trying to fight her way through them.

She heard the shouts of merpeople, felt bodies thrashing in the water. The spectators were in a frenzy of fear – swimming into one another, pushing and shoving. Children, separated from their parents, were screaming in terror. A little girl was knocked down. A boy was battered by a lashing tail.

Unable to break through the Janiçari, Serafina pressed her face between two of them and glimpsed her mother. Isabella was still staring down at the arrow in her side. The Janiçari were trying to surround her as they had Serafina, but she angrily ordered them to leave her and go to the Matalis. With a swift, merciless motion, she pulled the arrow out of her body and threw it down. Blood pulsed from her wound, but there was no fear on her face – only a terrible fury.

'Coward!' she shouted, her fierce voice rising above the cries of the crowd. 'Show yourself!'

She swam above the royal enclosure, whirling in a circle, her eyes searching the Kolisseo for the sniper. 'Come out, bottom-feeder! Finish your work! *Here* is my heart!' she cried, pounding her chest.

Serafina was frantic, expecting another arrow to come for her mother at any second.

'I am Isabella, ruler of Miromara! And I will *never* be frightened by sea scum who strike from the shadows!'

'Isabella, take cover!' someone shouted. Serafina knew that voice; it was her father's. She spotted him. He was looking straight up. '*No!*' he shouted.

He shot out of the royal enclosure, a coppery blur. A split second later, he was swimming up over the amphitheatre – between his wife and the merman in black above her who was holding a loaded crossbow.

The assassin, barely visible in the darker waters, fired. The arrow buried itself in Bastiaan's chest. He was dead by the time his body hit the seafloor.

Serafina felt as if someone had just reached inside her and torn out her heart. 'Father!' she screamed. She clawed at the

Janiçari, trying to get to her father, but they held her fast.

More Janiçari, led by Vallerio, surrounded Isabella. The Mehterbaşi had ordered another group to the royal enclosure, where they'd encircled the Matalis and the court.

'*Bakmak! Bakmak!*' the Mehterbaşi shouted. *Look up!*

Out of the night waters descended more mermen in black, hundreds of them, riding hippokamps and carrying crossbows. They fired on the royal enclosure and on the people. Janiçari raced through the water to fight them off, but they were no match for their crossbows.

'To the palace!' Vallerio shouted. 'Get everyone inside! *Go!*'

Two guards took Serafina by her arms and swam her out of the Kolisseo at breakneck speed. Two more swam above them, shielding her. In only seconds, they were back inside the city walls and safely under the thicket of Devil's Tail. They continued on to the palace. When they reached the Regina's Courtyard, the guards broke formation and hurried her inside.

Conte Orsino, the minister of defence, was waiting for her. 'This way, Principessa. Hurry,' he said. 'Your mother's been taken to her stateroom. Your uncle wants you there too. It's the centremost room of the palace and the most defensible.'

'Sera!' a voice cried out. It was Neela. She'd just swum inside the palace. She was upset and glowing a deep, dark blue.

Sera threw her arms around her and buried her face in

her shoulder. 'Oh, Neela,' she said, her voice breaking. 'My father . . . he's *dead*! My mother . . .'

'I'm sorry, Principessa, but we must go. It's not safe here,' Orsino said.

Neela took Serafina's hand. Orsino led the way.

As they swam, Serafina realized Neela was alone. 'Where's Yazeed?' she asked.

Neela shook her head. 'I don't know. He and Mahdi . . . they swam away. I'm not sure where they are.'

*They swam away?* Sera thought, stunned. While her mother, bleeding and in pain, was daring her attacker to come forward? And her father was sacrificing his life?

'Bilaal and Ahadi? Are they safe?' she asked.

'I haven't seen them,' Neela said. 'Everything happened so fast.'

The wide coral hallways of the palace, the long, narrow tunnels between floors – they had never seemed so endless to Serafina. She swam through them as quickly as she could, dodging dazed and wounded courtiers. As she neared the stateroom, she heard screams coming from it.

'*Mum!*' she cried. Pushing her way savagely through the crowd, she streaked to the far end of the hall. A horrible sight greeted her there. Isabella lay on the floor by her throne, thrashing her tail wildly. Her eyes had rolled back in her head and red froth flecked her lips. She didn't recognize Vallerio, or her ladies, and was clawing at her doctor as he tried to staunch her bleeding. Serafina knelt by her mother, but her uncle pulled her away.

'You can't help her. Stay back. Let the doctor do his work,' he said.

'Uncle Vallerio, what's wrong?' Serafina cried. 'What's happening to her?'

Vallerio shook his head. 'The arrow—'

'But she pulled it out! I don't understand . . .'

'It's too late, Sera,' Vallerio said. 'The arrow was poisoned.'

# FOURTEEN

SERAFINA WAS CRAZED WITH FEAR.

'No!' she shouted at her uncle. 'You're wrong! You're *wrong*!'

Vallerio's tone softened. 'Sera, the doctor's certain it's brillbane. He recognizes the symptoms. It only comes from one source – an arctic sculpin.'

'An arctic sculpin,' Serafina repeated woodenly. 'That means—'

'—that Admiral Kolfinn has attacked us. The soldiers are wearing black uniforms – the colour of Ondalina. They're Kolfinn's troops, I'm sure of it. This means war.'

Serafina pushed him away, skirted around the doctor, who was pressing a fresh dressing over Isabella's wound, and sat down on the floor by her mother. She shrugged out of the costly mantle she was still wearing, balled it up, and put it under her mother's head.

'Mum? *Mum!* Can you hear me?' she said, taking her hand. It was covered in blood.

Isabella stopped writhing. It was as if Serafina's voice was a lifeline. She opened her eyes. Their gaze was far away.

'Your songspell was so beautiful, Sera,' she said. 'I didn't get to tell you that.'

'Shh, Mum, don't talk,' Serafina said, but Isabella ignored her.

'Everyone looks so beautiful. The room does, too, with all the anemones in bloom and the chandeliers blazing and your father and brother, don't they look handsome?'

Serafina realized that her mother thought the Dokimí celebrations were taking place. The poison was affecting her mind.

'Why are you here, Sera? Why aren't you dancing with Mahdi?' Isabella asked, agitated. 'Why don't I hear any music?'

'The musicians are taking a break, Mum,' Sera fibbed, in an effort to soothe her. 'They'll be back in a few minutes.'

'He loves you.'

*Wow. She's totally out of her mind*, Serafina thought.

'I glanced at him once or twice. In the Kolisseo. You should have seen his face while you were songcasting. I'm happy for you, Sera, and for Miromara. The bond between our realms will be even stronger if true love unites them.' She grimaced suddenly. 'My side . . . something's wrong.'

'Lie still, Mum,' said Serafina. 'You have to rest now. How about we trade places for tonight? I'll be regina, you be principessa. And my first act as monarch is to order you to bed. You are to put your fins up, listen to gossip conches, and eat plenty of shaptas.'

Isabella tried to smile. 'Neela brought them?'

'And wondas, bingas, jantees, and zee-zees. My chambers look like a Matali sweet shop.'

Isabella laughed, but her laughter brought on a terrible fit of coughing. Blood sprayed from her lips. She moaned piteously. Her eyes closed.

'Help her! *Please!*' Serafina whispered to the doctor.

But the doctor shook his head. 'There's very little I can do,' he said quietly.

After a few seconds, Isabella opened her eyes again. Their gaze was not far away now, but focused and sharp. She squeezed Serafina's hand. 'You are still so young, my darling. I haven't prepared you well enough. There's so much you still need to learn.' There was an urgency to her voice.

'Mum, stop talking. You need to be still,' Serafina said.

'No . . . no time,' Isabella said, her chest hitching. 'Listen to me . . . remember what I tell you. Conte Bartolomeo is the wisest of my ministers. Vallerio will be regent, of course, until you're eighteen, and Bartolomeo's the only one strong enough to put your uncle in his place.' Isabella paused to catch her breath, then said, 'Conte Orsino, I trust with my life. Keep a close eye on the Volnero and the di Remora. They are loyal now, but may work to undermine you if they sense an advantage elsewhere.'

'Mum, stop!' Serafina said fearfully. 'You're scaring me. I was only *joking* about being regina!'

'Sera, *listen* to me!' Isabella's voice was fading. Serafina had to lean close to hear her. 'If we are not able to fend off the attackers, you must get to the vaults. And then, if you can, go to Tsarno. To the fortress there—' She coughed again. Serafina wiped the blood from her lips with the hem of her gown.

Vallerio joined them. The doctor looked at him. 'Send for the canta magus,' he said.

Serafina knew what that meant. The canta magus was summoned when a regina was dying, to sing the ancient chants that released a mer soul back to the sea. 'No!' she cried. 'She's going to be all right! Make her be all right!'

'Your Grace,' the doctor said, his eyes still on Vallerio, 'you must send for the canta magus *now*.'

Vallerio started to speak, but Serafina didn't hear his words. They were drowned out by a deafening roar, a sound so big, it felt like the end of the world. The very foundations of the palace shook, sending shock waves up into the water. Serafina was knocked backwards. For a few seconds, she couldn't right herself; then, slowly, her balance came back. She looked up, still dazed, just in time to see a large chunk of the stateroom's east wall come crashing down. Courtiers screamed as they rushed to get out of the way. Some didn't make it and were crushed by falling stones. Others were engulfed by flames ignited by lava pouring from broken heating pipes buried inside the walls.

Janiçari swam to the breach in formation, armed and moving fast. '*Ejderha! Ejderha!*' they shouted.

*No*, Serafina thought. *It's impossible*.

Grasping the side of her mother's throne, she pulled herself up.

And then she saw it.

*Ejderha*. Dragon.

And she screamed.

# FIFTEEN

A MASSIVE BLACKCLAW DRAGON, her head as big as an orca, stuck her face into the gaping hole she'd made in the wall. She reached an arm through, swiping at Janiçari with foot-long talons.

The soldiers attacked the beast, but their swords and their spells were useless against the thick scales covering her body, her bronze faceplate, and the stiff frill of spikes around her neck. Mermen wearing black uniforms and goggles sat on her back in an armoured howdah, controlling her with a bridle and reins.

The dragon bashed her head against the palace wall and another large chunk of it fell in.

'Stop her! Stop her!' voices screamed.

But there was no stopping her. The stateroom was deep inside the palace. The dragon had already knocked through heavy outer walls to get here. An inner wall would be nothing to her. She would be inside the room in seconds.

'Get the regina to the vaults!' Serafina heard her uncle shout. 'The princesses, too! Do it *now*!'

She knew he meant the treasury vaults underneath the

palace, where the realm's gold was kept. The hallway that led to them was too narrow for a dragon, and the bronze doors enclosing them were a foot thick and heavily enchanted. Food and medical supplies had been stored within them in case of a siege.

Two Janiçari converged on Neela. Five more rushed to Isabella and tried to lift her. She screamed in pain and struggled against them.

'Mum, stop it. *Please*. You have to let them take you. You'll be safe there,' Sera said.

Isabella shook her head. 'Lift me onto my throne,' she commanded her guard. 'I will not die on the floor.'

Serafina's heart lurched at her mother's words. 'You're *not* dying. We just have to get you to the vaults. We just have to—'

Isabella took Serafina's face in her bloodied hands. 'I'm staying here to face my attackers. *You* will go to the vaults, Sera. You are regina now, and you must not be taken. *Live*, my precious child. For me. For Miromara.' She kissed Serafina's forehead then released her.

'No!' Serafina shrilled. 'I won't go without you. I—'

She was cut off by a rumbling crash as the dragon knocked more of the wall down. The creature pulled her head out of the hole she'd made, and dozens of soldiers, all clad in black, swam inside. Their leader pointed towards the throne.

'There they are! Seize them!' he ordered.

Arrows came through the water. Many of the Janiçari surrounding the princesses and the regina fell.

'Go! *Now!*' Isabella shouted.

'I can't leave you!' Serafina sobbed.

Isabella's tortured eyes sought Neela's. '*Please* . . .' she said.

Neela nodded. She grabbed Serafina's hand and yanked her away.

Isabella spotted a dagger next to the corpse of a fallen Janiçari. She conjured a vortex in the water, and sent the knife hurtling at the invaders' leader. The dagger hit home, knocking him to the floor. His men came to his aid, but he pushed them away. 'Get them!' he gurgled, drowning in his own blood. 'Take the princesses to Traho!'

But Sera and Neela were already gone.

# SIXTEEN

NEELA HAD NEVER swum so fast. She was a blur in the water, moving like a marlin, her hand gripping Serafina's like a vice. But the mermen who'd chased them out of the stateroom were gaining on them.

Serafina, in shock, was deadweight. She was slowing Neela down.

'Come on, Sera, snap out of it!' Neela yelled. 'I need you to *swim*!'

They moved through a hallway that twisted and turned. As they rounded a bend, Neela could see that it ended in a *T*.

'Which way to the vaults?' she shouted.

'To the right!' Serafina shouted back, rallying.

They turned the corner. Ahead of them, in front of the doors to the vaults, were at least thirty enemy soldiers.

Neela wheeled around and headed for the other end of the *T*, pulling Serafina after her. As they shot past the mouth of the hallway they'd just swum down, she saw the soldiers who'd chased them from the stateroom.

'There they are!' one of them yelled.

Neela sang a velo spell.

*Waters blue,*
*Hear me cast,*
*Rise behind us,*
*Make us fast!*

The water in the hall rose like a breaker, swiftly pushing the mermaids ahead of it. They'd outpaced their pursuers for the moment but still had to find a room where they could barricade themselves. Neela didn't live here, and she didn't know where to go. They were in another hallway now, one filled with portraits of Miromaran nobles. Neela recognized it. Suddenly, she knew where they were.

'Sera, we can make it to my room!'

Her suite was nowhere near as secure as the vaults, but it was all they had. Serafina, roused now, sped ahead and cut left. Neela was right on her tail. They swam down a narrow loggia and then through a coral archway.

Seconds later, they were at the door to Neela's suite. But it was too late. There was no time to get it open. The soldiers had cast their own velos and had gained on them. In a desperate move, Neela cast a fragor lux spell, hoping to slow the attackers with a small light bomb.

*Lava's light,*
*Now attack,*
*Cause my enemies*
*To fall back!*

She'd sung the spell too fast. It was weak. They were done for, she knew it.

But the spell *wasn't* weak.

All at once, every globe in the hallway dimmed. The light from each one swirled together into a brilliant, glowing ball. It hurtled through the water, hit the ground a foot away from the soldiers, and exploded, forcing them back. Serafina swung the door open. The two mermaids raced inside and pushed it closed. Neela threw the heavy bolt in the nick of time. Just as it shot home, a body thudded against the door.

'What kind of frag spell *was* that?' Serafina asked, panting for breath.

'I don't know,' Neela said. 'I've never done it before.'

There was another thud. The door shuddered.

'They're going to break it down,' Serafina said. 'We can't stay here.'

Neela swam to a window. The waters outside were thick with soldiers. 'Where can we go?' she asked frantically. 'They're everywhere!'

'We could cast a prax spell and camouflage ourselves against the ceiling,' Serafina said.

'They'll search every inch of these rooms. They'll find us.'

A pounding started, rhythmic and loud. The invaders were battering down the door. Neela saw that it was bowing out of its frame with every blow.

'Is there anything here we can use to defend ourselves?

A knife? Scissors?' Serafina asked. 'I'm not going without a fight.'

Neela rushed to her vanity table and started pawing through the bottles and vials on it, looking for any kind of sharp object. And then she saw it – Yazeed's whelk shell necklace. She'd taken it from him when she and Serafina had found him and Mahdi in the reggia.

'Sera, over here!' she said. 'Hurry!'

'What is it?'

'Yaz's transparensea pearls.'

Neela shook the pearls out of the shell. The songspell of invisibility used shadow and light and was notoriously difficult to cast. Spellbinders – highly skilled artisans – knew how to insert the spell into pearls that a mermaid could carry with her and deploy in an instant.

Neela and Serafina each held one between the palms of their hands. A second later, they were invisible.

'Come on!' Neela said, opening a window.

She couldn't see Serafina, so she felt around in the water for her, got hold of her arm, and pushed her out through the opening. Her own tail fin had just cleared the sill when the door came crashing in.

# SEVENTEEN

'I CAN'T GO ANY FARTHER. I have to rest. Just for a few minutes,' Serafina said.

She and Neela had been swimming fast for over an hour through dark waters and were almost three leagues west of Cerulea, heading for the fortress at Tsarno. A sputtering lava torch, picked up on the edges of the city, was their only source of light.

'We've got to keep moving,' Neela said, looking around warily. 'You're shimmering, Sera. The pearls are wearing off. Come on.'

'I will. I just need a minute,' Serafina said. She was exhausted. She sat down on a rock, leaned over, and vomited.

Painful spasms racked her body until there was nothing left inside her. Nothing but the images of the arrow burying itself in her mother's side. Of her father's body sinking through the water. Of the dragon tearing through the palace wall.

'Here,' Neela said, handing her a kelp leaf.

Serafina took it and wiped her mouth. A tiny octopus, spooked by their movements, shot out from the seaweed and swam off. As she watched him, she thought of Sylvestre. She'd left him sleeping on her bed when she'd departed for the Dokimí. She had no idea if he was dead or alive. She had no idea what had happened to Tavia. To the ladies of her court. Or even of her mother's final fate.

Neela sat down next to Sera and put an arm around her. Sera leaned her head on Neela's shoulder. Some of the numbness she'd felt was wearing off and she realized she owed her friend a great deal.

'We'd be prisoners right now if it wasn't for you,' she said. 'Thank you.'

'Don't thank me until we're in Tsarno,' Neela said. 'Who are they? Who did this?'

'Ondalina. That's what my uncle said. He was worried this would happen. He wanted my mother to declare war on Admiral Kolfinn. I wasn't supposed to know, but I overheard them talking.'

'Why would Kolfinn do such a thing?' Neela asked.

'I don't know,' Serafina said. 'All I know is that he broke the permutavi without any explanation. And now hundreds are dead. My father. Maybe my mother. We don't know where Ahadi and Bilaal are. Or Mahdi and Yaz.'

Neela uttered a stifled cry.

'What is it?' Sera asked.

'Oh, Sera. One of the last things I said to my brother was that he was a tube worm,' Neela said, tears shimmering in her eyes. 'It might be the last thing I ever say to him.'

'It might be the last thing you ever say to *anyone*,' a deep voice rumbled, making both mermaids jump up. 'You're bait if you stay here. Soldiers rode through earlier. Mermen in black uniforms.'

'W-who are you?' Neela stammered.

'*Where* are you? Serafina said, peering through the gloom.

'They're asking about two princesses. That would be you, I assume. They're asking everyone they see, which is why they didn't ask me.'

A small movement close to where they'd been sitting caught the mermaids' attention. It was a merman who looked like a scorpion fish. With his spots and bands of colour, and the weedy frills of skin on his face, he was perfectly camouflaged against the algae-covered stone he was sitting on.

Just then, they all heard something, faint and faraway. It sounded like fins churning the water.

The merman rose from his rock, the better to listen. 'Hippokamps. Probably the same patrol,' he said tersely. 'They're coming this way.'

'We've got to hide,' Neela said.

'There's an abandoned eel cave about a hundred yards north of here. You'll see the wreck of a blue fishing boat. The cave's another ten yards past it. Swim fast and you'll make it.'

'Thank you. I don't even know your name,' Serafina said. His kindness heartened her. It was good to know there were still merpeople who cared, allies who would help her.

'Zeno. Zeno Piscor.'

'Thank you, Zeno. We won't forget this.'

Zeno flapped a fin at her. He settled himself back on his rock, eyes open, watching the waters. Serafina and Neela swam fast. The sound of hippokamps grew louder.

'Where's the blue boat?' Neela asked anxiously, a few minutes later. 'It should be here. Did we miss it?'

Serafina spotted it. She led the way to the eel cave. Its entry was littered with the bones of its former occupant's meals. The cave itself was narrow and dark, with a low ceiling. A minute later, they heard hippokamps and mermen. Neela, who was carrying the lava torch, quickly buried it in the silt.

'Why are we stopping, Captain Traho?' a voice called out. 'We searched this area on the way out.'

'To rest the animals,' came the reply.

Serafina heard the mermen dismount. They were very close. 'There's a cave here!' one shouted.

Her heart pounding, Serafina looked at Neela.

'It's empty. We checked it before,' another soldier said.

'Check it again!' the captain bellowed. 'They could have passed through here after we did. Be careful. I want them alive.'

Neela gasped. Serafina swam to the back of the cave, pulling Neela with her. She sang a prax spell to camouflage them. She sang it fast and low, but it was still strong enough to blend them into the grey stone wall.

The soldier, holding a lava torch, swam halfway into the cave, glanced around, and swam out again.

'Empty!' they heard him call out.

The captain swore. 'They *can't* have made Tsarno,' he said. 'No one swims that fast, even with a velo. Someone must be hiding them. Ride on!'

The mermaids didn't move a muscle until the hippokamps were gone. Then they both collapsed on the cave floor.

Serafina was the first to speak. 'Why do they want us alive? What do they want with us?'

'I'm guessing that whatever it is, it's not good. Come on, let's go. It's not safe here.'

'I have to rest first, Neela. Just for a little while.'

'Is that a good idea?' Neela asked.

'It's okay. We're out of sight. I just need a few minutes to get my strength back. Then we'll head out and follow Plan A – swim like mad to Tsarno.'

Neela looked sceptical. 'That's going to be a challenge with soldiers on hippokamps hunting for us.'

'You have a Plan B?'

'No, but I have a Plan Zee. Because never *ever* have I needed a sugar fix more than I do right now. Murderous sea scum invaders sure ratchet up the stress levels.' She reached into a pocket in the folds of her sari skirt and pulled out two zee zees. 'Here,' she said, handing one to Serafina. 'Candied clam with wakame crunch. So good.'

Serafina smiled wearily. She unwrapped her sweet and ate it. She was glad to have it.

She was even gladder to have Neela.

# EIGHTEEN

'GET UP.'

Neela heard the words, but they seemed so far away. She didn't want to get up. She'd fallen asleep and wanted to stay that way.

'I said, *get up*!'

She felt a stinging slap on her tail.

'Ow, Sera! What is it?' she mumbled, opening her eyes.

But it wasn't Serafina who'd slapped her. It was the wiry, eel-like merman who was leaning over her. He was wearing a black sharkskin vest. A row of stiff spikes ran from his forehead to his neck. A lantern glowed nearby.

'Who are you?' Neela cried, scrambling up. 'Where's Serafina?'

The merman swam aside and Neela saw her friend. She was sitting on the floor of the cave, her hands tied behind her and her mouth cruelly gagged.

'Sera!' Neela shouted. She tried to go to her, but was grabbed from behind. Like living ropes, two moray eels threaded themselves through her arms, binding her tightly.

'Let me go!' she shouted, struggling against them.

Another moray, bigger than the rest, swam to her. He wound his thick body around her neck and squeezed. His monstrous face floated only inches from her own. He hissed at her, baring his long, curved teeth. Neela couldn't breathe.

'Stop struggling and he'll let go,' the merman said.

Neela, gasping, did as she was told. The moray uncoiled himself and swam to his master.

'Good boy, Tiberius,' the merman crooned.

'What do you want with us?' Neela asked angrily.

The eels binding her arms tightened themselves, making her cry out in pain.

'Easy, my children, easy,' the merman said to the eels. 'They'll fetch a fine price for us, but only if they're alive.'

'You have to let us go. You don't know who we are,' Neela said.

The merman smiled darkly. 'Baco knows *exactly* who you are. He also knows that Captain Traho has put a bounty on your heads. Baco Goga is going to be *very* rich.'

'You can't do this! We're going for help. Cerulea's under attack. It may fall!' Neela said.

'It *has* fallen, little merl,' he said. 'Tsarno has fallen. And every town in between.'

'No!' Neela said. 'You're lying!'

The merman laughed. With his hand, he made a motion of a fish swimming away. 'Gone. All gone. As you're about to be. But first, you must pay Baco rent for staying in his cave.'

He signalled to the morays. They swam to the mermaids and began divesting them of their jewellery. Neela closed her eyes, revolted. She felt them tugging at her necklace, heard their teeth clicking against her earrings, felt their tongues sliding over her fingers, removing her rings. They'd just started on her bracelets when she heard Serafina scream behind her gag.

Neela's eyes flew open. One of the eels had dropped the necklace he'd taken from Serafina and had thrust his head down the front of her gown to retrieve it. Sera, lashing her tail furiously, caught another eel with her fins, and sent him spinning into a wall. He hit the stone hard and fell to the cave's floor, motionless. The other eels were on her immediately, snarling. Tiberius sank his teeth into her tail fin. Sera screamed again, and tried to pull away.

'Stop it!' Neela yelled. 'Leave her alone!'

Baco swam across the room and grabbed Serafina's chin. 'That was my Claudius!' he hissed furiously, his fingers digging into her flesh. 'You'd better be sorry. Are you? Are you sorry?'

Serafina, her eyes huge with fear, nodded.

'You lumpsucker! Take your hands off her!' Neela shouted, struggling against the eels who were still holding her.

'Get me something to shut her up,' Baco ordered. Tiberius brought him a length of sea silk. Baco jammed it into Neela's mouth and tied it tightly behind her head.

'These two are trouble. I want them gone. Go to Traho right away,' Baco told Tiberius. 'Tell him I have what he's after.'

The moray nodded and swam off.

'Tiberius, wait!' Baco said.

The moray turned. Baco flipped him a doubloon. He caught it in his mouth.

'Give that to Zeno. With my thanks.'

# NINETEEN

THE SOLDIERS REMOVED Baco's flimsy restraints. They shackled Serafina's wrists with iron cuffs and blindfolded her. They forced an iron gag into her mouth and wrapped a net around her. Then, one of the soldiers slung her over the back of his hippokamp and rode fast. The others followed. The ride was agony. The net's filament bit into Sera's skin. The gag, with its bitter taste of black metal, made her retch.

An hour later, they arrived at what sounded like some kind of camp. Sera couldn't see anything through her blindfold, but she could hear hippokamps whinnying, orders being shouted, and the blood-chilling roar of Blackclaw dragons. One of her captors carried her a short distance, then dumped her on the ground. She tried to free herself but soon stopped, for she was slapped – hard – whenever she moved. She tried to call out for Neela but couldn't because of her gag.

Lying on her side, she strained to hear all that she could, sifting the conversation for clues to her whereabouts.

'. . . on Traho's orders . . .'

'. . . pockets of fighting, but they can't hold out . . .'

'. . . find the prince. Just dangle a siren or two . . .'

*Who are they?* she wondered. *What do they want with me?* She didn't have long to wonder, for she was soon hoisted up and set down again. This time, in a chair.

'The principessa, sir,' a voice said.

'Remove the net.'

Several hands pulled the netting away. Serafina's shackles were removed, her blindfold, too, but not her gag. She looked around warily, her eyes adjusting to the light of lava lanterns. It was still dark. *Probably close to midnight*, she guessed. She was inside a well-appointed tent. There was a large campaign table in its centre. A bed stood in one corner and several chairs were scattered about.

A woman – obviously unconscious, her head lolling – sat in one of them. Serafina was horrified when she realized who she was.

Thalassa's beautiful grey hair was down around her shoulders. Her face was bruised. She held her manacled hands close to her chest. Blood swirled above them, pulsing from the stump of bone where her left thumb used to be. Serafina tried to swim to her but was roughly pushed down in her chair.

'Do you wish to help her?' a voice asked. The same voice that had instructed the others to remove her net.

Serafina searched for its source and saw a merman floating in the corner. He wore the black uniform of the Ondalinian invaders. His thick brown hair was cut short.

He had a compact build and a cruel face.

'My name is Markus Traho,' he said. 'I'm going to remove your gag. You are to use your voice only to speak. And only to me. Attempt to use magic and the canta magus loses her other thumb. Do you understand?'

Serafina glared at him but did not reply.

Traho pulled a dagger from a sheath at his hip. With a quick, fluid motion, he drove it into the arm of the chair in which Thalassa was sitting.

'I *said*, Do – you – understand?'

Serafina quickly nodded.

'Very good.'

Traho retrieved his dagger, then swam to her. He worked the tip of the knife under the strap of her gag then jerked the blade towards him.

Serafina spat out the gag. 'What have you done to her?' she shouted.

'It wasn't me, Principessa. It was the canta magus who cost herself a thumb,' Traho said, putting his dagger back in its sheath.

'Who are you working for? Kolfinn?'

'All in good time,' Traho said. 'You've been summoned, have you not?'

'*Summoned?* I've been brought here against my will,' Serafina said, furious.

Traho smiled thinly. 'Very clever, Principessa.'

Serafina gave him a look of contempt. 'I'm not trying to be clever. I'm trying to get answers. First Kolfinn breaks the permutavi. Now he attacks Cerulea, murders our merfolk—'

The blow was hard. And so quick Serafina never saw it coming. Her head snapped back. Light exploded behind her eyes. She stifled a cry. When the pain subsided, she sat up straight again and spat out a mouthful of blood.

Traho leaned over her, his face only inches from her own. 'Dear Principessa, I don't think you really *do* understand,' he said. '*I* ask the questions. *You* answer them.'

For the first time in her life, Serafina blessed her court and the hard lessons it had taught her. She fell back on those lessons now. Hiding her fear behind a mask, she forced herself to meet Traho's gaze.

'I can't answer a question I don't understand,' she said coolly. 'You didn't *summon* me, you kidnapped me.'

Traho swam to the campaign table, where a map lay, etched in squid ink on kelp parchment. He pushed tiny shell soldiers across it and as he did, he recited four lines:

*Daughter of Merrow, leave your sleep,*
*The ways of childhood no more to keep.*
*The dream will die, a nightmare rise,*
*Sleep no more, child, open your eyes.*

Serafina's heart hammered in her chest, but her face betrayed nothing. Those lines were from the Iele's chant. *But how does he know them?* she wondered. *It's not possible*. She'd only told her mother about the nightmare, and she hadn't told anyone about the chant.

Serafina didn't know why Traho had recited the lines, but a small voice inside warned her that she must not tell him anything.

'It is time to stop playing games,' he said now.

He took a conch from the campaign table and placed it on the arm of her chair. Sera realized he was going to record his interrogation.

'The Iele summoned you, daughter of Merrow. We know they have. We've heard their chant, too. We also know that they summoned Princess Neela – the one who keeps the light. They mentioned four others in the chant. We want to know who they are. And we want to know where the talismans are.'

Serafina laughed in disbelief, bluffing. 'I have no idea what you're talking about.'

'My forces destroyed Cerulea to take you and the Matali princess. We'll destroy every city in every realm if that's what it takes to get the talismans. You can prevent that.'

'You're insane. The Iele are make-believe. They aren't *real*.'

'No? Then why did you reach out to Vrăja when she appeared in your mirror?'

Serafina's heart lurched. *How did he know?* No one else had been in the room when she'd had that vision of the witch, and the terragogg with the black eyes.

Traho waited. A minute went by. Then two. Then he pulled out his knife again. Serafina steeled herself. She would not scream. He wouldn't take her courage and he wouldn't take her pride. She was Serafina, principessa di Miromara, and he was sea scum.

As Traho came closer, a tiny bubble floated past Serafina's face. She barely noticed it. Until it popped, softly, right inside her ear.

*Lie, child.*

Thalassa had regained consciousness, though she hadn't revealed it. Then she'd cast a bolla spell. Her magic was so powerful, she didn't have to sing. All she had to do was whisper, and tuck that whisper into a bubble.

'Who *are* they? Where do they live? I won't ask again,' Traho said.

Serafina looked down. She hoped it looked like she was struggling with her conscience, when really she was struggling to make up four names.

'Mitsuko . . .' she whispered.

'Louder, please. Speak into the conch.'

'Mitsuko Takahashi. From Shiroi Nami in the East Sea. Alice Strongtail from Cod Shoals in Atlantica. Natalya Kovalenko from the Volga. Lara Jonsdottir from Villtur Sjó.'

'Good. Very good,' Traho said nodding. He picked up the conch shell and listened to it, making sure everything she'd said had been captured. Then he looked at Serafina again. 'Now,' he said, 'where are the talismans hidden?'

'I don't *know* where they are. I don't even know *what* they are.'

'Vrăja, the witch—'

'Told me nothing,' Serafina said. She held out her hands, spreading her fingers wide. 'Go ahead. Cut them off. When you're finished, I'll say the same thing.'

Traho weighed her words, then turned to the two soldiers stationed by the doorway. 'Take them both to the prisoners' tent,' he said.

*He bought it*, Serafina thought. Relief washed over her. 'Let Thalassa go,' she said. 'I gave you what you wanted. I told you what I know. Let her go.'

'Not yet,' Traho said. 'Her powers will be useful to us. Yours, too, Principessa. But it's late now and you must rest. Good night. Sleep well.'

A guard handed Thalassa a rag to wrap around her hand and led her out of the tent. Another now led Serafina towards the doorway.

'Oh, and Principessa?'

Serafina stopped. She turned around.

Traho smiled. 'Gods help you if you've lied to me.'

# TWENTY

SERAFINA STRUGGLED when she saw the collar.

She flailed and tried to break away, but one of the guards grabbed her hair and pulled her head back, immobilizing her. All she could do was blink, eyes wild, as another guard closed the collar around her neck and padlocked it. Like the cuffs and gag used on her earlier, the collar was made of iron, and iron repelled magic. While it touched her throat, she could not songcast.

As soon as the guard released her, she thrashed about, stirring up silt from the tent's floor. The collar was heavy and cruel, and attached by a chain to a wooden post. She leaned forward and pulled against the chain with all her might. Slapped her tail against the pole. Threw her shoulder into it. But she only succeeded in hurting herself.

'Stop, child. It's no use.'

Serafina swam back to the wooden post. Thalassa had been chained to it also. She looked at her beloved teacher's face, mottled by violence. At her maimed hand, swaddled in a bloodsoaked rag. 'Magistra,' she said brokenly, '*why?* Why did he do that to you?'

'Because he believes the Iele are real. And he thinks that I might have some connection with them.'

'Sera?'

Serafina whirled around at the sound of the voice. 'Neela!' she said tearfully.

In the dim light of a single lantern, she saw her friend, curled up on the ground. She was chained to another pole only a few feet away. Her eye was swollen and bruised. Her skin was a sickly grey-blue. Serafina rushed towards her instinctively but was brought up short by her own chain.

Neela sat up and reached for Sera, but she was too far away to touch her. Serafina flattened herself on the seafloor and stretched herself out as far as the chain would allow. She patted Neela's tail fin with her own. Neela patted back.

'Did Traho do that to your face?' Sera asked.

'A soldier did it when I tried to escape.'

'Quiet in there!' a harsh voice ordered.

All three mermaids looked at the tent's door. A guard stationed outside was silhouetted against the flap.

Thalassa held a finger to her lips. Sera and Neela nodded. 'Traho will question you both tomorrow,' she whispered. 'Prepare yourself. Have *something* to tell him. There's no reasoning with him. He's a madman.' She shook her head. 'Attacking Cerulea over make-believe witches . . . brutalizing us over dreams and chants . . . it makes no sense.'

Neela stiffened. 'What dream? What chant?' she asked.

'A dream I had about the Iele. In it, they sang a chant. Traho knows about it. I have no idea how,' Serafina said.

'Sera,' Neela said urgently, 'what happened in your dream?'

'The Iele were chanting in a circle. And there was a monster in a cage. It wanted to get out. It almost *did* get out—'

'Abbadon,' Neela said. 'The monster's name is Abbadon. There's an older witch. She's the leader. Her name is Vrăja.'

Serafina shook her head. 'No way. *No. Way*. How do you know that?'

Neela, glowing a bright, electric blue, said, 'Because I had the very same dream.'

# TWENTY-ONE

'YOU COULDN'T HAVE. It's not possible,' Serafina said.

'Except that it *is*,' Neela said. 'Because I *did*. Remember when I told you – in the reggia – that I'd had bad dreams during the trip from Matali?'

'Yes, but you said you couldn't remember them.'

'I was too embarrassed to tell you that I was scared of make-believe witches.'

'How does the chant go, child?' Thalassa asked.

'*Daughter of Light, chosen one . . .*' Neela began to quietly sing.

Serafina stopped her. 'Mine was different. It started like this: *Daughter of Merrow, chosen one . . .*'

Neela joined her and they sang the rest of the chant together. Except for a few lines, the words were exactly the same.

'For me, when the chant gets to the *find the five* part, instead of *One whose heart will hold the light*, the Iele sing *One who will rule from Merrow's right*,' Neela said. 'That's you, Sera. You're descended from Merrow and the heiress to the

Miromaran throne. You're one of the five the witches were telling me to find.'

'And you're one of the five they were telling *me* to find. I'm supposed to look for *One who keeps the light*,' said Serafina. 'That's you, with the blue light you give off.'

'Um, right,' Neela said. 'Except for one thing – the Iele don't want us to find anyone, because the Iele aren't *real*. They don't exist.'

Serafina was silent for a few seconds, then she said, 'What if they *do*?'

'The invaders think they do,' Thalassa said. 'Because of this chant, they've destroyed Cerulea and killed countless of its citizens. They'll kill more. You heard Traho, Serafina. He said they'd destroy every city in every realm if that's what it took to get the talismans.'

Dread gripped Sera. It was all starting to make sickening sense.

'You're right, Magistra,' she said grimly. 'And I think I know why. Kolfinn wants to free the monster. That's what's behind all of this. Remember the lines about the talismans? *These pieces must not be united / Not in anger, greed, or rage / They were scattered by brave Merrow / Lest they unlock destruction's cage*. He's trying to find them. He wants to harness Abbadon's power.'

A cold rage flared inside her. The destruction, the bloodshed, the terrible suffering of her parents and so many innocent people . . . they were all because of one merman's insane quest for power.

'Did you tell Traho anything, Sera?' Neela asked.

Sera shook her head. 'I lied. I gave him made-up names.'

'What about the talismans?' Thalassa asked. 'Do you know what they are?'

'I have no idea,' Serafina said.

'In the morning, when Traho questions you, make something up, or gods only know what he'll do to you,' Thalassa said worriedly. 'There's no other way.'

'There *is* another way. We escape,' Neela said.

'How? We can't get out of these collars. We need keys to unlock them. Which we haven't got,' Serafina said.

'Keys,' Neela said thoughtfully, 'or a pick.'

'Which we also haven't got,' Serafina said.

But Neela didn't hear her; she was busy undoing her belt. It had a jewelled buckle with a long prong. The buckle had been hidden by the folds of her sari. Baco Goga's eels had missed it when they'd robbed her.

'Once, when we were little, Yazeed locked Mahdi in a trunk,' Neela said. 'Then he lost the key. Aunt Ahadi was beside herself. The royal locksmith came. We watched him. He said locks have pins inside them. All you have to do is push the right ones.'

Stabilizing the prong between her thumb and forefinger, Neela inserted it into the lock on her collar and started twisting. Nothing happened.

'Neels, it'll never work. You're a princess, not a safecracker,' Serafina said.

'Thanks for your vote of confidence,' Neela said, adjusting

the angle of the prong. She twisted it again, and they all heard a metallic click. Sera glanced nervously at the door, but the sound hadn't carried to the guard.

'It worked!' Neela said excitedly. She threw the padlock down and pulled her collar off. 'Never underestimate the power of accessories!'

'Go, Neela, get out of here!' Serafina said.

'And leave you to Commander Sea Scum?'

'The guard could come in at any moment. You have to *go*!'

Neela ignored Serafina's words and focused on her padlock. After a few minutes, she got it open too.

'Work on Thalassa's. I'll see if there's a way out of here,' Serafina said, throwing off her collar. 'Maybe one of the tent pegs is loose.'

She started to push on the canvas, hoping they could pull up a section and swim under it. Neela applied herself to Thalassa's collar. The lock on it was bigger and harder to pick.

'You must go, both of you. Leave me,' Thalassa said.

'We're *not* leaving you,' said Neela. 'I can do this.'

She pulled the prong out of the lock and held up her hand. Her skin was glowing brightly, as it did when her emotions were running high. She used the blue light it gave off to illuminate the keyhole and saw that a tiny pebble was stuck inside. She dislodged it, then tried again. A few seconds later, Thalassa was free.

'Ha! *Yes*. We're *so* gone,' Neela said, but her triumph was short-lived.

'Shh!' said Thalassa.

They heard the sounds of fins in the water. Someone was coming.

'I can't find a way out!' Serafina said frantically.

'Put the collars back on! Pretend you're asleep!' Thalassa hissed.

The three mermaids quickly fumbled their restraints back around their necks and threaded the locks' hasps through the collars without engaging them. Then they lay on the ground, letting their hair fall over the padlocks.

'Everything good?' a voice asked.

'They were noisy at first, but they've quieted down,' the guard at the door replied.

The flap opened. Two guards swam in. One shone a lantern over the mermaids. The other stayed in the doorway. Sera was sure they could hear her heart pounding.

'Getting their beauty sleep,' one guard said.

'They'll need it,' the other said. 'Traho's getting impatient, and when Traho gets impatient, he stops cutting off fingers and starts cutting off heads.'

The guards laughed and left the tent. One continued on his rounds, the other resumed his position by the door.

The mermaids sat up and removed their collars. 'Swim to the top of the tent,' Thalassa said. 'Maybe there's a vent, a hole, something you can rip—'

She was silenced by a short, sharp noise outside the tent, as if a shout had been cut off. It was followed by a soft pattering, like raindrops on sailcloth. Before Sera's mind could process what the sounds were, the flap was flung open, and a merman swam inside – dragging a guard behind him. The guard's throat had been cut. He was arching his back, flailing his tail. His eyes, pleading and desperate, found Sera's. She gasped and backed away.

The merman dragging the guard was tall and bronzed, with short blond hair and a blue tail. He was followed by two more. One had red hair and a green tail. Another grey eyes and a grey tail. They all had daggers in scabbards on their hips.

Neela lunged at the dying guard. She grabbed the sword from his belt and held it out in front of her.

'Get away from us,' she said. Her voice was steady, but her hand was trembling.

'You need to come with us. Right now,' one of the mermen said.

'Who are you?' Neela demanded.

'I'm Blu,' the blond said after a second. 'This is Verde and Grigio.'

'Yeah, those are some real convincing names,' Neela said. 'Why are you here? What do you want?'

'To get you out of here,' Verde said.

'Who sent you?'

'A friend. We'll explain later.'

Suddenly shouts were heard from the other end of the camp. Orders were yelled. A rush of fins churned the water.

Grigio swore. 'Time to move, kids.'

Neela made her decision. She threw her sword down and

swam to the mermen. Thalassa joined her. Sera, her eyes on the dying guard, did not. His lips formed a final word: *Please*. And then he was gone.

'Let's go!' Grigio hissed.

Sera, traumatized, didn't move.

Blu swam to her. He took her chin in his hand and turned her face to his. 'Look at me . . . look at *me*, not him.'

Sera met his eyes. 'H-he needed help. He reached for me,' she said, her voice breaking.

'And he would have killed you, too, if he was told to,' Blu said. 'Traho's coming. We've spooked him, so he won't wait until tomorrow morning to get his answers. He'll force you to tell him right now. Right here. And then he'll kill you. That's what he's doing in Cerulea. Either you come with us or you stay with him.'

'Please, child. We have no choice,' Thalassa said.

Sera nodded woodenly. Blu offered her his hand. She took it and he pulled her out of the tent and through the blood-dark water.

# TWENTY-TWO

'FIVE MINUTES,' Verde said, pointing to a cave. 'That's it.'

'She needs more than five minutes! Look at her!' Serafina said. 'She can't breathe!'

'Five minutes.'

The cave was on top of a seamount. Serafina and Neela swam inside. Blu and Grigio followed, each with one of Thalassa's arms around his neck. They lowered her to the floor, eased her against a wall, then left to keep watch. Thalassa's face was grey. Her chest was heaving. There was quite a bit of bioluminescent plankton in the cave. Neela sang a quick illuminata and it started to glow.

'Stay with her,' Serafina said to Neela. 'I'll be right back.'

Serafina found Verde hovering at the cave's mouth, scanning the seabed below for movement. 'We shouldn't have stopped,' he said. 'Dawn's only a few hours away. We need to keep moving while it's still dark.'

There were five other mermen with him, including Blu and Grigio. One of them shook his head. 'Had to, boss. The old lady's in bad shape.'

'Who are you?' Serafina said. At last there was time to ask.

'Friends,' Verde replied.

'Why are you helping us?'

Verde turned away without answering. He signalled to the others and all but one followed him, fanning out across the face of the seamount. Blu stayed by the cave, a lone sentry.

Serafina sat down in the cave's mouth. She didn't know how she was going to get up and swim again in five minutes – or how Thalassa would. She was tired and hungry. The bite on her tail fin was bleeding again. She'd been swimming flat out ever since she'd left Traho's camp, over an hour ago. They were heading north. Verde had navigated through the night waters.

They'd all only just made it out. An alarm had gone up as they were escaping, and soldiers had spread out in all directions, torches blazing. The mermaids and their mysterious rescuers had swum over a huge coral reef, hiding themselves on the other side. One of the mermen had poked his head up, a pair of binoculars in hand, to see how many were giving chase.

'Forty, at least,' he'd said. 'On hippokamps.'

'Quick, give me something. Each of you. A belt, a piece of cloth, anything,' Verde had ordered.

When Thalassa asked why, he tore a sleeve off her gown. Neela quickly gave him her underskirt. Serafina tore off a chunk from her hem. As she did, she heard the sound of baying.

'What is that?' she'd asked, frightened.

'Hound sharks. Big, ugly, and good at tracking,' Verde'd replied, tying the items together. Another merman, tall and rangy with a golden tail, took the bundle.

'They'll know we're heading to the Lagoon,' Verde told him. 'But they won't know which current we're taking. Swim due north with this bundle, then cut over to the Lido inlet. We'll head west, then loop over on the *alta* flow to Chioggia. Once we're in the Lagoon itself, the hounds will lose the scent. Meet us at the palazzo.'

The merman nodded and shot off.

'We're going to move fast now. Very fast. *Keep up*,' he'd said to the rest. 'If we don't make Chioggia before Traho's riders figure out what we've done, it's all over.'

No one had said a word until Thalassa had started to gasp. Serafina begged them to slow down to let her rest, but they wouldn't. Two of them took her arms and helped her along. They kept moving until she could barely breathe at all, until Serafina had shouted at them to stop.

Serafina stretched now, first her back, then her tail, trying to ease her sore muscles. As she stretched her arms, she looked at her hands. Her beautiful rings had been stolen. All but the little shell heart Mahdi once made for her. Had he survived the attack? Had Yazeed? She wondered if she'd ever see either of them again.

Serafina slid the ring off her finger. It was so simple and innocent that just looking at it hurt. It reminded her of everything she'd lost. Mahdi. Her parents. Cerulea. Her entire life.

'You belong to another Sera, not to me,' she whispered. She threw the ring away, watching as it sank through the water until she couldn't see it any more. Then she buried her face in her hands.

A minute later, a voice said, 'Are you okay?' It was Blu. He sat down beside her.

'Yeah, I'm great. Never better,' she replied, lowering her hands.

'We're not so far from the Lagoon now. We're going to make it. You'll be safe there.'

Serafina laughed bitterly. 'Safe? I'm not sure I know what that means any more, Mr Blu.'

'Just Blu is fine. And Grigio. And Verde. We don't swim on ceremony. What's wrong with your tail?' he asked, pointing at it. 'It's bleeding.'

'Eel bite.'

'You need to wrap it so that there's pressure against the wound. Otherwise it won't stop.'

He put his hands under the end of her tail and gently raised her fins, peering at the bite. The eel's teeth had torn a long, jagged hole in the soft tissue.

'This is a mess,' he said.

Serafina blushed. She wasn't used to strange mermen touching her tail.

'Um, I'm fine. Really,' she said, trying to pull away from him.

'Sorry, but this is no time for modesty. We can't have you bleeding into the water with hound sharks after us.' He lowered her fins, then tore a wide strip from the bottom of her gown.

'Hey!'

'You have a first-aid kit that I'm not aware of?'

'No, but—'

'Then this is the best we've got,' he said, tearing off two more strips.

He wadded up one strip and packed it against the bite. Then he wound another around her fin, securing the dressing. He worked quickly and expertly. Serafina watched as he carefully wrapped the third strip around the end of her tail, then over the dressing, tying it in such a way that it wouldn't slip off. His skin was light brown and smooth; his chest and arms were muscular. His hair had streaks of pure gold in it. He glanced up at her once and she saw that his eyes were the same deep blue as his tail. They met her gaze and held it. She looked away before he did, blushing again.

'There,' he said when he'd finished. 'It's not ideal, but it should hold you until we get to the Lagoon.'

'Thank you,' she said.

He shrugged. 'It's nothing.'

'Not just for the bandage,' she said. 'For saving us. I hope you'll tell me who you are. When I'm back in Miromara and all of this—'

Blu cut her off. 'That's not going to happen. The city's in ruins. The invaders control it. The dead are piled up in the squares. They . . . they can't even bury them. . . .'

He stopped talking and swallowed. Hard.

'Did you lose someone?'

'My parents,' Blu said tersely.

Serafina instinctively took his hand. 'I'm so sorry,' she said, squeezing it.

He squeezed back. 'Thanks,' he said softly. 'You can't go back there. Promise me you won't.'

'I have to go back. It's my city.'

'Not any more. It's Traho's now. He's been going through it current by current, interrogating people.'

'What people?'

'Nobles. Courtiers. Servants. Grooms. Anyone who might've had contact with you. Anyone he suspected of hiding you. If they didn't give him information, he had them executed.'

'Those poor people,' Serafina said, heartsick. 'They died because of *me*.'

'No, they died because of Traho,' Blu said firmly.

She looked down and realized she was still holding his hand. What was she doing? He was a total stranger. 'I should go. I need to check on Thalassa,' she said awkwardly, then swam off.

Thalassa's face was still deathly pale. She was sitting very still, with her eyes closed. Neela shook her head in response to Serafina's unspoken question.

A minute later, Blu joined them. 'We can't stay here much longer,' he said. 'We have to—'

'Praedatori!' a voice, harsh and ringing, called from

outside the cave. 'I have one of yours! Give me the mermaids and I'll let him live!'

'*Praedatori?*' Serafina repeated, stunned. She turned to Blu. 'You're *outlaws*?'

'According to some,' he said.

Serafina remembered Neela telling her that Bilaal had been worried about attacks from the Praedatori during their journey.

'Is that why you helped us? So you can ransom us to the highest bidder?' she asked accusingly. 'We trusted you! And you betrayed us!'

'Think about that for a minute,' Blu said. 'The highest bidder in this scenario would be Traho, right? We took you *from* him, remember?'

Sera was still suspicious. 'Then where are you taking us? To your leader? To Kharkarias?'

'Yes,' Blu said.

'What does he want with us?'

'To help you.'

Sera looked into Blu's eyes, searching for the truth. She wanted to trust him, but she was afraid. She had trusted Zeno Piscor and ended up as Traho's prisoner.

Grigio appeared. 'Trouble. Big-time,' he said.

Blu swam back outside. Serafina and Neela followed him. On the flats below were mermen on hippokamps, carrying torches. In their light, Serafina could see huge grey fish – hound sharks – circling. One of the riders moved forward. He was dragging something behind him. As he swam out in front of the others, Serafina could see what it was. Or rather, *who*: the merman who'd swum off earlier to lure the hound sharks away.

'Praedatori!' their leader called out. 'Bring me the mermaids or I'll kill the boy!'

Serafina started for the flats. Blu grabbed her arm.

'Let me go! I won't be the cause of anyone else's death!' she said.

'Don't be stupid. He's already dead,' Verde said.

'No, he's not! He's alive! He's right down there!'

'The minute I hand you over, the riders will kill him, me, and all my men.'

'Why is he bargaining with us?' Neela asked. 'Why hasn't he attacked? They totally outnumber us.'

'Because he's afraid. As well he should be. He knows I no longer have an iron collar around my neck.'

It was Thalassa, slowly making her way towards them.

'Magistra!' Serafina exclaimed. 'Oh, thank gods! Traho's soldiers are below. We have to go. Can you swim?'

Thalassa shook her head. 'I am the canta magus of Miromara, not some sneak thief scuttling off into the night. It's high time the sea scum chasing us learned that.'

She and Verde looked at each other. Something passed between them. An understanding.

'You could put a giant vortex behind us,' he said. 'Or a silt storm.'

'Child's play.' Thalassa sniffed. 'I'll do better.'

'A vortex would hold them off,' Serafina said excitedly.

'We're not far from the Lagoon, Magistra. We can make it now that you've caught your breath.'

'I can give you thirty minutes, possibly a bit longer,' Thalassa said, still talking to Verde. 'Swear to me you'll get them to safety.'

Verde nodded. 'On my life,' he said.

And then Serafina understood. They were leaving, but Thalassa was not.

'No, Magistra,' she said frantically. '*No!*'

'Serafina . . .' Thalassa said.

'You can't stay behind. You *can't*!' said Serafina, choking back a sob. 'You're all I have left of Miromara.'

Thalassa cupped Serafina's cheek with her good hand. 'And you, child, are all Miromara has left,' she said.

Thalassa's words hit her hard. She hadn't had much time to think about what was going to happen, only what had happened already. But what Thalassa said was true: the city of Cerulea had fallen, her mother was a prisoner – if she was even still alive. Her father was dead. She had no idea what had happened to her uncle. Or if her brother was still at the western borders. That meant that she was her realm's only hope.

'I can't do this, Magistra. I don't know how.'

'Never forget what I told you. Show what's in your heart and all hearts will be with you,' Thalassa said. She hugged Serafina tightly, and then let her go.

Serafina would go to the Lagoon. Because she had to. She had to stay alive. She couldn't help her people if she was taken. And Thalassa would stay here. Because *she* had to. She would rather die protecting Serafina than be the reason she was captured.

'We have to go,' Verde said.

Serafina shook her head, her eyes still on Thalassa.

'Not yet. *Please*.'

Thalassa swam out of the cave. She looked down at the riders for a few seconds, as if taking their measure, then she lifted her head and started to sing. Everyone stopped still, spellbound. Serafina, Neela, Blu, even Verde. No one said a word. Thalassa was battered and bloodied, she was facing certain death, and yet she had never sounded more magnificent. Her voice was the sound of the sea itself – the whirl and crash of breakers, the howl of a gale, the roar of a tsunami.

She pulled wind down into the water and spiralled giant vortexes one after another, until she'd raised a wall of spinning typhoons. She was no longer a mere mermaid. She was a storm system, a category five. And she was bearing down on the enemy.

'Serafina,' Blu said gently.

Sera nodded. She would leave now. She would swim away hard and fast. With the sound of Thalassa's voice forever in her head. Forever in her heart.

# TWENTY-THREE

FACES LOOMED OUT of the grey murk of the Lagoon. Voices, broken and desperate, begged for help.

'Please, can you spare some currensea?'

'My son is injured. He needs a doctor!'

'My husband is missing. His name is Livio. He's tall with black hair. Have you seen him?'

The Lagoon was only four leagues north of Cerulea, just over ten nautical miles. Refugees from the city, wounded and dazed, swam through its narrow currents. They huddled in doorways and slept in alleys.

'My children are hungry, do you have any food?' a mermaid begged. She had two little ones clutching her tail and a baby in her arms.

Serafina stopped. She had no food and no money to give. She turned to Blu.

'We need to keep moving,' he said. 'The waters are lightening. It'll be dawn in another hour.'

'You must have something on you . . . a drupe or a cowrie,' said Serafina. 'Give her something, or I won't budge.'

'*Keep moving!*' Verde hissed.

Blu pulled off his earring – a gold hoop – and handed it to the mermaid.

'Sell it,' Serafina told her. 'It should bring you a few trocii.'

The mermaid hugged Blu. She took Serafina's hand and kissed it. 'You're the principessa, I know you are! I saw you in the Kolisseo. Thank you! Oh, thank you, Principessa!' she said.

A merman, overhearing her, turned around. 'It's her! The principessa!' he said.

'Take back Cerulea!' a mermaid shouted. 'Avenge us!'

An oily-looking merman who'd been watching them from a doorway turned and swam off.

Verde yanked Serafina away. 'Word's travelling,' he said. 'And that's not good. There are Lagoonas, plenty of them, who would sell you to Traho for two cowries.'

'Are you going to sell us for more?' Serafina asked archly.

Verde didn't bother to answer her.

Serafina still wanted to trust him, to trust all of them. Thalassa had trusted them, it seemed. But they were Praedatori. Outlaws. Why would they help two princesses?

The group swam on, though ancient archways, down dimly lit currents. Serafina looked around, wondered where Kharkarias's lair was. She had never been to the Lagoon, but had heard many stories. It bordered the human city of Venice, and was part of Miromara, but belonged only to itself. Home to criminals, sirens, con artists, and spies, it was also a favourite haunt of swashbucklers – young mer who flipped a fin at society by dressing like pirates.

As they approached the heart of the Lagoon, the dingy currents gave way to squares lined with cafés and clubs. Lava bubbled in garishly coloured globes outside of them. Loud music spilled into the streets through their open doors. Serafina saw shops where one could buy anything – songspell pearls, shipwreck silver, rare sea creatures, posidonia wine.

Then the narrow currents of the Lagoon led to humanmade canals, and the clubs and cafés to Venetian palazzos. Her uncle had told her that wealthy terragogg nobles and merchants had built these grand dwellings centuries ago upon wooden piles driven deep into the Lagoon's hard clay, and that equally wealthy mer had built their palazzos underneath them. These merfolk, exquisite in dress and elusive in manner, swam in and out of their dwellings now. Many wore masks. Serafina saw white faces with red lips. Golden faces with delicate black tracery. The face of a water bird, with a curved, cruel beak. A harlequin. A crescent moon. The face of death.

She found the effect unnerving. The masks themselves were still and impassive, but the eyes behind them were lively and appraising. It was said that these palazzo-dwellers had gained their riches by giving secret concerts for humans. Consorting with terragoggs was illegal. In the Lagoon, however, the only crime was being stupid enough to get caught at it.

'That's the Grand Canal,' Verde said, pointing ahead. 'The palazzo isn't far.'

'It smells bad here,' Neela said, making a face.

'It's the goggs,' Grigio said.

A quarter league up the Grand Canal, Verde turned off into a smaller canal, or rio. 'This is it,' he said. 'Calliope's Way.' He swam a few yards down the rio, then stopped in front of a white marble building with a soaring gothic doorway. Lava torches glowed brightly at either side of it. Below them were carved stone faces with blind eyes and open mouths. An image of the sea goddess Neria, flanked by lesser gods, was carved in relief above the door. Above that was a loggia of pointed arches, decorated with a delicate frieze of sea flowers, fish, and shells.

Blu lifted a heavy iron knocker and let it drop.

'*Qui vadit ibi?*'

It was the stone faces. They'd spoken in unison.

'*Filii maris*,' Blu said.

*Ancient words. Spoken when the palazzo was built*, Serafina thought. She understood the Latin. *Who goes there?* was the question. *Sons of the sea*, the answer.

The doors opened outward.

'This way,' Verde said. 'He's expecting you.'

Serafina and the others followed him inside. The doors closed behind them with an ominous boom. The lock's tumblers turned. A bolt slid home. She looked up and saw light spilling over the water. Verde swam towards it. Serafina and Neela looked at each other, then did the same. When they surfaced, they found themselves in a large rectangular pool that took up most of a cavernous room – a room that also contained furniture, a fireplace, electric lights, and air.

A room for a terragogg.

'I – I don't understand,' Serafina said. 'I thought this was a mer dwelling.'

'You'll be all right,' Blu told her. 'We've got to go.'

'My gods, Blu,' Serafina said, realizing what the Praedatori had done. 'You sold us to *humans*?'

'*What?* No! You can't do this!' Neela said, her voice shrill with fear.

Blu was already under the water. All the Praedatori were.

'Blu, *wait*!' Serafina shouted.

It was too late. The mermaids were all alone.

# TWENTY-FOUR

'WHAT *IS* THIS PLACE?' Serafina asked, looking around warily.

'A seriously huge mistake,' Neela said. 'We've got to get out of here.'

'We can't. We're locked in,' Sera said.

Fins prickling, she swam to the far side of the pool. These wide, flat steps angled into the pool's wall led out of the water into the terragogg room. Using her tail, she pushed herself to the top of them, then peered into the room. The air, so rich in oxygen, made her feel momentarily light-headed.

The room's walls were covered in ornate mosaics. Logs were burning in a huge stone fireplace. Thick wool rugs covered the stone floor. On the mantle, on stands and on tables, were artifacts – amphorae, statuary, tablets with carvings, chunks of terracotta. Leather-bound tomes filled the tall shelves on the far wall.

'It's a terragogg ostrokon,' Neela said. 'Look at all the blooks.'

'I think they're called books,' Serafina said.

Old oil paintings hung on the walls – portraits of long-dead gogg nobility. One captured Serafina's attention. It was a picture of a young woman, not much older than she was. She was wearing a jewelled crown and dressed in an embroidered silk gown with a stiff lace collar. Around her neck she wore ropes of flawless pearls, a ruby choker, and a magnificent, teardrop-shaped blue diamond.

'Maria Theresa, an infanta of Spain, and an ancestor on my mother's side,' a voice said.

In a heartbeat, Serafina and Neela were back under the water. When they surfaced – well in the centre of the pool – they saw a man sitting at its edge. He was of a slight build, with thick grey hair that he wore swept back from his forehead. His blue eyes were shrewd and penetrating behind his spectacles. A tweed jacket, vest, and silk cravat gave him an old-fashioned elegance. His trousers were rolled, and his feet were in the water.

'Her jewels are exquisite, no?' he said, looking at the painting. 'They were handed down through many generations, from Spanish queens to their daughters. Alas, they were lost when the infanta was, in 1582. She was sailing to France in a ship called the *Demeter* to marry a prince. Pirates attacked the vessel and sank it.'

Serafina, alarmed, began to sing a confuto – a canta prax spell that made the goggs sound insane when they talked about merpeople. It was the first thing any mermaid did upon finding herself face to face with a human – but Sera's voice sounded tinny as she sang it, and her notes were flat.

'Please do not tax yourself unnecessarily, Your Grace,' the

man said, turning back to her. 'Confutos don't work on me.' His Mermish was flawless.

'Who are you?' Serafina demanded. 'Why did you buy us?'

'My name is Armando Contorini, duca di Venezia, leader of the Praedatori. This is the Praesidio, my home. And I haven't *bought* you. Good gods! What on earth gave you that idea? You are my honoured guests and are most welcome to stay or go.'

'You're the leader of the Praedatori?' Neela said. 'But that means you're Karkharias, the shark.'

The duca chuckled. 'I'm afraid so. A very silly nickname, no?'

'You don't look like an outlaw,' Serafina said.

'Or a shark,' Neela said.

'I'm a lawyer, actually, the worst kind of shark,' the duca said, laughing. 'My apologies, dear merls. Courtroom humour. Allow me to explain. The duchy was created by Merrow. For four millennia, the duchi de Venezia have carried out the duty she entrusted to us – to protect the sea, and its creatures, from our fellow terragoggs. I control a cadre of fighters on land and in the water. On land, we call ourselves the Wave Warriors and—'

'Um, Duca Armando? Are you actually saying you have terragoggs fighting other terragoggs on behalf of the seas?' Neela asked, a dubious look on her face.

'Oh, yes. Many humans cherish the seas as much as you do – and fight hard to protect them. The Wave Warriors collect evidence against pillagers and polluters, and then I go to court to stop them. In the water, our fighters are known as the Praedatori, and we are a bit . . .' He paused. 'Well, let's just say we don't do things the usual way.'

Neela narrowed her eyes. 'Excuse me very much, but in Matali, you're called *āparādhika*. Criminals. A few weeks ago – and don't even *think* about denying it – the Praedatori stole Foreign Secretary Tajdar's collection of shipwreck silver. It's worth nearly three hundred thousand trocii.'

The duca snorted. 'Deny it? I'm proud of it! It was a brilliant heist. Tajdar's collection *wasn't* salvaged from shipwrecks. It was given to him over the course of several years by a captain of a super trawler in exchange for information on the movements of yellowfin tuna. My spies saw the goods passing between the two on several occasions. Need I remind you of the yellowfins' precarious state? Their numbers have been devastated by overfishing. Your foreign secretary is as crooked as a fishhook, my dear. The Praedatori merely robbed a robber.'

'Are you *serious*?' Neela said.

'Usually.'

'What did you do with the swag?'

'I sold it to fund covert operations. We cut nets and longline hooks. We set up field hospitals for the turtles, dugongs, sea lions, and dolphins injured by them. We jam propellers, tangle anchors, puncture pontoons – whatever we need to do to preserve aquatic life. It takes a great deal of currensea to fund it all.'

'But Duca Armando, robbery is robbery,' Serafina said, still mistrustful of this man. 'It's a crime no matter who's doing the stealing. Or why.'

'Tell me, Principessa, if you were poor and had a child, and that child was starving, would you steal a bowl of keel worms to save her life? What is the greater crime – stealing food, or allowing an innocent to die?'

Serafina didn't answer right away. She couldn't argue with his reasoning, or the rightness of his cause, but she didn't want to admit it. Not before she understood exactly why she and Neela were here.

Neela answered for her. 'She'd *totally* steal the worms. Anyone would. What's your point?'

'That sometimes we must fight a greater evil with a lesser one. The waters of the world are in the greatest peril. We have had some success in the courts of the terragoggs against the worst offenders, but not enough. So we rob robbers to further our cause. I am more than happy to relieve Tajdar, and all like him, of their ill-gotten gains, if it saves one species from being fished to extinction, one more garbage lake from materializing in the Pacific Ocean, or one magnificent shark from being murdered for its fins.'

'Who are the Praedatori?' Neela asked.

'That I cannot tell you. Their identities are kept secret to protect them. Faces, bodies, voices – they're all disguised by powerful songspells. They come from all swims of life and they pledge themselves to the defence of the earth's waters.' His expression grew solemn. 'It is not a pledge to be taken lightly. The risks they face are enormous. Many are killed in the line of duty. In this day and age, friends of the water have many enemies. Just last week, two of my soldiers died sabotaging a seal cull. I grieved for them as I would my own children.' Sorrow filled his eyes and anger filled his voice. 'We have not yet recovered from that loss, and now we face this . . . this *butchery* in Miromara.'

At the mention of her realm, Serafina's fins prickled again.

'Duca Armando, why are we here?' she asked, unable to contain her fears any longer. 'You say the Praedatori exist to fight the terragoggs, but the attack in Miromara was made by mer, so why are you involving yourself? This is not the Praedatori's fight.'

'Oh, but it is,' the duca said.

'But it was Ondalina who attacked us. The arrow that wounded my mother was tipped with poison from an Arctic sculpin. The uniforms the attackers wore were black – Admiral Kolfinn's colour. They were *mermen*, Duca Armando, not humans,' Serafina said.

'You saw what Kolfinn wanted you to see,' the duca said. 'He had help.'

'From whom?' Serafina asked, frightened by the thought of another mer realm aligning with Ondalina. 'Atlantica? Qin?'

'No, my child. From a terragogg. The very worst of his kind. Rafe Iaoro Mfeme.'

# TWENTY-FIVE

'IT *CAN'T* BE,' Serafina said, stunned. 'The terragoggs have *never* been able to find us, or our cities. We have spells to keep them away; we have sentries and soldiers.'

She was practically babbling with fear. She wouldn't accept what the duca was saying. *Couldn't* accept it. For millennia, only magic had protected the mer from marauding terragoggs. Humans couldn't break the protective spells the mer cast, but other mer could. Is *that* what Kolfinn was doing?

'If the terragoggs can get to us, they'll destroy us,' she continued. 'Duca Armando, there's no way that Ondalina would be in league with the terragoggs. Even Kolfinn couldn't commit such a betrayal. No mer leader could.'

'*Think*, Principessa,' the duca urged her. 'Where did the attackers come from?'

Serafina cast her mind back to the Kolisseo. She could see it all so clearly, as if it had happened only minutes ago. She saw her mother wounded. Her father killed. And thousands of troops descending on the city.

The answer hit her like a rogue wave. 'From above,' she

said. 'Mfeme transported them. In the hold of a trawler.'

The duca nodded. 'Three, to be exact. The *Bedrieër*, the *Sagi-shi*, and the *Svikari*. They were all sighted in Miromaran waters the day of the attack.'

'But that makes no sense,' Neela said. '*How* could he transport them? The attackers were mer. They can't just walk up a gangplank.'

'We think he filled the holds of his trawlers with salt water, then lifted the troops aboard in enormous nets. Weaponry was loaded the same way. The sea dragons followed the ships.'

'What was his price?' Serafina asked bitterly. 'Mfeme gave Kolfinn speed and stealth. What did Kolfinn give him?'

'Information, we believe,' the duca replied. 'Most likely the whereabouts of tuna, cod, and swordfish shoals. Shark. Krill. Seal breeding grounds. Mfeme plunders the sea for any creature of value.'

'But Duca Armando,' Neela said, '*why* would Kolfinn want to attack Miromara?'

'Dissatisfaction with the terms of the peace treaty between the two realms. Ondalina still resents losing the War of Reykjanes Ridge.'

At that moment, a door opened and a small, stout woman walked in carrying a tray. Spooked, the mermaids dived again.

Armando calmed them when they resurfaced. 'This is Filomena, my cook,' he explained.

Filomena set her tray down at the top of the steps. She

looked at the mermaids, at Serafina in particular, then turned to the duca and spoke rapidly in Italian.

'*Sì, sì,*' he said sadly.

'*Ah, la povera piccina!*' she said, dabbing at her eyes with her apron.

Sera understood Italian, but Filomena spoke so fast, the duca had to translate.

'She asked me if you were Isabella's daughter. She says you have her manner. Isabella is a great favourite of hers,' he explained.

'My mother comes here?' Serafina asked. 'That can't be. It's forbidden.'

'Good leaders know when to follow rules and when to break them,' the duca said. 'She comes to find out about the doings of the terragoggs and how they might affect her realm.'

Serafina couldn't believe what he was telling her. Her mother broke the rules? That wasn't possible. He was lying, trying to gain her trust. But then she recalled something she'd overheard when she was outside Isabella's presence chamber. Conte Orsino had mentioned that the Praedatori had been sighted near a recently raided village, and Isabella had said: *The Praedatori take valuables, not people. They're a small band of robbers. They don't have the numbers to raid entire villages.* At the time, Sera had wondered at her mother's dimissive tone. Now she understood it: Isabella knew the Praedatori's leader, and she knew he and his soldiers would never harm the mer.

The duca was telling the truth.

'Do you have any news of my mother?' Serafina asked, fearful of the answer. 'My uncle? My brother?'

'Or my family?' Neela asked.

'There are rumours – and I stress they are only rumours – that your uncle escaped, Serafina. And that he's heading north to Kobold waters.'

'To the goblins? Why?' Sera asked.

'To raise an army. The Kobold are fearsome fighters, and the mer's only source of weaponry,' the duca said.

His reasoning made sense to Serafina. The mer depended on the goblin tribes to mine and forge metals for them. The goblins made mer weapons and tools, and cast their currency: gold trocus, silver drupe, and copper cowrie coins. Neria had forbidden the ability to shape metal to the merpeople, so as to prevent them from using magic to create wealth.

'We can at least hope these rumours are true,' the duca said. 'Eat now. Please. You must both be famished.'

Serafina looked at Neela and saw her own thoughts mirrored in her friend's eyes. *Can we trust him? The food could be poisoned.*

'I understand your concern,' the duca said, as if he had read their minds. He rose, crossed the room, and took an ivory conch from a shelf.

'If you listen, you will hear your mother's voice,' he said, handing the shell to Serafina.

Sera held it to her ear.

*Serafina, my darling daughter, if you are listening to this conch, it means you are in the Praesidio, and I am captured or dead. You must put your faith in the duca now. His family's relationship with our kind goes back for thousands of years. I trust him with my life, Sera, and with yours. Let him help you. He is the only one who can.*

*I love you, my child. Rule wisely and well. . . .*

Serafina lowered the conch, blinking back tears. It was hard to hear her mother's voice, to know that these echoes in a shell might be all she had left of her.

Neela gently took the shell from her and listened to it, too. When she finished, she put it down on the edge of the pool. 'Sera, if he wanted to kill us, he would have by now. I doubt the food is poisoned.'

'Quite true,' the duca said. 'Poison is too slow. They' – he pointed to the back of the pool – 'get the job done much faster.'

Neither mermaid had noticed, but half a dozen dorsal fins were sticking out of the water. The mako sharks to whom they were attached circled lazily at the far end of the pool. Sera knew that makos were keen predators.

The duca leaned down, stuck his hand in the water, and rapped three times against the side of the pool. The sharks immediately swam to him and raised their noses. He scratched the head of the largest one.

'The best possible alarm system,' he said. 'Smart, quick, and able to sense the tiniest vibrations in the water.' The shark whose nose he was scratching butted his hand impatiently. '*Sì, piccolo. Sì, mio caro. Che è un bravo ragazzo?*' the duca crooned. He tossed them sardines from a bucket.

The tenderness that the duca, a human, showed the sharks dispelled Serafina's last doubts. *Anyone who pets a mako and calls it 'little one' and 'my darling' and 'good boy' is for real*, she thought.

Ravenous, she swam to the steps and hoisted herself up them. Neela followed her. There were all manner of delicacies on the tray Filomena had brought. Pickled limpets. Walrus milk cheese. A salad of chopped sea cucumber and water apple. Sliced sand melon.

Neela ate a piece of sand melon. And then another. She pressed a hand to her chest, closed her eyes and said, 'Positively invincible.'

The duca looked puzzled. 'Is that a good thing?' he asked.

'A very good thing,' Serafina said, smiling. 'Thank you, Duca Armando,' she added, reaching for a limpet. It was all she could do not to bolt down the entire bowl.

'You are most welcome,' he said, looking at his watch. 'It's nearly five a.m. You must be very tired. I have rooms prepared for you and I hope you will find them comfortable. Before you retire, I wonder if I might ask you one more question . . . one that is very much puzzling me. Why did the invaders allow you to live?'

'We were wondering the same thing,' Serafina said, helping herself to a piece of cheese.

'*Were?*' the duca said. 'Did something happen to give you answers?'

Serafina and Neela traded uncertain glances.

'Please. You must tell me. Anything and everything. No matter how minor it may seem.'

'It wasn't minor. Not to Traho,' Serafina said.

The duca sat forward, suddenly alert. 'What was it?'

'The Iele,' Serafina said.

The duca blinked. 'I beg your pardon?'

'The Iele,' Neela repeated. 'As in: scary river witches.'

'Yes, I'm familiar with them. The stuff of myth,' he said. 'Simple stories our ancestors invented to explain what thunderstorms were, or comets. Traho obviously isn't interested in make-believe witches. The word must be code for something, though it hasn't come up in any intelligence.'

Serafina hesitated, then said, 'It's *not* code. We had a dream, Neela and I. A nightmare, actually. It was the same, though neither of us knew the other had had it until we were in Traho's camp. The Iele were in the dream. They were chanting to us. And Traho knew about it. He knew the exact words to the chant. He wanted more information and thought we had it.'

The duca nodded knowingly.

'You are *so* not believing us,' Neela said.

'I believe that in times of duress, the brain – human or mer – does what it must to survive. You may *think* you had the same dream, because your violent and terrifying captor said you did and going along with him saved your lives. His suggestion became your reality. I've seen it happen before to Praedatori who've been taken.'

'*Duca Armando, signorine bisogno di dormire!*' Filomena

said sharply. She'd bustled back into the room to retrieve her tray.

'*Sì, sì*,' the duca said to her. He turned to the mermaids. 'Filomena is right. Young ladies *do* need their sleep. You've both suffered terribly. You must rest now. We shall talk more tomorrow. I shall call for Anna – she's the housekeeper for the water quarters of the palazzo – to show you to your rooms.'

'Thank you again, Duca Armando,' Serafina said. 'For the meal, for freeing us, and for giving us a place to stay. We're very grateful to you.'

The duca waved away her thanks. 'I shall see you both later in the day. While you're resting, I'll send messengers to the leaders of Atlantica, Qin, the Freshwaters – and to your father, Princess Neela, who rules Matali now in the absence of the emperor and crown prince – advising them of Kolfinn's treachery. I know they'll come to your aid. Sleep well, my children. Know that you are safe. The doors through which you entered have been locked and barred. The Praedatori are here to guard you. Your ordeal is over. Nothing can harm you here.'

# TWENTY-SIX

'THIS WAY, PLEASE, Your Graces,' Anna said, smiling.

Serafina and Neela followed her. They passed the canalside doors through which they had entered the duca's home and swam down a dimly lit hallway.

The underwater walls of the ancient palazzo were shaggy with algae. Fleshy orange starfish and spiky blue urchins – their bright colours a warning – clustered on the ceiling. Tube sponges dotted the floor, their bloated fingers brushing against the mermaids' tails. Twining ribbon worms and tiny baglike salps, frightened by the bright light of Anna's torch, wriggled into cracks and seams. Feather stars and sea whips – things with mouths but no eyes – strained towards the mermaids as they passed, drawn by their movements.

Serafina was so desperately tired, she could've slept on the floor. Her stomach was full, but her mind was foggy, and her body was bruised and sore. 'Is the duca right?' she asked Neela as they swam. 'Do we only *think* we had the same dream?'

'I don't know, Sera. I'm so exhausted I can't think at all.

We'll figure it out later. We're safe. We're alive. For now, that's enough.'

'My quarters are just down the hall, should you need anything in the night,' Anna said, as she opened the door to Serafina's room. 'The Praedatori are also nearby. Sleep well. Princess Neela, your room is here. Just across the hallway.'

Serafina thanked Anna, then hugged Neela hard. Neela hugged her back. Neither mermaid let go of the other for quite some time. 'Love you, merl,' she said. 'Would never have made it here without you.'

'Love you, too,' said Neela.

Serafina entered her room, then closed the door. A canopied bed, carved from yellow amber and lined with blue anemones, greeted her. It looked so lush and inviting that it was all she could do not to flop down in it right away, but she didn't. She wanted to find the grotto first and scrub herself clean. As she crossed the room, she glimpsed walls painted with coloured squid inks, a gilt bamboo desk and chair, a tall looking glass in a corner, and a blue sea-silk dress hanging from a stand. A note on a table near the dress informed her that it was for her. She couldn't believe how thoughtful the duca was.

The doorway to the grotto was on the far side of the room. Serafina swam through it. It was tiled in shimmering, oceanhued mosaics. An ivory robe hung from a hook. On a marble table were glass jars filled with sand for scrubbing skin and scales. Serafina saw black sand from the shores of Hawaii, white from Bora Bora, and pink from the Seychelles.

It seemed almost too much to ask for after all she'd been through – a good, long scrub and a soft robe to wear.

As she was about to undress, a movement in the grotto's mirror caught her eye. She glanced at it and saw a figure looking back at her, wraithlike and haggard. A vitrina, she thought. But no. She swam closer and realized that she was looking at herself.

The left side of her face was mottled purple and black, thanks to Traho. Her hair was a tangled mess, her skin and scales filthy. Her once-beautiful gown was torn and bloodstained. As she stared at the blood, she started to shake. The images started coming at her, one after another. The arrow piercing her mother's side. Her father's body falling through the water. Dragons attacking the palace. Traho. The dying guard. Thalassa singing her last songspell. The refugee mother and her children.

She pulled off her gown and threw it on the floor. Naked and shivering, she grabbed a jar of black sand. She poured some into her hand, then scrubbed herself mercilessly until her skin was pink and her scales gleaming. Next, she took the robe from its hook and wrapped it around herself. Her body was stinging from the harsh scrubbing, but she didn't care. She welcomed the pain. It kept the images at bay.

'Take a deep breath,' she told herself, swimming into the bedchamber. 'It's going to be okay.'

But it wasn't.

A few strokes away from the bed, Serafina crumpled. With a cry of grief, she sank to the floor.

A second later, the door opened and Blu swam inside. 'Serafina, what's wrong? I heard a cry. Are you all right? Are you hurt?' he asked, kneeling by her.

'Yes,' she said through her sobs. She'd held herself together for so long, but she couldn't do it any more.

'Where? What happened? Show me,' Blu said, sitting her up.

'Here!' she said, pounding her hand against her heart. 'Everything I loved is gone, my parents, my home, my city. . . .' Her voice caught. The rest of her words were drowned in a torrent of tears.

Blu lifted her off the floor, pulled her to him, and held her silently. There was nothing he could say, nothing anyone could say, to make it better.

When there were no more tears left inside her, Serafina raised her head. 'I'm sorry, Blu. I'm so, so sorry. Here I am crying and carrying on, and you lost your parents too.'

'It's okay. You're in shock. You've had no time to absorb what's happened, and now it's all hitting you,' Blu said. 'You need to sleep. It's the only way to get your strength back. Rest now. I'll be right outside.'

Serafina clutched his hand. 'No! Please don't go. Talk to me. Tell me something. Anything.'

'If I do, will you get into bed?'

'Yes,' she said.

'You need to let go of my hand.'

'Okay,' Serafina said.

She climbed into the bed. The anemones caressed her

weary body. Their touch was soft and lulling. She turned on her side, folding one arm under her head. Blu pulled a chair close to the bed. Having him near calmed her, but she was still desperate for distraction.

'Tell me the scariest thing that ever happened to you, Blu. Or the best thing. Or your favourite food. Do you have a sister?' she asked him.

'No,' Blu said.

'Do you have a merlfriend? Tell me about her.'

Blu hesitated.

'Oh, no. Oh gods, I'm sorry. I put my fin in my mouth, didn't I? Please tell me she's not dead.'

'No, she's not dead. She's not . . . well, she's not my merlfriend any more.'

'You split up?' Serafina asked.

'Yeah, I guess we did.'

'What happened?'

'Stuff.'

'*Stuff?*'

Blu looked at the ceiling. 'Being in the Praedatori is tough. It demands a lot from you. Family, friends, merlfriends, you can't tell them about it and they don't understand the sacrifices you have to make, the double life you lead.'

'Maybe you'll get her back.'

He shook his head. 'Not likely.'

'What's she like?'

'Smart. Beautiful. Good.' He paused, then said, 'And brave. Really brave.'

'Sounds like you're still in love with her,' Serafina said.

'Um, yeah. Guess I am.'

There was an awkward silence. Then Serafina said, 'Tell me why you joined the Praedatori.'

'Why I joined the Praedatori . . .' Blu said thoughtfully.

'For fun and adventure? To see exotic places?' Serafina joked, desperate to keep him talking.

He looked at her then, with an expression of such intensity and passion, it made her catch her breath. 'I joined the Praedatori because I love the sea more than my own life,' he said. 'Bad things are happening. Oceans are being destroyed by the goggs. Sea creatures are being hunted to extinction. Mer are attacking mer. The duca says some mer are even aligning with the goggs now. I want to do everything I can to stop it. All of it.'

His eyes held Serafina's, just as they had outside the cave, when he'd bandaged her tail. And once again, she found herself unable to look away from them, caught by their depths like a swimmer in a riptide. *Who* are *you?* she wondered. She forced herself to break his gaze and said quickly, 'I owe you an apology.'

'For what?'

'Earlier, when you brought us here, I was certain you'd sold us to a terragogg. Now I see you would never do that. You're a very upstanding outlaw, Blu. Thank you for rescuing us. We owe you our lives.'

Blu shook his head, embarrassed. 'Anyone would have done it,' he said. 'How about you? You have anyone?' he asked, obviously wanting to change the subject. 'Wait . . . of course you do. You were about to be betrothed to the crown prince of Matali, weren't you?'

'Before everything happened, yes,' Serafina said. 'Before he disappeared.'

'I'm sure he's trying to get back to you.'

Serafina smiled sadly. 'He might be trying to get back to a nightclub. Or a siren. But not to me.'

'Why? What happened? Was he—'

'Just not that into me?'

'A beautiful princess? And kind of funny too? He's totally into you. I'm sure of it,' Blu said.

'I *thought* he was. He made me believe he was. But he wasn't. Parties, other merls . . . they all became more important to him. And now I just . . . I wish I knew *why*. The last time we talked . . . well, we *didn't* talk, really. I swam off. I didn't want to have anything to do with him. I guess I'll never know now.'

'You don't know that he's dead.'

'Chances are good, though, aren't they?'

'Maybe we should change the subject again.'

'To a topic that's cheerful and uplifting,' Serafina said. 'Too bad there isn't one.' She propped herself up on one elbow.

'Hey, you're supposed to be going to sleep,' Blu said. 'If the duca finds out I'm in here keeping you awake . . .'

'Keep talking. *Please*,' she said.

'I don't know what to talk about.'

'Tell me a story, then.'

Blu snorted. 'Do I look like a nursery shoal teacher?'

'Tell me one about Trykel and Spume. You must know one about them. Everyone does.'

Trykel and Spume were the gods of tides, twin brothers who were always fighting over the beautiful goddess Neria. One lived on the shore, the other in the water. Many stories were told of their schemes to win her.

'All right. But I have a condition. You stop talking. Not—'

'—another word,' Serafina said.

'Once upon a time,' Blu began, 'the sea goddess, Neria, fell in love with Cassio, god of the skies. She made a plan to steal away from her palace and meet him on the horizon. Trykel found out and was jealous. He went to Fragor, the storm god, and asked him to fill the sky with clouds so he could hide in them, pretend to be Cassio, and steal a kiss . . .'

Blu's voice, rising and falling, lulled Serafina. She felt so safe here, with him nearby. *He's kind and brave and good. So different from Mahdi*, she thought wistfully. *The mermaid he loves is very lucky. I hope he gets her back some day.*

Serafina continued to listen to Blu's story and before she knew it, sleep was carrying her away like a gentle sea swell. Her eyes closed. Her breathing deepened. She was out.

Blu stayed where he was, remaining very still so as not to wake her. He gazed at her face for quite some time. When he was certain she was fast asleep, he raised her hand to his lips and kissed it.

# TWENTY-SEVEN

*Daughter of Merrow, leave your sleep,*
*The ways of childhood no more to keep.*
*The dream will die, a nightmare rise,*
*Sleep no more, child, open your eyes. . . .*

IT WAS THE SAME NIGHTMARE. The same chant. Only the monster was stronger now. When it shook the bars of its cage, they groaned and cracked, and ice fell from them.

Suddenly, the elderly witch, Vrăja, stopped chanting. She turned and stared at Serafina, her eyes wide with fear.

*He's coming. . . .*

'No,' Serafina mumbled in her sleep.

*He's close, child – you must flee!*

There was a booming crash then, so powerful that it shook the walls of the palazzo.

Serafina sat bolt upright and reached for Blu. He was gone, but she wasn't alone. Someone else was here. She could feel it. She stared into the grey, early morning light, her eyes sweeping across the room, her heart pounding. It was there. In the corner. A dark, hooded figure.

'Who are you?' she asked, terrified. And then she realized the figure was not in the room; it was in the mirror. A pale hand was pressed against the inside of the glass. 'Baba Vrăja!' she whispered. 'Am I still dreaming?'

She got out of bed, swam to the mirror, and pressed her hand to Vrăja's. The glass, cold and hard at first, shimmered, then gave way ever so slightly. Sera felt as if her hand was sinking into thick soft mud. She cried out as Vrăja grasped her hand. The witch's skin was warm, her talons hard and sharp.

'Leave this place, child! *Quickly!* He's coming, and even the Praedatori won't be able to stop him.'

'*Who*? Who's coming?'

'I must go. It's too dangerous. He's using me to find you. You must come to us. Both of you. Please, Serafina!'

'How? Where are you? How do I find you?'

'The River Olt. In the black mountains. Two leagues past the Maiden's Leap, in the waters of the Malacostraca. Follow the bones.'

At that very second, the door to Serafina's bedchamber burst open.

Blu swam inside. He had Neela with him. 'Get dressed, Sera. Hurry,' he said.

'What is it? What's happening?'

'I don't know. Something's going on topside. We may have to get you and Neela out of here. For now, stay here and lock the door. Don't open it for anyone but me,' he said. Then he was gone.

'Sera, it happened again,' Neela said. 'The nightmare. I saw her – Baba Vrăja.'

'I did too. In the nightmare and in my room. Inside the mirror.' She turned back to the glass, but it was empty.

'The duca's wrong, Sera. It's real. It has to be.'

Serafina remembered Vrăja's sharp talons against her skin. 'Yeah, Neela, it is,' she said softly.

Neela was already dressed. Sera shrugged out of her nightclothes, took the blue dress from its hanger, and pulled it over her head. A split second later, she and Neela both heard shouting.

'What's going on?' Neela asked anxiously.

'I don't know, but we need to find out,' Serafina said.

The mermaids left Sera's room. They swam down the hallway, past the canal-side doors, and up to the pool. As they surfaced, they saw the duca, still in his robe and pajamas, shouting orders to a dozen Praedatori. Someone was trying to break down the palazzo doors, he was telling them. They were to take the princesses to safety. The makos were agitated, swimming to and fro. Wary of them, the mermaids hugged the edge of the pool. As they neared the pool's steps, there was a shattering crash from the floor above, and a scream.

'Filomena?' the duca shouted. '*Filomena!*'

There was no answer, just the sound of feet on the stone steps. The duca ran to a table, grabbed a small cloth sack that was on it, and threw it to Serafina.

'There's some currensea in there. Get to a safe house. The Praedatori will help you.'

'Duca Armando, what's happening?' Serafina said.

'Go! *Now!* Get out of here!' the duca shouted.

Serafina and Neela were about to dive when four human men rushed into the room. Their leader's face was obscured by sunglasses and the brim of a baseball cap, but the duca knew him.

'*You!* How *dare* you come into my home!' he shouted.

The man was carrying a speargun. As Serafina watched, he aimed it at the duca.

'*No!*' she screamed.

The man whipped round . . . and levelled the gun at *her*.

It happened so fast, she had no time to cast a deflecto spell. Luckily, the duca lunged at the man and grabbed his arm. The gun went off. Trailing a thin, nylon line, the spear hit a wall and fell into the water.

'Get them!' the man shouted. The duca threw a punch at him, but he deflected it, grabbed the duca, and hurled him against a wall. The duca crashed to the floor, motionless. The three other invaders, all armed with spearguns, dived into the pool.

Serafina felt hands on her, pulling her down through the water. It was Blu. Grigio had Neela. The attackers were in pursuit, but at a signal from Blu, high-pitched and piercing, the makos were on them. The sharks were fast, but not fast enough. All three men had time to get shots off. Two silver spears buried themselves deep into two makos, mortally wounding them. The third pierced Grigio's tail. He was jerked backwards by the nylon line. Serafina screamed as he thrashed against it. Blu swam to him, his knife drawn, and sliced through the line. There was a high, thin scream as a mako's teeth sank into an attacker's flesh.

'Cover us!' Blu shouted at the other Praedatori as he and Grigio pulled the mermaids down through the pool to the canal doors.

Grigio was about to slide the heavy iron bolt back and open them, when they all heard two deep voices say, '*Qui vadit ibi?*' Instead of answering, whoever was outside started battering on the doors. '*Cavete! Cavete! Interpellatores!*' the stone voices shouted. *Beware! Intruders!*

Grigio risked a quick look through a small barred window to the left of the door. He swore, then turned back to the others. 'It's Traho,' he said grimly.

'Go!' Blu shouted, pushing the mermaids down the hallway.

'Where?' Serafina shouted back.

'Into your room! Lock the door and stay there!'

Neela was already inside Sera's room when the outside door crashed in and a spear came hurtling through the water. Sera looked back in time to see it hit Blu's back with a sickening *thuk* and exit his body under his collarbone. His attacker yanked on the line attached to the spear, pulling the cruel, barbed head into his flesh. Blu thrashed madly against it. He twisted in the water, his knife in his hand, trying to cut the line. All Serafina could see was the blur of his powerful tail, frothing water, and blood.

'Blu! *No*!' she screamed, swimming back to him.

'Get her out of here!' he yelled.

Grigio shoved Serafina into her room. He handed her his knife. 'Take it!' he shouted. 'Lock the door!'

Neela pulled the door shut, slid the bolt, and backed away from it. 'If Traho got through the outside door, he can get through this one,' she said, her voice shaking.

'Neela, we've got to go back out there. We've got to help them!' Serafina cried.

'That's *Traho* out there, Sera! It's us he wants. The only way we can help the Praedatori is by getting out of here.'

'*How*? The window has bars on it!'

'Are they bronze? Can we melt them with a liquesco spell?'

Sera shook her head. 'They're iron.'

'Maybe there's a door that connects to another room,' Neela said, desperation in her voice. 'Maybe there's a secret passage, a trapdoor to a tunnel, or—'

Her words were cut off by the sound of pounding. Traho's men were on the other side of the door.

Neela cast a quick robus spell, hoping to shore up the door. 'Hurry, Sera, help me pull up the rug!' she cried.

Serafina slipped Grigio's knife into a deep pocket of her dress. Then she and Neela searched the floor frantically for an outline of a trapdoor, but there was nothing. They heard the sound of splintering wood. Neela's robus was no match for Traho's men. They'd be in the room any minute. She whirled around, desperately looking for a way out, but there was nothing. And then her eyes fell on the looking glass.

'Neela, remember when I said I saw Vrăja in the mirror?'

'How exactly does that help us right now?' Neela asked, her eyes on the door.

'She reached for me, and I reached for her, and my hand went through the glass.'

Neela looked at her. 'No way. Not even the canta magi can do that. We could *die* in there.'

'We'll die out here if Traho gets us.'

An axe blade cleaved the door.

'We have about two seconds, Neels.'

Neela took a deep breath, then grabbed Sera's hand.

Together, they dived into the mirror.

# TWENTY-EIGHT

IT WAS LIKE swimming through sea lily honey. Silver sea lily honey.

'Neela? Neels, where are you?' Serafina called out anxiously.

'*Here*. Yuck. I don't like this, Sera.'

Neela was behind her, trying to catch up. It was an effort just to breathe in the liquid silver, never mind to move.

Sera looked past her, at the mirror they'd just swum through. She could see what was happening on its other side. Traho was in her room. He was furious. His soldiers had ripped the doors off a wardrobe and flipped over the bed looking for them. As both mermaids watched, he peered into the glass, then pounded a fist against it. Serafina shuddered. Neela pulled her away.

'I think he can see us,' she said.

'Even if he can, he can't get to us. He can't swim through the glass.'

'Um, Sera? How did we?'

'I don't know,' Serafina said. 'Right now, the bigger question is, can we get out again?'

The two mermaids turned and stared out at the strange new place they'd just entered, a glittering high-ceilinged hall that seemed to go on forever. Vitrina were everywhere. They sat slumped in chairs or on benches. Or stood motionlessly, heads hanging. A few lay facedown on the ground on the marble floor, as lifeless as flung-away toys. Ghosts of vain terragoggs whose souls had been captured by the mirror, vitrina craved admiration. They became listless without it.

Crystal chandeliers hung from the ceiling, and mirrors of every shape and size adorned the walls. Some were incredibly ornate. Others were sleek and modern. Some boasted frames of precious metals, studded with jewels. Others were made of cheap plastic.

'There must be *thousands* of them,' Neela said wonderingly, touching one. 'Which one do we take? Where do we go?'

Sera didn't reply right away. Then finally she said, 'To the Iele.'

'Seriously?'

'It's time to stop swimming away from everything and start swimming towards something.'

'You know how to get there? Because I don't.'

'I do. Sort of. "The River Olt," Vrăja told me. "In the black mountains. Two leagues past the Maiden's Leap, in the waters of the Malacostraca. Follow the bones."'

'Okay, but how do we get there from *here*?'

'I don't know. I know this, though: I'm sick of being scared. Sick of being hunted. Sick of Traho, and those goggs with their spearguns. They don't get to decide what happens to us any more. We do. Come on.'

Sera led Neela to a mirror. They pressed their faces to the glass. It started to give way, melting around them just as the mirror in the duca's palazzo had. A human girl was on the other side, in her bedroom. They hadn't seen her, but she saw them – and let out an earsplitting scream. They quickly scrambled back from the glass.

'We'd better not do that again or we'll end up flopping around on some terragogg's floor,' Serafina said. 'If we want to get to the Iele, we need to find the mirror Vrăja used.'

'Good luck with *that*,' Neela said, looking at the endless hallway and its multitude of mirrors. 'We need directions, or a map.'

'Maybe we could ask the vitrina how to navigate in here,' Serafina said.

'Let's do it quickly,' Neela said, looking around uneasily. 'This place gives me the creeps.'

Serafina swam to a vitrina – a woman in a slinky golden dress, with bobbed hair and pouty red lips. 'Hello?' she said. 'Excuse me . . .' She got no reponse. 'Oh, isn't she pretty!' Sera added, knowing how to perk up a vitrina. 'And her dress is *gorgeous*.'

The vitrina drew a breath and opened her eyes. Colour came into her cheeks. 'Oh, thank you!' she said, sitting up in her chair. She frowned. 'But what do you think of my hair?'

'It's *so* beautiful!' Serafina said. 'Please, Miss . . .'

'Josephine.'

'I know why this place creeps me out,' Neela suddenly said. 'There aren't any children here.'

'Of course there aren't,' Josephine said. 'Rorrim Drol *hates* children.'

'Why?' Neela asked.

'Because they're strong and fearless. Their little backbones are made of steel. It takes years for them to soften. Fear only sets in as one grows up, you see.'

'Backbones?' Neela echoed, looking confused.

'Who's Rorrim Drol?' Serafina asked.

The vitrina looked past them. 'Shh! Here he comes! Be careful!' she said. 'Don't let him get close or he'll bind you to the glass too.'

The mermaids turned and saw a fat bald man in a red silk robe and blue velvet slippers shuffling towards them.

He held out his arms, smiling wide. '*Food! Food! Food! Feed me! Feed me! Oh, yes! Oh, yes!*'

'Is that, like, a caballabong cheer or something?' Neela whispered to Serafina.

'*Both of them full of fear, I bet! Lovely, tasty, juicy fear!*' the man said, rubbing his plump hands together.

'I'm very sorry, sir, but we can't understand you,' Serafina said.

The man pressed a hand to his chest. '*Do* forgive me! I was speaking Rursus, the lingua franca of Vadus, the mirror realm.' He swept a bow. 'Rorrim Drol, at your service. Welcome to the Hall of Sighs.'

Serafina thought fast. She knew now how dangerous

it could be to reveal her real identity to strangers. 'I'm very pleased to meet you,' she said. 'I'm Sofia . . . and this is Noor.'

The man gave them an oily smile, revealing small, pointed teeth. 'No need to pretend *here*, my darlings! You're perfectly safe. *I* know who you are. Your fame precedes you,' he said. He nodded at Josephine. 'I see you've been talking to my vitrina. So kind of you. They *adore* admirers. Simply can't get enough compliments. Come, meet a few more.'

He walked over to a young woman wearing a damask gown with a square neckline and pointed bodice. Her face was deathly pale. 'This is our darling Katharine. She ended up here because her complexion was darker than was fashionable during her time, and she feared it hurt her chances of finding a husband,' he said.

Katharine smiled and Serafina saw that her teeth were black. Rorrim ran a finger down her cheek, then showed them the tip. It was covered with a white, satiny substance. 'Venetian ceruse. Used by Renaissance ladies to whiten the skin. And it *did*, my dears! Unfortunately, it also caused their teeth to rot and their bodies to wither. It was absolutely *full* of lead and it poisoned them,' he explained happily.

He moved to another woman. She wore a high-necked dress with puffy sleeves. Her eyes, sunken and empty, were like two black holes in her head. 'And of course there's the lovely Alice, who ate arsenic mixed with vinegar to improve *her* complexion. She was getting on in years – all of twenty-three! – and feared losing her beauty. Arsenic was all the rage in the nineteenth century. The vomiting and convulsions it brought on were a bit daunting, but I'm happy to say that Alice persevered and succeeded. There's *nothing* paler than a corpse, is there?'

Smiling, he glided over to a third vitrina. Her blonde head lolled sickeningly on her shoulder. 'And we musn't forget our sweet Lydia. *Bel-la-don-na*,' he said, relishing each syllable. 'It means *beautiful lady*. Lydia feared losing her beau to another, so she put drops of belladonna into her eyes to make her pupils dilate. Victorian men found doe-eyed women oh so alluring, you see. Though, I must say, it wasn't so pretty when she lost her eyesight to the poison, fell down a stairwell, and broke her neck.'

Rorrim smiled at Serafina. He circled her. 'I wonder, little principessa, what do *you* fear?'

Sera felt a chill and realized Rorrim was running his cold fingers down her spine.

'Oh, this is no good at all,' he said. 'Much too strong. I'll have to soften this up or I'll starve.'

'Stop it!' Serafina said angrily. 'Take your hands off me!' She tried to swim away from him but found she couldn't. Her tail was suddenly as heavy as stone. The liquid silver held her fast.

'Neela, I can't move!' she cried, panic-stricken.

Neela started towards her.

'No! Don't come near me! He'll get you, too!'

'Hang on, Sera!' Neela said. She cast a depulsio, a songspell used to move objects, hoping to push Rorrim away, but nothing happened.

'You're wasting your breath, my dear,' Rorrim said. 'Early mirrors were made of polished iron. There's a great deal of it in the Vadus, I'm afraid.'

'Find the way out, Neela! Hurry!' Sera urged.

Neela hesitated, torn, then she swam off.

'Wait a moment . . . what have we here?' Rorrim said, probing the spaces between Sera's vertebrae. 'You hide your fears well, Princess, but I've found one. Ha! Got you!'

Sera felt a strange popping sensation in her back, and then Rorrim swam out from behind her. He had something soft and dark pinched between his fingers. It was fluttering and squealing. 'What is that?' she asked, horrified.

'It's called a dankling. It's a little piece of fear. They burrow into backbones. A few of them will infest a nice strong spine, and then as the bones weaken, more come,' Rorrim explained. He put it in his mouth and swallowed it. 'Mmm! Simply divine!' he said, licking his fingers. 'There's nothing, absolutely *nothing*, as tasty as fear. Doubt is delectable, of course. Insecurities, anxieties – all delicious, but fear? Oh, fear is exquisite! And that one was especially piquant . . . fear for the luscious Mr Blu! That *was* a rather bad injury he sustained on your behalf, wasn't it?'

Desperate to escape, Serafina struggled harder to break free.

'Don't bother. It's pointless,' Rorrim said. 'There's a lot of mercury here, too. The older mirrors are full of it. It weakens you.'

He was behind her again. She could see his reflection in the mirrors on the walls. He'd grown fatter.

'Fight him, Sera!' Neela shouted, as she moved from mirror to mirror, frantically peering in each one. 'He's feeding on your fear! Don't let him!' Getting nowhere, she swam to the broken-necked vitrina. 'Lydia, hey,' she said, cocking her head to meet the ghost's eyes. 'I need to get to the Olt River. Can you help me?'

Lydia closed her doe-like eyes.

Neela swam to Alice. 'Alice, please,' she begged.

Alice frowned. 'Paler. I could be paler still. Don't you think? I know I'd find a husband then.'

Neela started towards Katharine, but Rorrim spoke before she could reach her.

'My dear, dear, Princess Neela, do slow down! You look *so* stressed. Here, just for you. A shapta,' he said, holding out a sweet on his palm. 'Swallow it, darling. Just like you swallow all your fears and frustrations. They leave such a bitter taste, don't they? This is much sweeter.'

Neela stopped dead.

'It gets so tiring, doesn't it? Always having to smile and agree. Never being able to speak your mind. The sweets make up for it all. Cram a bag of bingas into your mouth and you forget for a while how much you hate pink. And the palace. You forget how much you fear your future – the boredom, the longing to do something else, to *be* something else.'

'H-how . . . how do you . . .' Neela stammered.

'*Know*? Why, I've seen you, darling. In your room. Alone at night. Cutting and sewing dresses you'll never wear. Stashing them in the back of your closet. Suma knows about that, by the way. Watch out for her.'

As Rorrim continued to speak, Neela's face changed. Her expression became vulnerable and raw, and Serafina knew Rorrim was getting to her, too. He'd turned Neela's heart inside out for anyone to see, just as he'd done to hers.

Then Neela abruptly shook her head, as if clearing sea foam from her ears. 'Nice try, lumpsucker,' she said. She swam down the hallway and kept searching.

Watching her, Serafina rallied and almost freed her tail, but before she could, Rorrim said, 'I wonder if we can go deeper. Yes, there's something right there . . . oh, it's *very* deep. Ah! Here we go!' There was another popping sensation in her back and then: 'Lovely! Fear of failure! It has such a wonderfully sharp flavour to it. You're terrified of proving yourself a disappointment, aren't you? I can see why. Your mother is – forgive me, *was* – an incredible leader. Strong, smart, *so* dedicated. You're *nothing* like her, darling. Not at all.'

Serafina felt weaker. Rorrim was right – it was pointless. Everything was pointless. It didn't matter if she broke free or not. Why should she even try? She would only fail.

Rorrim prodded her spine again. 'This will soften soon. Fear rots backbones like cavities rot teeth.' He smiled, his eyes glittering, then said, 'And you, my dear, are *full* of it.'

'Principessa!' a voice shrilled.

Serafina looked up. It was Josephine. She was walking towards Serafina and she was furious.

'Principessa, tell your friend to stop being so annoying! She's making a spectacle of herself and taking everyone's attention off *me*!'

'Not *now*, Josephine,' Rorrim warned.

'Yes, *now*, Rorrim,' the vitrina said, stamping her foot. 'Nobody's looking at *me*! Everyone's looking at *her*!' She turned to glare at Neela.

Neela was far down the hall of mirrors. She was waving her arms over her head, trying to get Serafina's attention. As soon as she had it, she pointed to a mirror on the wall and gave her a thumbs-up. Then she cupped her hands to her mouth. 'Don't *listen* to him, Sera! You faced down Alítheia! You faced down Traho! Fight this tube worm!' she shouted.

Neela's words were like a powerful undertow, pulling Sera out of her torpor. *She's right*, she thought. *I have faced worse things than Rorrim*. She straightened her back, picked up her head, and shook off the hopelessness that had descended on her. With a great, wrenching cry, she pulled herself free of the silver.

'Swim, merl, *swim*!' Neela yelled.

Sera did. She raced down the hall to her friend. When she was only a few feet away, Neela dived through the mirror she'd been pointing to, shouting, 'Follow me!'

Serafina put on a burst of speed, ready to dive after her, but Rorrim was right behind her, surprisingly fast for a man of his size. He grabbed her hair and yanked her back. The pain was electric. She screamed and tried to pull away, but he only tightened his grip.

'Not so fast, little princess. You're mine now.'

Blu flashed into her mind. She saw him as Traho's soldiers shot the spear through him. She saw him trying to cut the line attached to it. Then she remembered the dagger Grigio had given her. In a flash, she pulled it out of pocket, reached behind her head, and sliced through her tresses.

A split second later, she shot through the mirror, leaving Rorrim Drol holding a handful of hair.

# TWENTY-NINE

'UM . . . SO, NEELS,' Serafina said, looking down at her tail fins, which were submerged in a low, wide stone bowl, 'the Iele live in a toilet?'

They were in a tiny grotto, no more than three feet by four. They'd tumbled out through a narrow mirror in the wall and Sera had landed tailfirst in the bowl.

'Wow. I think something went wrong,' Neela said, jammed painfully between the toilet and the wall.

'You think?' Serafina said, pulling her fins out of the bowl. She gave them a shake. 'Yuck. *So* gross.'

'Sera, your *hair*!' Neela said.

'That bad?' Serafina asked. She glanced into the mirror and winced. 'Oh, wow. That bad.' The edges were all different lengths. Some chunks grazed her chin, others were up around her ears.

'What happened?'

Serafina explained.

'No one has hair like that except swashbucklers,' said Neela. 'You'll attract attention.' She sang a prax spell – an illusio – and Serafina's long hair was temporarily restored.

'That should hold you for an hour or so. Now, where exactly are we?'

The door was closed. They could hear voices and the sound of clattering dishes coming from the other side.

Neela opened it cautiously. 'It seems to be a café,' she said, swimming out of the grotto. Sera followed her.

The two mermaids looked around. The place was bustling. Bright morning light filtered in through the windows. Merfolk were sitting at tables or at the bar, eating breakfast. A mermaid wearing a red jacket glanced at Serafina and Neela, then returned her attention to her bowl of seaweed. Serafina pointed at a large plate-glass window. It had the café's name on it.

'The *Old* River?' she said. 'Nice going, Neels. We need the *Olt* River.'

Neela squinted at the letters. 'Oops.'

'You have no idea where we are, do you?' Serafina asked.

'Well, I'm fairly confident we're in, or close to, a river.'

'Really? What gave it away, detective? Couldn't be the café window, could it?'

'Ha. So funny, Sera. What gave it away is the smell of freshwater.'

She sneezed. 'It always does that to me.'

Just then, a graceful turtle swam past them.

'Let's ask him where we are,' Neela said.

'I don't know Tortoisha,' Serafina said.

'I don't either. I'll sing a loquoro,' said Neela. Loquoro spells enabled a mermaid to temporarily understand another's language. 'Excuse me, sir,' she called out after she'd cast it.

The turtle stopped and turned around – v-e-r-y slowly. Neela knew that turtles did *everything* v-e-r-y slowly. He raised his head and looked at her with his large eyes.

'Hello,' she said brightly. 'Do you know what town this is?'

The turtle frowned. He scratched his spotted head. Blinked. Thought hard. Took a deep breath. Blew it out. Scratched his head again. Flapped his flippers. Then, finally, he spoke.

'*Z-d-r-a-s-t-i*,' he said slowly.

'Does he know? What did he say?' Serafina asked.

'He said *Hi*,' Neela replied.

'*Hi*? All that for *Hi*? It'll take a *week* to find out where we are! Forget this. Let's ask someone else.'

Neela shook her head. The mermaid in the red jacket was looking at them again. 'We're attracting attention. Let's get out of here.'

As they opened the door, they heard more voices.

'Shipwreck silver! Right off a gogg yacht! All first-rate!'

'Songspell pearls! Transparansea pearls! Best quality! Cast to last, folks!'

'Keel worms here, plump and juicy! Ribbon worms, sweet and slimy!'

The café was on the town's main current and a morning market was in full swing. Its stalls were hung with all manner of goods. Foodmongers sold freshwater fare: braids of marsh grass, frog eggs, pickled crayfish, candied water spiders, and leech puffs. Saltwater importers displayed clams, mussels, scallops, walrus cheese, and the long, twining egg cases of whelks. There was a secondhand clothing stall and salvage stalls selling anything that could be scavenged from a shipwreck – dishes, clothing, lanterns, teapots, knives and swords, even the skulls of terragoggs for those who liked to collect them.

'Voice too small, ladies? Lift it up and push it out with our patented voice enhancer!' a merchant called. 'Totally discreet! Results guaranteed!'

As they swam down the main current, Serafina could see that the town they were in was poor and sprawling, nothing like Cerulea. It was a shabby place, made up of found things. The freshwater mer, living so close to the terragoggs, had an abundance of one thing no matter how poor they might be: garbage. And they made good use of it. Serafina and Neela swam down the current, saw a shop built from oil drums, another from plastic buckets. Others were made from wrecked boats, stacked tyres, or shipping containers that had fallen off freighters. Roofs were shingled with flattened tin cans or plastic bottles. Down at the end of the current was a department store that had been built from a sunken oil tanker.

'Sea cucumbers – still oozing!' a peddler called.

'Gooseneck barnacles – crunchy and sweet!' another cried.

And then the mermaids heard another voice, right behind them: 'They're coming.'

Neela whirled around. It was the mermaid from the café,

the one with the red jacket. Her tail and torso were white with brilliant orange patches, the colours of a koi fish. She had almond-shaped eyes and high cheekbones. Her black hair was coiled into two knots on top of her head. She carried an embroidered silk bag over one shoulder. A sword in a scabbard was slung over her back.

'They're coming,' she repeated. 'You should get out of here.'

'Who's coming?' Serafina asked.

'*Moarte piloti*. That's what the locals call them. It means *death riders*. Traho's men.'

'Who are you?' Neela asked warily.

'My name's Ling. I'm from Qīngshuǐ in Qin.' She called to a manta who was gliding above them and spoke to her in perfect RaySay. Then she asked something of a school of anchovies in Pesca. Finally a stickleback told her what she wanted to know.

'Fifty of them. On hippokamps,' she said. 'Three leagues off, but coming fast.'

Neela's fins began to prickle. 'You speak a lot of languages,' she said.

'I'm an omnivoxa,' said Ling.

Neela knew that omnis, who could speak every dialect of Mermish, and communicate with most sea creatures, were very rare. The prickling in her fins grew stronger. She suspected that Ling was more than some random mermaid from Qin.

'You haven't even disguised yourselves,' Ling continued.

'They'll pick you out in no time. Even with that really bad haircut.'

'Um, thanks,' Serafina said. 'Guess the illusio wore off.'

'How did you know who we are?' Neela asked brusquely.

'Because you stick out like sore fins. You're wearing dresses that probably cost more than most people here make in a year. That, and Traho's wanted signs. Your faces are everywhere. There's a price on your heads. Twenty thousand trocii each. Every bounty hunter and his brother is after you. If I recognized you, they will too. You've got to get out of here. I'm going to get some food, then hit the northbound currents, and find a cave till the death riders blow by. I suggest you do the same.'

'Do you know where we are?'

'Are you *serious*? You don't know where you *are*? You two are hopeless,' Ling said, shaking her head. 'Radneva. In the Black Sea. The Dunărea River is about a two-day swim from here. Then it's another two days, maybe three, to the Olt.'

'But how do you—' Serafina started to say.

'Know where you're going?' Ling finished. 'Because I'm going there, too.' Then she quietly sang the Iele's chant.

As she did, Neela's fins flared. Her suspicions had just been confirmed. Ling had heard the chant. She'd had the same dream. The Iele had called her, too.

'I'm the *One who sings all creatures' songs*. Vrăja summoned me, just as she summoned you, Daughter of Merrow,' Ling said to Serafina. 'Which one are you?' she asked Neela.

'*One whose heart will hold the light*,' Neela said, giving Ling a dark look.

'Of course,' Ling said cheekily. 'How could I have missed that?'

Neela glowered at her. She didn't want this. She didn't like it. It scared her.

'Forgive me for not shining my light at this particular moment. We've had just a teensy bit of a bad time. Nothing much, really. Just an invasion and a kidnapping. An attack by speargun-wielding thugs. Had to swim for our lives a few times. Got stuck in a mirror with a psycho. Maybe I'll get my glow back tomorrow,' she said waspishly.

Ling gave her a solemn look. 'You're going to have a worse time if you don't come up with a disguise and get out of here. . . . ' Her voice trailed off. Her face took on a distracted look, as if she was listening to another conversation.

'What is it?' Neela asked. 'Do you hear something else?'

'I don't know,' she said. 'Maybe it's just mackerel chattering.' She frowned. 'It sounds like laughter, though. Strange.'

'It's the monster,' Serafina said gravely. 'I hear it too.'

'But I've never heard it when I'm awake. Only in my nightmares. That means . . .'

'. . . it's getting stronger,' said Sera.

'Yeah,' Ling said grimly. 'I guess it does. Hey, see you at the Iele's maybe.' She started to swim away.

Sera put a hand on Neela's shoulder. 'I know what you're

feeling, but we need to go with her. She's one of us, Neels,' she said.

Her words struck a chill into Neela. *One of us*. Part of her still wanted to believe that none of this was real. Part of her still hoped that someone – her uncle Bilaal, her father, or one of the praedatori – would ride in on a big white hippokamp and tell her that it was all over, that Traho had been captured and everything was okay and she didn't have to face a dangerous journey, a bunch of freaky witches in a dark cave, and worst of all, that thing in the waterfire. Meeting Ling made that a lot harder.

'Neela?'

'Okay. Yeah. Let's go,' Neela said, her voice trembling a little.

'Wait, Ling! We're coming with you,' Serafina called out.

In her head, Neela heard the Iele's chant. She heard the grey-haired witch calling.

'One down, three to go, Baba Vrăja,' she whispered.

She and Serafina hurried to catch up.

# THIRTY

'I'D *KILL* FOR A BINGA RIGHT NOW.'

'When would you *not* kill for a binga, Neels?' Serafina asked.

The mermaids were swimming across a sandy shoal. It was early evening. They'd left Radneva two days before and had been on the move ever since, stopping only to sleep at night. They'd sang velo spells to speed them along at first, but stopped when they realized that velos, difficult enough to cast in salt water, required even more magic in freshwater. Using back currents, they'd worked their way north, up the coast of Bulgaria towards Romania and the mouth of the Dunărea.

'A wonda would be nice, too. Or a zee zee. Gods, I'd *love* a zee zee. I'd like a cup of sargassa tea, too. Clean clothes. Pretty hair combs. A massage. A soft bed. And a crisp, blue water apple,' Neela said.

'Here, have some shrivelled-up reef olives and stale walrus cheese instead,' Serafina said, handing her the bag of food they'd bought at the Radneva market.

'Olives and cheese *again*?'

'It's all we have left. We better hope we hit a village soon.'

'We will. Aquaba's at the mouth of the Dunărea,' Ling said. 'I'm sure we're close.'

It had been hard going on the currents, riding them – and sometimes fighting them – to get to where they were now. Neela was tired, dirty, hungry, and longing for home and its comforts. And though they were getting closer to the Dunărea, they still had leagues to go to reach the Olt.

'Did we go west around that sandbar off Burgas? Or east?' Serafina asked, looking around. She was holding a kelp parchment map in her hand. It belonged to Ling.

'West. Definitely west,' Ling said. 'That was the shortcut we took. Remember?'

Ling was a good navigator. She'd led the way out of Radneva to a back current and had found them a roomy cave to hole up in for their first night together. They'd avoided death riders and bounty hunters, and at Ling's urging, had changed the colour of their hair and clothing with illusio spells. The only problem was that an illusio, like any spell, eventually wore off. Maintaining it took effort and energy – energy that was going into the constant swimming they were doing. Ling was always reminding them to recast it. Neela was grateful when night fell and she could revert to her true appearance. She knew that she and Sera would have to come up with more permanent solutions, but that would require another village, where they could buy some clothes.

It felt strange to Neela to be three instead of two, and she wasn't always comfortable around Ling, as the merl could be blunt. She also had a disconcerting way of abruptly stopping a conversation to listen to a passing shoal of blennies, or interrupting it to say something like, 'Have you ever noticed the amazing overlap of sibilant clickatives in Dolpheen and Porpoisha?' Neela never really knew if Ling was listening to her or to a sea creature that happened to be swimming by.

Ling was smart and tough, though, and she'd saved them from being captured. She was also the one who knew the route to the River Olt, so Neela had no choice but to accept her.

The three mermaids had talked as they'd made their way north. Serafina and Neela had shared their backgrounds, and Ling had told them that she was from a large clan, most of whom lived in her village.

'Actually, we *are* the village,' she'd said with a laugh. 'Every house contains a relative of mine.'

'How big is your family?' Neela had asked.

'My extended family? There are over five hundred of us. My immediate family – my mother, sisters, and brothers, grandparents, aunts and uncles, and cousins – we're fifty-three. Maybe fifty-four by now. One of my aunts . . .' She paused, listening, then said, 'The size of the sea horse lexicon is incredible, don't you think?'

'Oh, totally,' Neela had replied.

'So, as I was saying, one of my aunts was expecting when I left.'

'And you all live in one house?' Serafina had asked.

'A very big house,' Ling had said, her smile fading. 'All of us but my father. We lost him a year ago. He went out to explore in the Great Abyss, as he loved to do, and he didn't come back. My mother has barely said two words since he disappeared.'

'I'm so sorry, Ling,' Serafina had said.

'What happened?' Neela had asked.

'I don't know,' Ling had replied. 'The entire village searched for him. For days and days. But he was never found. Maybe he went too deep and something attacked him. Or maybe he blacked out. All I know is that I miss him.'

'It must've been hard for your mother to let you go so far away from her,' Serafina had said. 'Especially after losing your father.'

'She didn't *exactly* let me go. In fact, she didn't want me to. But the legend of the Iele is very strong in my culture. My grandmother, Wen, is also our clan's shaman. She's very wise and a keeper of the clan's traditions. When I told her my dream, she said I must go. So I went. And here I am,' she said. 'I've been on the currents for two months. A few days ago, I started to think I was crazy for coming. And then I met you two—'

'—and now you *know* you are,' Neela had joked.

But Ling hadn't laughed. '—and I knew I *wasn't*. The things you told me about the attack and Traho, the fact that we've all had the same dream . . . the Iele are real. We've been called for a reason.'

'Yes, we have. But what is it? That's the big, scary question,' Sera had said. And then she and Ling, still poring over the map, continued across the shoal.

Neela watched them go, then reluctantly followed, knowing that every stroke they took brought them closer to the answer.

'I don't like it,' Neela said now, her hands on her hips.

They'd come to the edge of the shoal. It dropped away steeply to a broad seabed that was flat and open and planted with water apples, but all the trees were bare.

'It's too open. We can be seen.'

'We have no choice,' Serafina said. 'According to Ling's map, we can't go west towards the coast because the shoals are too high. We'd have to surface near gogg beaches. And we can't go east into deep water. The current's too strong there. It'll push us off course.'

'Let's make it quick, then,' she said.

The three mermaids set off. They followed the current into the seabed and made their way across it, attuned to movement, listening for the sound of voices or the swish of fins.

Neela kept looking behind them as they swam, expecting to see death riders crest the shoal at any second, but they didn't. She was just beginning to think they might make it through unnoticed when she heard Ling say, 'Uh-oh.'

Directly in their path was a merman holding a hoe. Its edge gleamed sharply, even in the evening light.

Neela looked left and right and saw several other mermen emerge from behind the trees, carrying scythes and pitchforks. They were ragged and thin, and their mouths were set in hard lines. 'They don't seem too pleased to see us,' she said.

'No, they don't,' Serafina said.

'Get ready,' Ling said. 'On my signal, swim straight up.'

'What if they follow us?' Neela asked.

'Hopefully we can lose them. They look like they don't have much stamina for a chase. Okay, ready? One, two . . .'

Suddenly the merman with the hoe lowered it and bowed his head. 'Long live Serafina, principessa di Miromara!' he shouted. One by one, the others followed his example. They made fists of their right hands, struck their chests, then saluted.

'Hail, Serafina, principessa di Miromara!'

'Long live the Merrovingia!'

'Death to the tyrant Traho!'

Neela glanced at Sera. The illusio spell she'd cast had worn off again.

The merman holding the hoe swam up to them. He bowed and told them his name was Konstantin. 'Forgive us, Principessa. At first we didn't know who you were. There are death riders in these waters.'

Serafina turned in a circle, looking at all those gathered around her. As she did, the other mermen approached. They took her hand and kissed it. They called on the gods to favour her. They told her their stories in voices that were halting and emotional.

'I was away visiting relatives. When I returned, the village was empty. It's the next one over. They were gone, all gone . . .'

'They came at night . . .'

'Where did they go?'

'Why, Principessa, *why* did they take my family?'

'Help us find them. Help us, please.'

Serafina, Neela, and Ling learned that the death riders had taken nearly everyone in their village. They'd left only a handful of mermen to work the orchards for them.

'They say your uncle escaped, Principessa. That he's raising an army of Kobold goblins in the north. Is it true? Have you any word from him?' Konstantin asked hopefully.

Serafina shook her head. 'No. Nothing.'

'And Regina Isabella?'

Neela saw her friend's eyes darken with pain at the mention of her mother.

'I'm hoping she's still alive, but I don't know for sure. We're on our own, I'm afraid. We're travelling to seek help against the evil in our waters,' Sera replied.

Konstantin nodded, trying to hide his disappointment. He reached into his pocket, pulled out a single cowrie, and gave it to Serafina.

'I can't take that,' she protested.

Konstantin didn't listen to her. Neither did the others. They gave her what they had. A few keel worms bundled up in a kelp frond – someone's only meal for the day. A precious silver drupe. Three small water apples hidden from the death riders. A handful of sand nuts.

Serafina looked at the gifts pressed into her hands, from mermen who had *nothing*, and swallowed hard. Neela knew she was swallowing her tears. She also knew that Sera didn't want to take their last few coins or scraps of food, but to refuse would wound them.

'Thank you,' Serafina said, her voice quavering. 'Thank you all. I promise, I *swear* to you, that I will do everything I can to help you. If my mother is still alive, and my uncle, I'll find them and tell them what's happened to you. They'll find your people, I know they will.'

Cheers went up. Serafina thanked the farmers again, said goodbye, and then she, Neela, and Ling resumed their journey. As they swam, Neela noticed that Serafina was strangely quiet. 'What's wrong?' she asked her.

'They bowed to me. They hugged me and kissed me. And I don't deserve it. I don't deserve any of it.'

'You gave them something they needed,' Neela said. 'You gave them hope.'

Serafina shook her head. 'I gave them empty promises, that's all.'

Ling turned to her. 'Hey, Serafina?' she said, an edge to her voice. 'Those mermen back there? They weren't cheering for your uncle. Or your mother. They were cheering for *you*.'

'It's a sign of respect for the crown, that's all,' Serafina said.

A large shoal of shad passed overhead, blotting out the sun. The sudden darkness seemed ominous to Neela. It added to the tension building between Sera and Ling.

Ling took a deep breath, then said, 'It's all wishful thinking, Serafina. You know that, right? What people are saying about your uncle being in the north, I mean. He was in the palace when it fell. Your mother, too. That much we know. The rest is only hearsay. Another thing we know is that your mother was very badly wounded. You told me so yourself. She might not have survived—'

'Don't,' Serafina said brokenly.

'I *have* to,' Ling said. 'Omnivoxas speak all languages. My grandfather was one too, and he told me that with the gift of language comes a responsibility to speak not only words, but truth. Right now, we've only got one goal – to get to the Iele. But what happens afterward? When the witches tell us whatever it is they want to tell us? Are you going to hide out with them forever? Everywhere we go in this realm, your realm, people are suffering. They need hope. They need a leader.'

'They have a leader,' Serafina said angrily.

'Serafina, you have to face the—'

'You're *wrong*. She's alive. I know she is!' Serafina shouted.

An uncomfortable silence fell over the group. Serafina was the one who broke it. 'I'm sorry. It's been a rough few days,' she said. 'There's a shoal above us. I'm going to join it. See you in a few.'

'You're going shoaling? *You?* That's so stupid only Yazeed would do it!' Neela said. 'We're near the mouth of a major river. There's a harbour. With boats. And goggs. This is *not* a good idea.'

But it was too late. Serafina was already swimming away.

'Cerulea has fallen. Villages are being gutted. If she doesn't lead Miromara, all of Miromara will fall,' Ling said. 'Once that happens, what's to stop Traho from taking Qin? Matali? The other waters?'

'Ling, being leader, at least in Miromara, means being regina. The one and only. There aren't two,' Neela said, with an edge to her voice. 'Do you understand?'

Ling nodded.

'Serafina can't accept being the leader of her realm, because it means accepting that her mother is dead. It's only been a few days. She's lost everything. *Everything*, Ling. She needs time.'

'I can see that, Neela. But the thing is . . . we don't have any.'

# THIRTY-ONE

SLEEK, QUICKSILVER BODIES flashed by her. Smooth, cool scales brushed against her skin. There were bright looks and laughter. Serafina was in the shoal.

She sped up, stopped, then turned. She dived down into the dark, cool depths of the sea, then spiralled back up to its warm, sparkling surface. One with the shoal, she forgot everything and everyone. She forgot her losses and her grief. Forgot Mahdi and all that he wasn't; Blue and all that he was. For a few precious moments, she forgot who *she* was.

The evening was soft and beautiful. The lengthening rays of the sun were playing over the water. Shad had moved up from the cool depths to feed on moon jellies floating on the warmer surface layers. Their movements exerted a powerful pull on Serafina – one that she, like most young mer, found hard to resist. It was magical, swimming with a shoal. It was wild and joyous, but dangerous, too. Predators followed shoals. A mermaid could be diving with thousands of sardines one minute only to find herself nose-to-nose with a shark the next. Mer parents repeatedly warned their children never to go shoaling.

But how could she resist? The shad called to her. Thousands of musical voices, like rain on water, beckoned. It was said that the goggs thought fish made no sound. Serafina wondered if it was because they listened only with their ears. She knew that those who truly loved the sea's creatures listened to them with their hearts.

*Sister*, they called her. *Seaswift. Come, coppertail. Come, beauty. Swim with us*.

Serafina swam faster and faster, her sleek body arching and turning, cutting through the water like a knife. There was only the shoal. Only the sea. Nothing else.

And then, 'Serafina!'

A voice from far away. Pulling at her. Dragging her back to a thousand questions she didn't know how to answer. A thousand demands she couldn't meet. Back to the fear and despair. To the broken voices asking her why, asking her for help, asking her to be something she could not.

'Serafina, come *on*!' It was Neela. She was close now.

'No,' she said, moving deeper into the shoal. 'No, Neela. I *can't*.'

A hand closed on her arm. It was Ling. 'We've got to go! Now!' she said, alarm in her voice. Serafina shook her off.

'Sera!' Neela shouted. 'There's a fishing net! Get out of there! *Hurry!*'

Like a merl emerging from a trance, Serafina slowly stopped. She looked around and her eyes widened in terror. A web of filament surrounded her. It was being hauled up by a winch and cinched around the top like a sack. The shad were no longer laughing and calling. They were frantically yelling to one another to swim clear.

Serafina shot to the top of the net. With a snap of her tail, she tried to propel herself through what was left of the opening. She didn't make it. The net closed around her hips and tightened painfully. She grasped the edges with her hands and pushed them down. At the same time, she thrashed her powerful tail with every bit of strength she had and managed to wriggle out just before the net broke the surface. Its edges had scraped off some of her scales. She was bleeding, but she was free.

'Neela!' she called out.

'Over here!' Neela shouted, swimming to her. 'Where's Ling?'

The net continued to rise through the water. The screams of the shad were deafening.

'I can't see her!' Serafina shouted. 'Ling! *Ling*!' she called, circling the net.

And then she saw it – a hand thrust through the net, reaching for her. A face pressed against the mesh, eyes wild with terror, mouth open in a scream.

It was Ling.

# THIRTY-TWO

'NEELA, GRAB THE NET!' Serafina shouted.

The two mermaids hooked their fingers in the bottom of the heavy net as it broke the surface, hoping the weight of their bodies would pull it back down into the water. The winch made a grinding noise. It slowed, but didn't stop. The net was out of the water and rising. The filament was cutting into their fingers, but still they hung on. It pulled them farther out of the water until only the tips of their tails were submerged.

'It's no use! Let go!' Neela shouted.

'We have to help her!' Serafina cried.

'Sera, let *go* before they get us, too!' Neela shouted again.

Serafina shook her head, but the net rose even higher, towards the deck of the fishing ship, a small trawler named *Bedrieër*. The shad gasped agonizingly for water. Ling's screams ripped through the air.

'*No!*' Serafina shouted. But her fingers couldn't hold her weight any longer. She dropped back into the water. Neela did too. The net rose even higher. Serafina and Neela stayed in its shadow, out of sight of the trawler's crew.

'What's going to happen to her?' Neela asked fearfully.

Serafina heard voices, the sound of goggs shouting to each other. There was a sudden silence, and then, 'What the *hell*? Mr Mfeme! Quick! Over here!'

'No. It *can't* be,' Serafina said. She only knew a smattering of the gogg language called English, but she knew that name. She swam as close to the edge of the shadow as she dared and looked up.

A shirtless, sunburned man caught hold of the net with a grappling hook and pulled it towards the ship. Another man joined him. He wore jeans, a faded black T-shirt, a baseball cap, and sunglasses.

Serafina gasped. 'Neela, that's *him*,' she said. 'The man who broke into the duca's palazzo. The one who attacked us. *He's* Rafe Mfeme!'

'Bring her aboard!' Mfeme shouted.

Ling's screams carried over the water.

'I'm going to try a vortex,' said Sera, desperate to save her friend.

She started to songcast, but struggled to project her voice. In the air, her spell sounded thin and strained. She managed to conjure a water vortex, though, about twelve feet tall. She aimed it at the trawler, hoping to hit it hard broadside and knock the net loose from the winch.

'A waterspout, Mr Mfeme!' one of the crew shouted, just as the vortex got within a foot of the ship.

As the man's words rang out, the vortex stopped violently, as if it had hit a wall. The whirling water flattened, then sheeted back into the sea.

'Let me try,' Neela said.

She cast a fragor lux spell using sunrays and threw it at the trawler, hoping to put a hole in it, but the frag exploded uselessly a foot away from the ship.

'A waterspout, and now a sun dog,' Mfeme said. 'What very strange weather we're having.'

As he spoke, he looked over the ship's railing, into the water, as if he knew they were there. Sera grabbed Neela and pulled her farther into the net's shadow.

'What's going on? Why aren't our songspells working?' Neela whispered.

'I don't know,' said Sera. 'It makes no sense. Terragoggs can't do or undo magic.' Then the answer hit her. 'I bet it's the ship's hull! I bet it's made of iron.'

'What are we going to do? How are we going to free Ling if we can't use magic?' Neela asked.

Sera had no time to reply.

'RAFE MFEME!' a voice suddenly boomed. The mermaids turned and saw that it had come from another ship, a fast, sleek cigarette boat that had just arrived off the trawler's starboard bow.

'Rafe Mfeme, this is Captain William Bowen of the vessel *Sprite*. The *Bedrieër* is in direct violation of the Black Sea Treaty. You are not permitted to fish in these waters. The Romanian Coast Guard is en route.'

'It's the Wave Warriors,' Mfeme growled. 'Start the engines.'

'Mr Mfeme, sir, the Warriors can't board us, but the coast guard can. We can't outrun them. Their vessel is lighter and quicker. If they come aboard . . . if they see what's in the hold . . .'

Mfeme cursed the air blue. 'I didn't even want the damned shad! I wanted jellyfish!' He strode over to the winch's control box and hit a lever. There was a loud, grinding sound as the winch released the net. It fell into the water and disappeared below the surface.

Mfeme faced the *Sprite*. 'What net?' he shouted at Captain Bowen. 'You have nothing on me!'

'We got it on tape, Mfeme!' Captain Bowen shouted, holding up a video camera. 'You're headed to court!'

Serafina didn't stay to hear any more. Neela was already underwater. Sera dived and joined her. Together, they pulled the net open, freeing Ling and the shad. The fish, coughing and gasping, quickly swam away. Ling sank to the seafloor, bruised and bleeding. Her wrist was bent at a sickening angle.

'I'm sorry, Ling,' Serafina said tearfully. 'It's all my fault. It wouldn't have happened if I hadn't gone shoaling. I'm so, so sorry.'

'The gogg's the one who should be sorry,' Ling said. 'He nearly killed me.'

'He's Rafe Mfeme,' Neela said. 'He nearly killed us, too. At the duca's.'

Serafina remembered what Duca Armando had told them about Mfeme: he was in league with Ondalina, and in his trawlers he'd transported the very troops that had invaded Cerulea.

'Stay with her, Neela. I'll be right back,' she suddenly said.

'Where are you going?' Neela asked.

'To see what I can learn about Mfeme.'

Serafina sped to the surface and cautiously poked her head up, wary of being seen. But no one was watching the water. Mfeme's crew had brought the *Bedrieër* alongside the *Sprite*, and Mfeme himself had boarded her. Serafina heard shouts and threats, and then Mfeme ripped the video camera out of the captain's hands and tossed it overboard. A young man rushed at him. Mfeme threw him overboard, too. As two of the young man's shipmates tried to haul him back into the boat, Mfeme advanced on a woman, grabbed a cell phone out of her hands, and pitched it into the water.

'You want to follow it?' he shouted at her. Frightened, she backed away from him.

A fast, powerful man, he seemed to be everywhere, all at once. Serafina quickly swam aft and saw him bring a heavy wrench down on the ship-to-shore radio. 'I'm warning you, all of you! Stay the hell away from me!' he yelled. He threw the wrench aside, reboarded his ship, and barked orders to depart.

As his crew made ready, Mfeme rested his hands on his ship's gunwale. 'She's headed for the Dunărea, Nils,' he said to a crew member. 'I want her. *Now*. Before she gets to the Olt. There are others with her. I want them *all*.'

Serafina dived. The waters of the harbour were shallow.

Neela and Ling were sitting on the seafloor about thirty feet below the ship.

'We're out of here,' she said, when she reached them.

'Ling can't swim. Her wrist is broken.'

Serafina looked at Ling. She was cradling her arm to her chest. Her face was grey with pain.

'You're going to have to,' she said to her. 'Mfeme wants you. Us, too. He knows we're heading to the Olt.'

'How?' Ling asked.

'I don't know. We've. Got. To. *Go*.'

'We need to help her, Sera. She's in a lot of pain,' Neela said.

Serafina looked around. Her eyes fell on the fishing net. 'We could lay her on the net and drag it behind us,' she said.

'Oh, I'm sure she'd love that, considering it almost killed her. And besides, it's hard to swim dragging a net! We won't be able to propel ourselves fast enough to—'

'Wait a minute, Neela . . . that's it!'

'What's it?'

'We can jam the propeller! That'll stop him. And give us a head start.'

'With what? Our magic doesn't work against this ship.'

'With the net. Ling, sit tight. Neela, give me a hand.' The two mermaids picked up the net, dragged it to the ship, and began to wind it around the propeller's fearsome blades.

'Hurry, Sera. If this starts up, we're chum,' Neela said.

As they worked, Sera thought she heard voices. Was it mer? They sounded strange – nearby, yet muffled. She stopped and looked around warily. There was no one else in the water.

'Neela, did you hear that?' she asked.

'I didn't hear any—'

And then they both heard it.

A wail, high-pitched and desperate. Coming from inside the *Bedrieër*.

Sera swam to the ship and pressed her ear against its hull. Neela did the same. But neither mermaid heard anything further.

'Maybe it's shad,' Serafina said uneasily. 'One of Mfeme's crew said they couldn't have the coast guard board them because of what they had in the hold. An illegal catch, probably.'

'Sera . . . oh, my gods. Oh, *Sera*.'

'What is it? What's wrong?'

Neela couldn't speak any more. Her hands were pressed to her mouth. Serafina followed her gaze. On the seabed below, maybe twenty feet off the ship's port side, were bodies. At least a dozen of them.

Serafina uttered a strangled cry. She swam down to them, hoping that what her eyes were telling her wasn't true. But it was. They were dead. Some were lying on their backs, others facedown. Some had the kind of open, gaping wounds that were made by a speargun. Others had bruises on their faces. Many had their wrists tied behind their backs. Almost all the women had braids in their hair, and all the men wore seaflax tunics – styles favoured by rural mer in these waters.

'No,' she moaned. 'Oh, great Neria, *no*.'

They were Miromarans. Her people. They weren't soldiers; they were civilians. And they'd been slaughtered. She felt a deep, tearing sorrow inside, and a white-hot fury.

'I think Mfeme's trying to capture *us* for Kolfinn. Because he wants the talismans and thinks we know where they are. But why would he kill innocent people? *Why?*'

Neela found her voice again. 'For information. He must've thought they knew something about the talismans. Or about us.'

Above them, a humming noise started. It grew louder, and then there was an enormous whoosh as the blades of the huge propeller started to spin.

'Come on,' Sera said, hoping against hope that their plan would work.

The blades made several revolutions – and sliced through the net effortlessly. Serafina's heart sank.

'Time to make wake,' she said.

'No, Sera, it's working! Look!'

As the mermaids watched, the shredded filament wound itself around the propeller's shaft and jammed it. The shaft strained, turned a few more time, then quit.

'We stopped him,' Neela said.

Serafina shook her head. 'We've only slowed him. He followed us here. He knows where we're going. As soon as he fixes his propeller, he'll come after us again.'

'Sera,' Neela said, 'Mfeme transports death riders for Kolfinn. The duca said so. What if they're on board right now? What if they come out to see why the propeller stopped?'

'If they were on the ship, Mfeme would have sent them out to get us by now. But that doesn't mean they're not patrolling nearby. We need to get moving.' She glanced at the dead once more. 'Before we end up like them.'

# THIRTY-THREE

'HI, KITTY! NICE KITTY! Please let us pass, nice little kitty-witty!' Neela said nervously to the catfish circling around her.

There were eight of them in the dusky water, and they were monsters. Six feet long, they had speckled grey backs and fleshy pink undersides. Long barbels stood out like whiskers on either side of their broad, flat faces. Their mouths were over a foot wide. Big enough to down a duck in one gulp, a mermaid in two or three. Neela reached out her hand to pet one.

'Um, Neela? I wouldn't do that,' Ling said.

'It's okay. He's purring,' Neela said.

'He's *not* purring. He's growling.'

The catfish snapped. Neela jerked her hand back.

'We don't have *time* for this,' Serafina said, casting a worried glance over her shoulder.

'Tell *him*!' Neela said, checking her fingers.

Death riders were on their tails. The mermaids had reached the Dunărea and had put a league or so between themselves and Mfeme's ship when they heard the soldiers coming. They'd been trying to find a place to hide. Instead, they found themselves surrounded by giant catfish.

'Get off my river,' a voice brusquely said.

Neela looked up. A freshwater mermaid floated nearby, brandishing a hockey stick. She was dark grey with beige stripes and spots. A spiky fin ran down her back. She wore dangly earrings made out of bottle caps and a necklace the likes of which Neela had never seen before. All sorts of goggish things dangled from it: a doll's head, a child's dummy, a bottle opener, a lighter, a small torch, and a golf ball. Her hair, bound into two hippokamp tails that stuck up on either side of her head, was dyed an alarming shade of red. Her mouth was painted a matching shade. She hadn't exactly coloured inside the lines.

'*Perfect*. Just what we need. A crazy lady with too many catfish,' Ling whispered.

The mermaid had come out of a house – kind of. Neela had never seen anything like *that*, either. It appeared to be made out of old, rusting car parts – doors, hoods, chrome bumpers. The windows were bicycle wheels. An old black umbrella, its edges hung with forks, knives, and spoons that clattered and chimed, was stuck at the very top. It twisted in the river's current like a weather vane.

'*Zi bună, doamnă*,' Ling said in Romanian, trying to smile as she held her broken arm to her chest. *Good day, madam*.

'Don't *madam* me, merl,' the freshwater retorted, in Mermish. 'Leave the way you came. Now.'

'We can't do that, Miss . . . Miss . . .'

'Lena,' the freshwater said. 'This section of the river,' she added, pointing with her hockey stick, 'from that rock all the way up to the next bend, is *mine*. And I don't like trespassers. Trespassers upset the kitties. Can't you see the line of pebbles I put out? You aren't supposed to cross it!'

Neela knew that freshwater merfolk were very territorial. They liked to be left alone, too. But this mermaid's behaviour . . . there was more to it than a dislike of strangers. Under the brusque words and aggressive posturing, there was fear. Neela could sense it.

'Could we please cross, Lena?' she asked. 'We'll swim right through and keep on going.'

Lena crossed her arms over her chest. 'That's what the mermaid who wanted to cross *yesterday* said!'

'Do you know who she was? Did you get her name?' Serafina asked.

'Sava or Plava or Tava . . . something like that,' Lena said.

Neela traded glances with Serafina and Ling. She could see they were thinking the same thing she was: could Sava, Plava, or Tava be one of theirs?

'Lena, *please*. We really need your help,' Serafina said.

'Why should I help you?' Lena asked.

'Oh, no reason,' Neela said. 'It's not like the fate of the oceans rests in our hands or anything.'

Sera nudged her with her tail fin. 'Because mermen are after us. Bad mermen,' she said.

Lena lowered her hockey stick. She was no longer making

any attempt to hide her fear. It was written plainly on her face.

'The same ones who took the folk?' she asked.

'What folk?' Neela asked, casting a nervous glance over her shoulder. The death riders were coming closer every second.

'The ones from Aquaba, a village near the Dunărea's mouth. It happened three days ago. More than four hundred disappeared. They just *vanished*. I've been afraid that whoever did it would come for me.'

'I don't know about that,' Neela said. 'But they're coming for the three of us, for sure.' She told Lena what Traho and the death riders had done to Cerulea, to Sera's family, and her own.

Lena's eyes widened. 'You think they'd take my kitties?'

Serafina shook her head. 'I don't—' she started to say.

She was about to say *I don't think Traho wants catfish*. Neela was sure of it. She was also sure the only way to get Lena's help was to make her think that Traho was a common enemy.

'—I don't doubt it for a minute,' Neela cut in. 'Traho *totally* wants those kitties. They are so . . . so incredibly . . .' She paused, at a loss for words.

'Beautiful?' Ling prompted.

'*Yes!* They are so *beautiful* he'd surely want them all.'

Lena nodded, her mouth set in a grim line. 'Well, I'd like to see him try. I have more, you know. A lot more. And they don't take kindly to bullies.'

She put her fingers in her mouth and blew a piercing whistle. Catfish materialized from behind rocks and downed trees. They came out of eddies and pools. There were at least fifty of them.

'Whoa,' Ling said.

'Thank you for warning me,' Lena said. 'This Traho might think twice when he sees how many I've got.' She frowned. 'I guess I owe you one for that. You can hide here until the soldiers pass. Better be quick about it. I hear hippokamps.'

The mermaids started towards her house.

'Not there. That's the first place they'll look. Hide with Anica.'

'Where is she?' Neela asked.

'In the nursery. Over there,' Lena said, pointing to a ramshackle shed made out of old tyres. 'Don't come out till I tell you.'

They opened the door, expecting a mermaid named Anica to greet them. Instead a dozen baby catfish charged out. One swam up to Neela and licked her face.

'Oh, yuck! *Gross!*' she said, batting the baby away.

A low, rumbling growl shook the walls of the nursery. The baby's mother, all three hundred pounds of her, rose menacingly from her nest. She made the catfish outside look like minnows.

'I think that's Anica,' Ling said.

Neela grabbed the baby back. 'Mwah!' she cried, kissing its nose. 'Oh, you little oodgie-woodgie! Aren't you the *cutest*?

Come and see your Auntie Neela!'

The baby gurgled happily. Anica's growl turned into a purr, and she settled herself back on her nest. The three mermaids swam around the back of it and ducked down behind her.

Only minutes later, the door to the nursery opened. A soldier dressed in black swam inside. Anica growled ferociously at the sight of his spear.

'More of the same, sir!' he called out. 'This one's bigger than the others. Uglier, too, if you can believe it.'

Another merman swam into the shed. Neela's blood turned to ice when she saw who it was. *Traho*.

'So it is,' he said, making a face. 'Only a lunatic would keep these things. Gods, how I hate the Freshwaters. Let's go. The faster we find those merls, the faster we get back to civilization.'

'Should we take the mermaid Lena with us, sir?'

'No, it's too dangerous. There are only ten of us, and many more of these things,' Traho said, nodding at Anica. 'They might attack. We don't need her. Mfeme has plenty of new captives. . . . ' His voice trailed off as he and his underling swam away.

A few minutes later, the door opened again. 'They're gone,' Lena said. 'You can come out now.'

Neela swam out from behind Anica's nest. Ling was right behind her.

Lena's expression was troubled. 'They've got a cage with them. For you,' she said. 'You shouldn't put mer in a cage.

You shouldn't put *anything* in a cage.'

'Thank you for hiding us, Lena,' Neela said. 'You took a big risk on our account. We'll be going now.'

'You can't go,' Lena said in a resigned voice. 'They only just left, and they're heading up river. Same as you. Much as I hate to say it, you'd better stay here for the night. I've got a pot of salvinia stew I was fixing to eat all by myself. Now I'll have to share it.' She nodded at Ling. 'I'll take a look at her wrist, too. Long as she doesn't howl.'

Neela blinked at her. 'Um, thanks. I think,' she said. She turned to talk to Serafina, but only Ling was there. 'Sera?' she called out. 'Where are you?' Her friend was still behind Anica's nest. She was staring straight ahead, motionless. 'What's wrong? You're as white as a spookfish. It's okay. They're gone. And Lena's letting us stay the night.'

Serafina turned to her. 'I know why Rafe Mfeme didn't want the coast guard to board his ship. I know what he's carrying in the hold of his trawler and it's not shad,' she said.

'What is it?' Neela asked.

'The stolen villagers of Aquaba.'

# THIRTY-FOUR

'MFEME'S BEEN BEHIND it all along,' Serafina said. 'He carries Traho's soldiers in his ships to the waters over the targeted villages. They descend, force the villagers into the ships, and then Mfeme carries them away. That's why it always looks as if they've vanished without a trace. And that's why he wanted jellyfish, not shad. Remember when he said that? Just after he caught Ling? Jellies are mer food. He needed them to feed to his prisoners.'

She was swimming to and fro in Lena's kitchen, angry and upset. Neela leaned against a wall, watching her. Ling was sitting at the table, cradling her arm.

'But these raids have happened in all the waters, not just Miromara's. Thousands of merpeople have been taken. Mfeme can't keep them *all* in his trawlers. So what's he doing with them?' Neela asked.

'I think he's taking them to Ondalina. So Kolfinn can use them as hostages. No one will attack Ondalina if doing so means killing their own people,' Serafina said. 'We have to do something. We have to stop him.'

'How?' Neela asked.

'I don't know. We could go to your father. After we find the Iele. He's emperor now. We can tell him what's happening. He'll stop it. He'll get a message to the other rulers of the water realms—'

Ling cut her off. 'Um, Sera? *You* are a ruler of a water realm,' she said.

Serafina looked away. No one spoke. The tension between the two mermaids was palpable, and just as prickly as it had been before Serafina had swum off to join the shoal.

Sera had apologized and Ling had said it was not her fault, but none of that changed what had led to the disaster – the fact that Sera couldn't accept that her mother was likely dead, or that she was now the ruler of Miromara.

Lena was the one who broke the tension. She came into the kitchen carrying sea flax bandages, pieces of a Styrofoam cooler, scissors, and several fronds of gracilaria weed, a painkiller. She dumped it all on the table.

'It's going to hurt bad. Real bad. You'll probably scream your head off, wet yourself, and pass out,' she said.

'Hey, Lena, ever hear of something called a little white lie?' Ling asked.

Lena didn't reply. She was looking down at a sickly kit who was swimming around her. 'What's the matter, Radu?' she said, scratching the creature's head. 'Still not feeling well? Hang on, little one. I'll get you your medicine in a minute.'

Ling looked at the heap of supplies on the table. 'Have you ever done this before?' she asked.

'No, but I've set more duck wings than I care to

remember,' Lena said cheerfully.

'Duck, mermaid . . . same thing,' Ling said. She lifted her arm away from her chest. Her wrist flopped. 'At least it's not my sword hand.'

Lena let out a low whistle. 'Looks like both bones are broken,' she said. 'Neela, take hold of her forearm and hold it still.'

Neela was horrified. '*Me?* Why me? I can't do that!'

'You have to,' Lena said.

Neela held her hands up. 'Wait . . . I need a zee zee. I won't get through this without one.'

'*You?* What about Ling?' Serafina asked.

'Ladies, can we please just do this?' Ling said, through gritted teeth.

'Neela, steady Ling's arm. Serafina, when I say so, pull her hand. Straight out. Slowly and gently,' Lena said. 'We've got to separate the broken edges.'

'Did you *have* to say that?' Neela asked, turning green. 'The bit about the broken edges?'

Serafina took Ling's hand. 'I'm sorry. This is all my fault. I'm so sorry,' she said softly.

'Just *do* it,' Ling said.

'Neela, you ready?' Lena asked.

Neela nodded. Lena placed a frond of gracilaria weed on the table in front of Ling. Neela stuffed it into her mouth and swallowed it.

'That was for *Ling*,' Lena said.

'Oh,' Neela said. 'Sorry.'

Lena handed Ling another frond; Ling chewed it.

'Okay, Serafina, go,' Lena said.

As Serafina stretched Ling's arm, and Neela supported it, Lena worked on the break. With sure but gentle fingers, she found the edges of each bone and fit them together. Neela gasped as she did. Ling, however, didn't make a peep. Furrowed lines on her forehead were the only signs of the terrible pain she was in.

'You are one tough merl,' Lena said admiringly.

When Ling's arm was straight again, Lena splinted it with the Styrofoam, then secured the splint with lengths of sea flax. Next she made a sling out of an old scarf. When she was finished, she gave Ling another frond of gracilaria.

'Thank you,' Ling said, her voice ragged with pain.

'Are we through here? Because I am *really* light-headed, people. I need to sit down,' Neela said.

Ling rolled her eyes. Serafina cleaned up Lena's supplies. And Lena asked if anyone was hungry. They all were. She complained how they'd eat her out of house and home, then served them heaping bowls of stew thick with salvinia leaves, frogspawn, and river root. Darkness had fallen, but Lena had turned up the lava globes on her wall. It was cozy in her overstuffed kitchen, and Neela felt immensely grateful to be inside it. She shuddered to think of what would have happened if they hadn't found her.

After the dinner was eaten and the dishes cleared away, Lena sat in a rocking chair she'd made out of an old terragogg baby carriage, scooped Radu into her lap, and crooned to him. The kit was obviously in pain.

'What's the matter, *bibic*?' she said worriedly. 'Is it your stomach? Why don't you eat?'

The kit mewled piteously. Ling, watching him, waggled her fingers in the water and caught his attention. Then she started making a strange series of clicking and popping sounds. The kit clicked and popped back at her.

'It's not his stomach. It's his left gill. He's not eating because the pain's so bad, it's put him off his food,' Ling said.

Lena, wide-eyed, stopped rocking. 'How do you know that?' she asked.

'I just asked him. I speak Dracdemara, his language. I'm an omnivoxa.'

Lena gently folded back the kit's gill. 'Oh, my. He has a stagnala leech!' She hurried to get a pair of tweezers and in no time had removed the parasite. Almost instantly, the little kit perked up and spoke to Ling.

Ling smiled. 'He says he feels much better and he's hungry,' she told Lena.

Lena fixed Radu his dinner, and when he was done, she kissed his nose and put him to bed in a crate lined with marsh grass by the lavaplace. 'There, *bibic*. There, my sweet boy. Sleep now.'

She turned to Ling 'You saved him,' she said. 'I have something for you. A gift. To say thank you. All I have to do is find it,' she said.

'Lena, it's okay, really,' Ling said. 'You've done so much for me, for all of us. I'm glad I could help you out.'

'No, I insist. It's a game the goggs play. A word game. You're an omni and omnis like words,' Lena said. She took down a box from a shelf, and started rifling through it. She pulled out a dress, a coat, a mixing bowl, a necklace, and an eggbeater. 'I've seen them playing this when they have picnics on the riverbank.' She dug some more. Out came a bicycle horn. A brass lantern. A plastic dinosaur. 'One got really mad once when he lost – I saw him. He chucked the game into the river. That's how I got it. Where *is* it?'

She got up, leaving the mess she'd made, and took down another box. A raincoat came out of it. A trumpet. A steering wheel. As she pulled out more stuff, Neela remembered the difficulties she and Sera had in keeping their illusio spells going.

She got up and started to sort through the things Lena was strewing around. She picked up a dress and a tunic. A bolt of cloth. A jacket. Some jewellery. A messenger bag. A packet of fishhooks. There were possibilities here. That cloth – it was just the right colour. And that dress – how would it look with the sleeves cut off? Neela started to feel tingly and excited, as she always did when she had fabric in her hands and ideas in her head.

'Ah, *here* it is!' Lena declared, after she'd dumped out her tenth box.

She handed a little plastic sack to Ling, who opened it, then tipped the bag upside down. Dozens of small white plastic tiles, all with black terragogg letters on them, poured out on the table.

'*So* cool! Thank you, Lena!' Ling said, and immediately started making human words with the tiles.

Neela, who was still bent over the piles of junk, straightened and pointed to the things she'd found. 'Lena, can I buy these from you?' They still had some currensea left from the coins the duca had given them.

'Buy them? Why?'

'We need disguises, Sera and I. There's a bounty on our heads. I was thinking I could use this stuff to turn us into swashbucklers,' Neela said hopefully. 'Sera's already hacked her hair off, so we're halfway there.'

'No,' Lena said firmly.

'Please, Lena. We'll pay you well,' Neela said. 'We can't go around the way we are. Someone will recognize us.'

'I mean, I won't sell them to you. Just take them. And then stop the bad men. The ones who came here today. Stop them from hurting people.'

Lena looked at Neela, then looked away. But not before Neela had seen the fire in her eyes. Lena was shy and awkward and not very tactful. She was better with catfish than people, but she was also kind and brave. Very brave. If the death riders had found them here, she would have paid a high price.

'We'll do everything we can,' said Neela, swallowing the lump that had risen in her throat. 'Could I borrow some scissors, a needle, and some thread?'

Lena nodded. As she opened a drawer to get them, Serafina said, 'I'm tired, everyone. I'm going to turn in.'

'I'm right behind you,' Ling said.

Serafina and Ling said their good nights. Lena went outside to settle her catfish down for the night, then went to bed herself. And Neela stayed up, working into the small hours by lava light in Lena's kitchen.

She was battered and bruised. She felt heartbroken and lost and scared of what lay ahead. And yet, alone at her work, with cloth in her hands, and a sense of purpose in her heart, she felt something else, too.

For a few hours, she felt wildly, defiantly happy.

# THIRTY-FIVE

'HALF A LEAGUE to the river's mouth, max,' Ling said, squinting against the bright rays of the noontime sun.

'*Two leagues past the Maiden's Leap, in the waters of the Malacostraca. Follow the bones*. Those are the landmarks Vrăja gave me, but we haven't seen any of them yet,' Serafina said anxiously.

She and Ling were consulting Ling's map again.

'The landmarks probably only start in the Olt,' Ling said.

'Does this water make me look fat?' Neela asked.

Ling looked at her over the top of the map. 'You're kidding, right?'

'I feel like a whale! It's so hard to float in water without any salt in it,' said Neela.

'Death riders could appear at any moment and you're worried about how you look? This isn't a beauty contest!'

'Life's a beauty contest,' Neela said. 'Just ask my mother. Or either of my grandmothers. Or any of my aunts. Are we any closer to the Iele's cave? I could really use a cup of sargassa tea, people.'

Ling rolled her eyes. 'I hear singing. That's the river's mouth. Has to be,' she said. 'Come on, we need to keep moving.'

The mermaids had set off from Lena's house three days earlier, with food she'd packed for them. 'Goodbye! It's been awful having you!' she'd called out cheerfully, waving them off. 'Don't even *think* about coming back!'

They'd hewed close to the dark riverbanks, trying to stay out of sight, and had holed under tree roots or behind rocks during the night. It had been a lot easier to blend in with their surroundings since Neela had turned them into swash bucklers, dressed in grey and black.

Sera glanced at her friend and smiled. She was almost unrecognizable. Same with Ling. Sera knew that she, too, looked nothing like her old self. She and Ling had gone to sleep at Lena's house, and had woken to new clothes, new accessories, and new identities.

'Did you get *any* sleep?' she'd asked Neela when she saw all the work her friend had done.

'Not much, but it's okay. I'm not tired. And before you try on your new clothes, we've got to do something about that hair,' Neela had said, patting one of Lena's kitchen chairs.

Serafina sat down in it. In all her sixteen years, her hair had never been cut, not even trimmed. Before Rorrim had knotted his fingers in it, it had hung halfway down her tail. As Neela snipped away, letting the chopped locks fall to the floor, Sera had the oddest feeling that parts of her self were falling away with them. The part that trusted blindly. The part that followed all the rules. The part that always let others take the lead.

After Neela had cut her hair and dyed it black with a bottle of squid ink, she'd led Sera to Lena's bedroom mirror. Sera had quickly checked to make sure Rorrim wasn't lurking inside it, then peered at her reflection. Neela had transformed her raggedy mop into a sleek, edgy pixie cut. A spiky black fringe fell over her forehead and tapered to points at her cheekbones. The cut emphasized her long, slender neck, and enormous green eyes. She was speechless.

'Totally swash? Totally genius? Or totally both?' Neela said.

'Totally *wonderful*! I love it, Neela – thank you!' Serafina said.

'Of course you do,' Neela said. 'Now, put these on.'

She handed Serafina a long, clingy grey dress. She'd cut the arms off it and slashed the neckline. A loosely-knit black tunic went over it. Neela looped bicycle chains around Serafina's hips and slid Grigio's dagger through them. She put silver hoops in Sera's ears.

Next, she outlined Sera's eyes and stained her lips with more black squid ink. Her cheeks got a silvery dusting of ground abalone shell.

'You look so awesome, I don't recognize you,' Neela said, when she'd finished.

'I look so awesome, *I* don't recognize me,' Serafina said, still staring at herself.

Neela had also made herself a disguise, using a tattered

lace top, a voluminous sea-silk skirt fashioned from Lena's bolt of fabric, and a military jacket that had lost its buttons – all in black. She'd torn the collar off the lace top, and pinned the jacket together with rusty fishhooks. She'd found herself a terragogg messenger bag and inked *Anne Bonny Roolz* across it in silver. After she bleached her hair blonde, she coiled it on top of her head and secured it with a swordfish's bill. A pair of fishhooks served as earrings and a shark's tooth threaded on some fishing line as a necklace. She stained her lips black and brushed shimmering blue-black mussel-shell powder over her eyelids.

Ling got a makeover, too, though she hadn't wanted one, to make it look as if the three of them had always been together. Death riders looking for two princesses wouldn't glance twice at three swashbucklers, Neela reasoned. Ling's braids received purple streaks. A torn black cape replaced her red jacket and covered her sling. Long turitella-shell earrings, a necklace made of old skeleton keys, and the sword she wore slung over her back completed her outfit.

'No princesses here, Mr Death Rider,' Neela had singsonged, laughing. 'Only some swashbucklers on their way to see Skwall play the Marshlands.'

Sera and Ling had thanked her profusely. She'd told them it was nothing, but Sera had seen how brightly she'd glowed. She'd also seen how well Neela's strategy had worked. The few mer they'd come across on their way upriver had glanced at them, then quickly crossed to the other side of the current.

*Neela's right in a way*, Sera thought, swimming behind

Ling. *Life* is *a beauty contest. And I'm sick of competing in it, sick of being a smiling, nodding, pretty little princess*. There was another contest that mattered now – a contest for Cerulea, one of life and death.

She was done with heavy silk gowns that got in the way. Of jewels so valuable they required their own security detail. Of gold crowns and diamond tiaras that weighed heavily upon her.

Now she wore clothing that allowed her to move and to blend in. Her hair was so short that no one could grab it and hold her back. Instead of jewels around her neck, she carried a dagger at her hip.

For the first time in her life, she didn't look like royalty. She looked fierce, edgy, and troublesome. A merl not to be messed with.

And she liked it.

The three mermaids rounded a bend in the Dunărea now.

'Look! There it is!' Ling said, pointing.

Fifty yards ahead of them was the Olt. It was rushing heavy and fast into the Dunărea, whirling into swift eddies, and thick with silt. Like all rivers, it had a voice. The Olt's was earthy and low, and it sang about the black mountains it came from; the wolf, bear, and deer that drank from it; the tall trees that grew on its banks; and the sweet breezes that blew across it. The mermaids swam into the mouth, then through its rough, churning waters. They emerged a few minutes later, coughing and sneezing and the worse for wear. Serafina shook silt out of her hair. Ling pulled a frog out of her sling. Neela spat out a minnow.

Dazed, Serafina scrambled away from the river's mouth towards its bank, trying to get out of the rushing water. She rested her back against a network of gnarled tree roots.

And didn't see the thing lurking behind them until it was too late.

'Sera, look out!' Neela cried.

All at once, Sera was jerked against the tree roots. She heard a snarl and smelled a gut-wrenching stench. She screamed and tried to pull away, but was pulled back.

'Hang on, Sera!' Ling shouted, pulling her sword out of its scabbard.

The blade came down to the right of Sera's head. An instant later, she was free . . . and a human arm was lying on the ground. She whirled around to see what had attacked her.

It was a terragogg. Or what was left of him. He was dead. His clothes were in tatters and so was his skin. His nose was gone. Teeth showed through a lipless mouth. He had only one arm now. And only one eye. It moved rapidly in its bony socket as he raged back and forth in his tree root prison.

'Holy *silt*!' she said, gasping. 'What *is* that?'

'A rotter,' Ling said. 'There's some serious malus at work here, merls.'

Serafina knew that very powerful mages could reanimate the human dead and make them do their bidding using canta malus, or darksong, a forbidden magic.

The creature growled low in his throat. He swiped at them with a decayed hand.

'I wonder if he's a sentry for the Iele,' Ling said. 'He saw us, but we never would have seen him if Sera hadn't got so close.'

'What a welcoming touch,' Neela said, grimacing.

'And there's another,' Ling said. With her sword she pointed at some white objects, half-buried in leaves and mud. They were small bones. From a hand, most likely. They were arranged in an oval with crossed lines running through it. 'It's Greek. A theta in its archaic form,' she said. 'It means death.'

'Death?' Neela said. 'How about *Hi*? Or *Hey, there!* Or *Nice to see you?*'

'It's a warning, I think. Meant to scare off the uninvited,' Ling said.

'*Follow the bones*,' Serafina said. 'That's what Vrăja told me. I think we're on track.'

The rotter stopped growling. He turned towards the mouth of the Olt, listening.

'Come on,' Ling said, putting her sword back in its scabbard.

'This is no place to hang out.'

The three mermaids continued up the river Olt, and the rotter stood where he was.

Listening.

Watching.

And waiting.

# THIRTY-SIX

BY LATE AFTERNOON, the mermaids had put another five leagues behind them and were coming to the Olt's first bend. They'd used no velo spells in the Olt, as they were afraid of speeding past landmarks. They'd encountered more freshwater mermaids, defensive and territorial, and had pleaded with them to be allowed to cross their patches of river. As they approached the bend, they heard voices, raised and shrill.

'What *now*?' Neela said wearily.

Serafina, worried, held a finger to her lips and hooked a thumb towards the bank. All three flattened themselves against it, then inched forward. As they rounded the bend, an alarming sight greeted them – three ghosts were attacking a mermaid. The ghosts had once been terragogg girls. They were wearing clothing from another time. The mermaid was young, too. She had curly red hair, blue eyes, and a smattering of freckles across her face. She wore gold-rimmed glasses that were hanging off one ear.

'How dare you come here!' one ghost shrilled at her.

'After what you did!' the second shrieked.

'Stealing him from me!' the third shouted.

The ghosts were pinching the mermaid. Slapping her. Pulling her hair. She was fighting back hard.

Ling sighed. 'Is *everyone* in the freshwaters a *tǐngjǔ*?' she asked.

'What's a—' Serafina started to say.

'A jerk.'

The three rushed to the red-haired mermaid's aid.

'Leave her alone! Get out of here!' Ling shouted.

'Shoo!' Neela said.

But instead of scaring the ghosts off, they only made them angrier. So angry, in fact, that the ghosts started to attack *them*. They were everywhere at once. Their slaps and pinches hurt. The mermaids outnumbered them four to three, but they were still taking a beating.

One, a buxom blonde, ripped Neela's messenger bag off her arm and rifled through it. When she found that there was food in it, she greedily ate it. It slowly fell all the way through her transparent body to the riverbed – which made her furious. Another ghost pulled the redhead's combs from her hair and her pearls from her neck and tried to decorate herself with them. But they, too, fell to the riverbed. The third tried to pull Ling's sword off her back.

'What do you want?' Neela shouted.

'I want my Gregory back!'

'My Fyodor!'

'My Aleksander!'

'Merls, I'm getting my tail kicked here!' Serafina shouted

as one of the ghosts ripped the neck of her tunic.

'What are we going to do?' Neela yelled. 'I can't get them off me!'

'*Meu Deus!*' a new voice said. 'I just *saw* him! He's with *her*!'

All three ghosts stopped short.

'What?' the first said.

'You saw him?' the second said.

'With *her*?' the third said.

A new mermaid – wearing glasses with round silver lenses, a lot of fuchsia, and holding a piranha on a leash – nodded gravely. Her skin was a warm chocolate brown. She had dozens of glossy black braids.

'I *did*. Swear to gods. He was kissing her. And they were laughing so hard. At you, *querida*. What's your name again?'

'Elisabeta!'

'Ileanna!'

'Caterina!'

'Oh, yeah. That's the name I heard him say. It was you, *mina*, for sure.'

The three ghosts threw down the things they'd taken and screeched with rage. 'Where *is* he?' they all shouted at once.

The mermaid pointed downriver. 'That way. Just past the last village.'

The ghosts raced off.

'*Tão louca!*' the mermaid said with a chuckle, watching them go. Then she said, 'I'm Ava. *Tudo bem, gatinhas*?'

'Um . . . still alive . . . I think,' Ling said. She turned to the others. 'Ava just asked us how we are. In Portuguese.'

'I'm not sure,' Neela said, her hair hanging in her eyes. 'What *was* that?'

'*Rusalka*, they're called. Here, at least,' Ava said. 'They're the ghosts of human girls who've jumped into a river and drowned themselves because of a broken heart.'

'The Maiden's Leap!' Serafina said excitedly. 'It's one of Vrăja's landmarks!'

'Maiden's Leap,' Ava said, shaking her head. '*Maluca!* Must be something irresistible about rivers to sad girls. They just *have* to throw themselves into them. I've seen a lot of river ghosts. They're like vitrina, only mean. We have them in my river, the Amazon, but they have a different name.'

'What do you call them?' Neela asked.

'Idiots!' Ava said, cracking up. 'Can you imagine? Killing yourself over some guy?' She made a face. '*Ekah! Não faz sentido!* And I don't care how hot he is!'

The others laughed too. Serafina introduced herself, followed by Neela, then Ling.

'And you, *mina*?' Ava asked the red-haired mermaid.

'I'm Becca. From Atlantica,' she replied. 'Thanks for the backup.'

Becca was kneeling on the riverbed, collecting her possessions and putting them neatly back in her travelling case.

'They gave you some nasty cuts. Your cheek's bleeding,' Ling said. 'I can't believe you were fighting them off by yourself.'

Becca, smiling, shrugged off Ling's concern. 'It's only a scratch,' she said. 'I've had worse.'

'You're brave. You'd have fought them all day long,' Ava said.

'If I had to,' Becca said. Her eyes narrowed. 'And *they'd* have come out the worse for it . . . eventually.'

'*One with spirit sure and strong*,' Ava said. 'Felt that the second I met you, mina.'

Becca stopped repacking her things and looked at Ava. 'How do you know those words?' she asked.

Ava was about to answer her, when there was a loud snapping sound.

'He tried to bite me!' Neela screeched. 'I was only trying to pet him!'

'Careful,' Ava said. 'He has lots of teeth and no manners.'

'What, exactly, are you doing with a piranha on a leash?' Neela asked huffily.

'He's my seeing-eye fish. I'd be lost without him. Wouldn't I, Baby?' Ava said, smiling at the growling piranha.

Baby stopped growling and smiled back.

'Wait, you're . . . you can't . . . I mean you're . . .' Neela stammered.

'Blind? Yeah. Totally. Can't see a thing.' She lowered her glasses. Her eyes were pale and clouded.

'But you just saw us. You saw the ghosts,' Serafina said.

'I *heard* you. And the ghosts. Felt you, too. My eyes don't work, but I still see. Just in a different way. I *feel* things. Sense them. Like a . . . *tubarão*. How you call it, *querida*?'

'Shark,' Ling said.

'Like a shark. I felt the three of you days ago.'

'You're the one Lena saw, aren't you?' Neela said. 'She told us you'd crossed her patch of the river. . . . But you were ahead of us. How'd you get behind us?'

'I sensed you coming and I didn't know if that was good or bad. So I ducked out of sight. Let you pass. Felt you out. You' – she nodded in Serafina's direction – 'are Merrow's daughter. I can tell by the way you got between those ghosts and your friends just now, like a warrior-princess. You' – she nodded at Neela – 'you keep the light. I feel it coming from you, as warm as the sun. And you' – she nodded at Ling – 'speak all creatures' tongues. Talk to Baby, will you? Tell him to behave himself.'

Serafina and Neela looked at each other. '*One possessed of a prophet's sight*,' they said together.

'Becca makes four, and Ava makes five,' Ling said. 'Where's our sixth?'

'Let's ask the Iele,' Becca suggested. 'Maybe they can tell us.'

'*Maybe? Que diabo!*' Ava said. 'Witches *better* tell us where the sixth is, and a lot more, too. Think I came all the way over from Macapá to this cold, gloomy, *repulsivo* river to hear *maybe*?'

Becca snapped the lid of her travelling case closed. She rose and brushed the mud off her scales. 'We should get going,' she said briskly, pushing her glasses up on her nose. 'Patrols could be near and we're still two leagues away, which

– by my calculations – should put us there by evening *if* we swim at a moderate pace and don't encounter any more ghosts, strong currents, waterfalls, mermen in black uniforms, or—'

There was another snapping sound. And an indignant '*Hey!*' from Ling.

'Baby, what is *wrong* with you? Cut it out! She's a friend, not dinner!' Ava scolded.

Serafina and Neela traded glances. 'I think we'd be safer with Traho, the death riders, and Rafe Mfeme all put together than we are with Baby,' Neela whispered.

Serafina laughed. The others set off and she followed at a little bit of distance, watching Neela swim with Ling, and Ava with Becca. She'd taken an immediate liking to colourful, laughing Ava, and was intrigued by Becca, who seemed so organized and efficient.

Death riders were somewhere behind them, and the Iele were somewhere in front of them, and both scared her. But as she watched her oldest friend, and her three new ones, swim ahead of her, she felt surer and stronger about facing what was to come.

Neela turned around. 'Sera, what was the next landmark again?' she asked, motioning for her to join them.

Sera swam to catch up, and the five mermaids continued up the Olt. Together.

# THIRTY-SEVEN

THE RIVER GREW murkier and colder, the farther the mermaids swam up it.

'We're close now,' Serafina said, as they put the last two leagues behind them. 'We have to be. *Two leagues past the Maiden's Leap* – that's what Vrăja said. *In the waters of the Malacostraca*.'

'What's a Malacostraca?' Neela asked.

'I have no idea.'

Serafina looked around anxiously for any sign of a cave, a doorway – anything that might lead to the Iele. The sun was starting to set. Looking up through the water, Serafina saw a flock of crows pass overhead. Their dark silhouettes seemed ominous to her. She returned her gaze to the waters in front of her, sweeping her eyes left to right, alert for danger. There were hollows in the river's banks. Creatures darted in and out of them. She felt them watching as she passed and hoped there were no more rotters lurking.

'We're getting closer every minute, aren't we?' Neela said. 'Please say we are. This river gives me the creeps.'

'We better be,' Ava said. 'I feel something now. Coming

up behind us. Coming up fast.'

'Great,' Ling said, looking over her shoulder.

'By my calculations, the cave should be right here,' Becca said, glancing around.

'As much as I want to get there,' Neela said, 'I don't want to get there.'

'I know what you mean,' Becca said. 'I just can't believe this. I travelled thousands of miles, on the spur of the moment, all because of a dream. I don't do things like this. *Ever*. I told my parents I was checking out a college in the Dunărea. How could I tell them the truth? 'Mum, Dad . . . I'm going to visit some witches. I don't know for sure where they live, or if they actually exist, or what I'm supposed to do once I find them. But hey, I just have to do it. Don't ask me why.' I had to take time off my after-school job as well.'

'Where do you work, *mina*?' Ava asked.

'In a songpearl shop. As a spellbinder. I take ready-made spells, then heat pearls – Caribbean pinks – in a lava forge until they expand, and insert the spells. We export the pearls all over the world. The shop's called Baudel's.'

'Baudel's?' Neela squealed. 'I know Baudel's! I *love* their stuff. My family orders *tons* of their songpearls – decorating spells, party spells, hairstyling spells, makeup spells. What's coming out for the new season?'

Serafina could hear the worry in their voices under the chattery excitement. They were talking about anything – anything at all – to take their minds off their fears. The goggs had a good expression for it: whistling in the dark.

'Well,' Becca said, 'I'm *really* excited about the new Whirlpearl Glitterbomb. It's part of our Cast-to-Last line.'

'I love it!' Neela said. 'What is it?'

'We take a pink pearl and we pack it with glitter spells in ten different colourways. When you cast it, your hair, eyelids, lips, and fins will sparkle silver, blue, green – whatever you choose – for two weeks. No dulling, no fading. Guaranteed.' She smiled shyly, then added, 'It was my idea. The first one I ever pitched.'

Neela pressed a hand to her chest. 'Darling, *when* can I get them?'

'Um, merls?' Ling said, stopping short.

'They're coming out this winter,' Becca said.

'Do they come in fuchsia, *mina*?' Ava asked. 'Everyone tells me that's my colour.'

'Ladies? *Hel-lo!*' Ling said. 'I think we've arrived.'

She pointed ahead – at the biggest crayfish any of them had ever seen. The chatter stopped. There were two of them. They were dark brown with shiny black eyes, and powerfully built. As the mermaids watched, they rose up and pressed their claws against a large rock. It rolled a few feet through the river mud, revealing a passageway. A freshwater mermaid, her body stippled in a hundred shades of brown and grey, swam out of it. Her face was pale; her hair was dark and flowing. She wore a necklace of fox teeth and a fitted gown of grey herons. Snake skeletons twined around each arm.

Serafina recognized her. She was one of the witches who'd

chanted in her dream. One of the Iele. At last.

They'd made it. With the help of the others. They were finally here. Soon they would learn why they had been summoned.

The witch spoke briefly with the crayfish. Their bristly mandibles opened and closed rapidly. Their long antennae waved. The witch nodded, then turned to the mermaids.

'I am Magdalena, of the Iele. The Malacostraca tell me that they sense enemies half a league south and moving fast,' she said. 'This way, please. Hurry.'

Serafina, Ava, Ling, and Becca swam inside. Neela followed them, but at the very last second, shied. 'I can't,' she said. 'Once I go in, there's no way out again. This is real. *You're* real. All this time, a part of me was hoping you were only a dream.'

The witch cocked her head. '*Only* a dream?' she said mockingly. 'Long ago, a great mage dreamed of stealing the gods' powers. Abbadon was born of that dream. Atlantis died because of it. Now, because of a new dreamer, all the waters of the world may fall. There is *nothing* more real than a dream.' She nodded at the waters behind Neela. Silt was rising in the distance, a great deal of it. 'The merman Traho knows this. He's coming. If you do not believe me, perhaps he can convince you.'

Neela, paralyzed by fear, stayed where she was, eyes squeezed shut. The sound of beating fins was growing louder. The death riders were closing in.

Serafina pushed past the witch and swam back out of the

tunnel. She took Neela's hand. 'We go in together, Neels,' she said. 'Together, or not at all.'

Ava joined them. 'Together,' she said, placing her hand over Neela's and Sera's. Ling and Becca did the same.

Neela opened her eyes and Sera saw that the fear was gone. It had been replaced by something else: faith. Faith in her. Faith in the others. Faith in the bond between them, however new and fragile.

'Together,' Neela said.

She swam into the tunnel. The others followed. As soon as they were all inside, the Malacostraca moved the rock back into place and used their tail fins to sweep away the tracks it had made in the mud. When they finished, the creatures hid themselves – one under a submerged tree trunk, one under a blanket of rotting leaves.

Half a minute later, Traho and fifty death riders thundered by.

# THIRTY-EIGHT

As THE MALACOSTRACA rolled the heavy stone back across the entrance to the Iele's caves, blocking off the light from above, Serafina felt like she was being sealed inside a tomb.

'I will take you to the obârşie now, our leader,' Magdalena said.

She led them down a murky passageway. It was lit by sputtering lava globes and spiralled downward, branching into a network of tunnels carved into the rock by the river. As her eyes adjusted to the gloomy waters, Serafina saw that many guards – tall, golden-eyed frogs – flanked the passageway. They held long, steel-tipped spears at an angle from their bodies, creating an X between them. As the witch approached, they snapped their spears back smartly, allowing her to pass. Serafina and the others hurried along behind her. It was quiet in the passageway.

'No one will be able to get in, at least. Not with that giant rock blocking the entrance,' Becca whispered. 'That's a comfort.'

'And no one will be able to get out,' Ling said. 'That's not.'

'Anyone have a spare zee zee?' Neela asked in a shaky voice.

No one answered her, and the witch led them farther down the passage. Just as it seemed she would lead them straight to the centre of the earth, she stopped in front of a wooden door heavily carved with runes. A fierce-looking sturgeon, his back knobby and spiked, his barbels so long they touched the floor, pulled it open. Magdalena led them inside.

Serafina looked around. The room appeared to be someone's study. A huge stone desk, its top intricately inset with onyx, stood at the far end. Behind it was a tall chair made of antlers and bones. More chairs, all made of driftwood, were scattered about. Shelves hewn out of the rock held animal skulls, freshwater shells, and stone jars with odd creatures half in and half out of them, blinking and slithering. Plump black leeches inched up the walls. A spotted salamander skittered across the ceiling. Becca put down her travelling case. Neela dropped her messenger bag on the floor.

'Wait here. Baba Vrăja will see you shortly,' Magdalena said. She swam out of the room and the sturgeon closed the doors behind her. The mermaids were alone.

Or so they thought.

The room was filled with so many curious things that it took a few seconds for Serafina to see that there was another mermaid in it. Her back was to them. She wore a long sealskin vest embroidered with silver thread. A scabbard made from eelskin hung from her waist. Her tail had the bold black and white markings of an orca. Two ornate braids ran along the sides of her head; the rest of her white-blonde hair flowed long and loose. She turned suddenly, and Serafina gasped as she looked into a pair of icy blue eyes.

It was Astrid.

Admiral Kolfinn's daughter.

From Ondalina.

# THIRTY-NINE

SERAFINA'S TAIL thrashed furiously. Alarms went off in her head.

*It's a trap!* she thought. *How could I have been so stupid?*

'Coward!' she snarled at Astrid. 'Ambushing us like this! Did you come alone? Or did you bring your assassins?'

'*You!*' Astrid spat. 'This is typical Merrovingian treachery. Good thing you brought backup, Principessa. You'll need it!'

Astrid lunged, fins flaring. Serafina dodged her. The two whirled around a chair, poised to attack. Baby went wild. Ava could barely contain him.

'Merls, hey . . . that's *enough*,' Ling warned, but Sera and Astrid ignored her.

Serafina's fury was alive. She could feel it, roiling and twisting inside her, wrapping its red tentacles around her heart. She could hear its laughter – gurgling and low.

'First your spies try to kill my father by putting a sea burr under his saddle – one that only grows in Miromaran waters,' Astrid hissed. 'You'll be disappointed to know he only broke some ribs, not his neck. Then they mixed poison into his supper. Venom from a Medusa anemone. You know those, don't you, Sera*fienda*? *They* grow in the reefs off Cerulea!'

'Don't accuse Miromara of using Ondalina's methods! The assassin's arrow that wounded my mother was dipped in brillbane. Cerulea was attacked by soldiers wearing the uniforms of Ondalina. I was there. I *saw* them!'

'Stop, both of you! *Please!*' Neela begged.

'Your father's soldiers destroyed my city!' Serafina shouted. She swept a handful of water into a ball and hurled it at Astrid, casting a stilo songspell as she did. Spikes sprouted from the ball as it neared its target.

'Isabella ordered my father's death!' Astrid yelled, deftly ducking the missile. She did not fire back with a spell of her own. Instead, she pulled her sword from its scabbard, and swung it at Serafina.

'Kolfinn killed hundreds of innocent people!' Serafina spat, parrying the blade with a deflecto spell. It crashed down across the water shield she'd conjured, spraying droplets like shrapnel.

A door located behind the stone desk suddenly banged back on its hinges. An elderly mermaid swam through it. She was dressed in a long black cloak, a ruff of ebony swan feathers at her neck. Her grey hair was coiled at the back of her head. On her hands she wore rings carved from amber. Their prongs held eyeballs that swivelled and stared. Her own eyes blazed with anger.

'You *fools!* How *dare* you behave this way in the presence of the Iele!' she thundered.

Serafina and Astrid stopped still, the red trance of rage broken.

'You were not summoned here to fight. That's exactly what the monster wants. It wants you to destroy each other.'

'You're Baba Vrăja, aren't you?' Neela said, her eyes wide, her voice hushed with awe. 'Oh. My. *Gods*. I can't believe it. I saw you in my dream. But Duca Armando said the Iele are only myths, like the ones ancients told to explain thunderstorms. He said you were just a story.'

'Then your duca's a fool,' said the witch. 'Stories don't tell us what a thunderstorm is, they tell us what *we* are.' She looked each of the six mermaids over in turn, her black eyes glittering. 'Come. Follow me and I will show you an adversary worth fighting.'

Before anyone could respond, Vrăja turned and swam back through the doorway. Neela, Ling, Serafina, and Becca were right behind her. Ava warned Baby to stay put, then followed the others. Astrid brought up the rear. Vrăja led them down a winding tunnel. They had to move fast to keep up with her. Some young river witches were swimming up the tunnel in the opposite direction. They touched their steepled hands to their foreheads as they approached her. One was bruised. Another bloodied. One, nearly unconscious, was being carried.

'Tell me again why we came here?' Neela whispered nervously.

'I think we're about to find out,' Serafina said.

'I hear chanting,' Becca said.

‘Me too,’ Ling said. ‘Ava, can you see anything?’

‘Not so much as a minnow,’ Ava replied. ‘Is there iron nearby?’

‘Yes. An iron door. Up ahead of us,’ Ling said.

‘Where does this crazy little tour end, anyway?’ Astrid called out from the back.

‘At the Incantarium. Turn back if you are afraid,’ Vrăja said, stopping by the iron door.

‘*Afraid?* I’m not afraid,’ Astrid scoffed. ‘I just want to know where I’m—’

Vrăja cut her off. ‘A moment ago, I said that stories tell us who we are. There is something behind this door, and its story will tell you who *you* are. Before I open it, be sure you truly want to know.’

No one turned back. Vrăja nodded, then swung the door open. As she did, the sound of chanting grew louder. A scream of rage echoed off the thick stone walls. The water was heavy with the scent of fear.

‘Oh, gods,’ Serafina whispered as she looked into the room.

In front of her eyes, a nightmare came to life.

# FORTY

IN THE CENTRE of the room, the waterfire burned.

Eight river witches – incanti – swam counterclockwise around it, chanting, hands clasped, just as they had in Serafina's dream. Their faces were grey and gaunt. Blood streaked the lips of one, and dripped from the nose of another. Bruises mottled the face of a third. Sera could see that the magic cost them dearly.

Vrăja circled the witches, her eyes on the waterfire. '*Du-te înapoi, diavolul, înapoi!*' she shouted at the thing inside it. *Go back, devil, back!*

As Serafina swam closer to the witches, she saw an image rippling within the ring of waterfire. She recognized it; it was the bronze gate, sunk deep underwater and crusted with ice. Behind it, something moved with a feral grace. An eyeless face appeared at the bars. Above it rose a pair of cruel-looking, jet-black horns.

'*Shokoreth!*' it howled, as if it somehow knew Sera and the others had come to hear it. 'Apateón! Amăgitor!' The monster threw itself against the gates. They shuddered and groaned. The ice encrusting them cracked. '*Daímonas tis Morsa!*'

'*Aceasta le vede! Consolidarea foc! Ține-l înapoi!*' Vrăja ordered. *It sees them! Strengthen the fire! Hold it back!*

The witches' voices rose. One, summoning the last of her strength, closed her eyes and leaned forward. Closer to the waterfire. Closer to the rippling image. It was a mistake.

The monster opened its lipless mouth in a snarl. As Sera watched in horror, a sinewy black arm, streaked with red, shot through the bars of the gate, through the waterfire, and into the Incantarium. The monster grabbed the witch by her throat. She screamed in pain as its nails dug into her flesh. It jerked her forward, breaking her grip on the incanti at either side of her. The waterfire went out.

'*E a rupt prin! Condu-l înapoi! Închide cercul înainte să ne omoare pe toți!*' Vrăja shouted. *It has broken through! Drive it back! Close the circle before it kills us all!*

There were more screams. There was blood in the water, terrror and chaos in the room. Serafina was right in the midst of it, yet somehow, she was suddenly above it. Her hearing sharpened; her vision focused. She could see the monster's next move, and the one after that, as if watching pieces sweep across a chess board. And she could see how to block them.

'Becca!' she shouted. 'We need a deflecto spell!'

'I'm on it!' Becca shouted, then started to songcast a protective shield.

'Ling! Take the witch's place!'

Ling joined the incanti, crossing her wrists so she could grip hands with them despite her sling. She grimaced in pain as one of the witches took hold of her bad hand, then started to chant. As she did, slender fingers of waterfire rose from the ground in front of the prison. Serafina knew the blue fire took time to conjure. She would have to draw the monster off.

'Hey!' Serafina shouted, clapping her hands loudly. 'Over here!'

The monster whirled around. More hands came through the bars. In the centre of each palm was a lidless eye.

'Come on! Right here, sea scum! Let's go!' Serafina shouted.

The monster released the incanta and struck at Serafina. It was fast and powerful, but Becca's deflecto, well-sung and solid, protected her.

While Serafina distracted the creature, Becca tried to pull the wounded incanta clear of the waterfire. The monster saw her.

'No!' Serafina shouted. Without thinking, she swam around the deflecto and slapped the water noisily with her tail.

The monster turned from Becca and rushed at her again. She shot backwards, but not fast enough. Its claws caught her tail, opening three long gashes in it.

Serafina bit back the pain. 'Ava, talk to me!' she shouted. 'Can you see anything? What's it afraid of?'

'Light, Sera! It hates light!'

'Neela, frag it!'

Neela bound the lava's light tightly, then hurled it through the bars of the gates. It hit the floor and exploded, forcing the monster back. Only seconds later, though, the creature was reaching through the gate again, seemingly unharmed and fuelled by a new fury. The bronze bars groaned as it shook them. One started to bend. The waterfire was rising, filling the room with blue light, but it was still weak. Becca, cradling the wounded witch, added her voice to the incanti's and the waterfire flared higher.

'It's going to get out!' Neela yelled. 'The flames aren't strong enough!'

Suddenly, a blur of black and white flashed past them. It was Astrid, moving with the deadly speed of an orca. 'Not if I can help it,' she growled.

'Astrid, *no*! You're too close!' Serafina shouted.

But Astrid didn't listen. With a warrior's roar, she swung her sword at the monster, the muscles in her strong arms rippling. The blade came down on one of its outstretched arms and cut off a hand.

The monster shrieked in pain and fled into the depths of the prison. Its severed hand scrabbled in the silt. Astrid drove the point of her saber through it. The fingers clutched at the blade, then curled into the palm, like the legs of a dying spider.

Becca, eyes closed, songcast with all her might. As her voice rose, the flames of the waterfire leapt. Astrid backed away from it.

'Of all the *stupid* moves!' Serafina shouted at her. 'You could've been killed!'

'It worked, didn't it?' Astrid shouted back.

'Songspells do, too. Ever hear of those?'

Astrid didn't reply. She swam to a wall and leaned against it, panting. She had a deep cut across one forearm. Her left temple was bleeding.

*She saved our lives. All of us*, Serafina thought. *Even me*. It wasn't what she expected from the daughter of the man who'd invaded Cerulea and it made her feel off-balance and unsettled.

Becca was sitting on the floor with Vrăja, who was cradling the wounded river witch.

Serafina turned her attention to them. 'How is she?'

Becca shook her head. The incanta's eyes were half closed. Blood pulsed from a deep gash in her neck. She was trying to say something. Serafina bent low to listen.

'. . . so many . . . in blood and fire. . . . I heard them, felt them. . . . Lost, all lost. . . . He's coming. . . . Stop him . . .'

And then her lips stopped moving and Serafina saw the light go out of her eyes.

Vrăja raised her head; the grief in her heart was etched on her face. '*Odihne□te-te acum, curajos*,' she said. *Rest now, brave one*. Sera's own heart filled with sorrow.

More Iele, drawn by the creature's roars, hurried into the Incantarium. Vrăja asked two of them to carry their sister's body away and prepare it for burial, and for another to take Ling's place in the circle and keep the chant going. And then she rose wearily. Becca helped her.

'It has been growing stronger, but I had no idea how strong until just now,' Vrăja said.

'Was that—' Serafina started to say.

'Abbadon? Yes,' Vrăja said.

'It's *here*? In the Incantarium?' Becca asked.

Vrăja laughed mirthlessly. 'It's not supposed to be,' she said. 'Only its image. We watch over the monster with an *ochi* – a powerful spying spell. Abbadon broke through the ochi just now, and the waterfire, too. That is bad enough. But it also manifested physically in this room, which is far worse. Such a thing is called an *arăta*. Until now, it was a theoretical spell only. Though many have tried, no one – not even an Iele – has ever been able to cast an arăta. The monster's was weak, thank the gods. Had it been stronger, we would all be dead, not just our poor Antanasia.'

'I *knew* I should have stayed outside,' Neela said.

'Oh, no, bright one,' Vrăja said. 'If you had, I never would have seen it.'

'Seen what?' Neela asked.

'How magnificent you are together,' Vrăja said. 'It is just as I'd hoped. It's *more* than I'd hoped. Each one of you is strong, yes, but together . . . oh, *together* your powers will become even greater. Just as theirs did.'

'Excuse me?' Ling said. '*Magnificent?* One of your witches just *died*. The rest of us almost did. That thing nearly got out. If it wasn't for Astrid, it would have. We weren't magnificent. We were lucky.'

'Luck has nothing to do with it. Abbadon grows strong, yes. But you will, too – now that you are united,' Vrăja said.

'I don't understand,' Serafina said.

'Did you not feel what happened? Did you not feel your

strength? You, Serafina, marshalled your troops as cleverly as your great-grandmother, Regina Isolda, did during the War of Reykjanes Ridge. And you,' she pointed at Ling, 'you chanted as if you'd been born an incanta. Neela threw light as well as I do. Becca's deflecto didn't so much as crack under Abbadon's blows. Ava saw what it fears, when we, the Iele, have not been able to. And Astrid attacked with the force of ten warriors.'

Serafina looked at the others. From the expressions on their faces, she could see that they *had* felt something, just as she had. A clarity. A knowing. A new and sudden strength. It had felt so strange to feel so powerful. Disorienting. And a little bit scary. *How had it happened?* she wondered.

'You will do even more. We will teach you,' Vrăja said, swimming towards the door. 'Come! There is much to do. We will go back to my chambers now. We will—'

'No,' Astrid said, putting her sword back in its scabbard. 'I'm not going anywhere. Not until you tell us why you brought us here.'

Vrăja stopped. She turned, fixing Astrid with her bright black eyes. 'To finish what you just began,' she said.

'Finish *what*? I don't get it. You want me to cut off more of the monster's hands?'

'No, child,' she said.

'Good,' Astrid said, looking relieved. 'Because that was really tough.'

'I want you to cut off its head.'

# FORTY-ONE

ASTRID'S LAUGHTER rang out above the witches' chanting.

'*Cut off its head!* That's a good one, Baba Vrăja. I mean, did you see that thing? It's really strong and really mad. If it could have, it would've cut off *our* heads. So really, why did you summon us here?' she asked.

Vrăja was not laughing.

'Wait, you're not . . . You *can't* be serious.'

'I've never been more serious. You must go to the Southern Sea, where the monster lies imprisoned. Another seeks it for dark purposes. This other has woken it. You must find the monster and kill it before this other can free it. If you do not, the seas, and all in them, will fall to Abbadon.'

Serafina was speechless. They all were. The six mermaids looked at each other in wide-eyed disbelief, then all started talking at once.

'Go to the Southern Sea?' Ling said.

'We'll freeze to death!' Becca said.

'Kill Abbadon?' Ava said.

'How would we even *find* him? The Southern Sea is huge!' Neela said.

'This is totally insane,' Astrid said. 'I'm out of here.'

As Serafina watched Astrid swim towards the door, lines from her nightmare suddenly came back to her.

*Gather now from seas and rivers,*
*Become one mind, one heart, one bond*
*Before the waters, and all creatures in them,*
*Are laid to waste by Abbadon!*

And suddenly she knew what she had to do. Just as she had moments ago, when the monster attacked them. She had to keep the group together, no matter what. *One mind, one heart, one bond*. She couldn't let anyone leave.

'Astrid, wait,' she said.

Astrid snorted. 'Later,' she said.

'You're afraid,' Serafina said, sensing that the only way to stop her was to challenge her.

She was right. Astrid stopped dead, then turned around, eyes blazing.

'What did you say?'

'I said, you're afraid. You're afraid of the story. That's why you want to leave.'

'Afraid of what story? What are you *talking* about? You're as crazy as she is,' Astrid said, nodding at Vrăja.

Serafina turned to the river witch. 'Baba Vrăja, before you opened the door to this room, you said that what's inside it had a story,' she said. 'And that it would tell us who we are. We need to hear that story. *Now*.'

# FORTY-TWO

THREE EYEBALLS, set in three amber rings, twisted around in their settings and stared at Serafina.

Serafina stared back uneasily.

'You like them?' Vrăja asked, as she handed her a cup and saucer.

'They're very, um, unusual,' Sera replied.

Vrăja had led the mermaids back to her study. She'd invited them all to sit down, and had sent a servant for a pot of tea.

'They're terragogg eyes,' she said now.

'Did they drown or something?' Neela asked.

'Or something,' Vrăja said. She smiled and Serafina noticed, for the first time, that her teeth were very sharp. 'One dumped oil into my river. Another killed an otter. The third bulldozed trees where osprey nested. They live still – or rather, *exist* – as *cadavru*. I use them as sentries.'

'That rotter by the mouth of the Olt, is he one?' Neela asked.

'Yes. He has his right eye and I have his left. What he sees, I see. Very handy when death riders are about.'

She finished pouring the tea and sat on the edge of her desk. She'd poured a cup for herself, but didn't drink it. Instead she picked up a piece of smooth, flat stone that was lying next to the teapot and turned it over in her hands. Symbols were carved into its surface.

'The songspell to make a cadavru is called a *trezi*. A Romanian spell. Very old,' she said. 'I have many such spells. Passed down from obârşie to obârşie. These spells are how we, the Order of the Iele, have endured as long as we have. Merrow created us four thousand years ago, and we have carried out the duties she entrusted to us ever since, in order to protect the merfolk.'

'From what?' Ling asked.

Vrăja smiled. 'Ourselves.'

She held the stone out so that Sera, Neela, Astrid, Becca, and Ling could see it, then handed it to Ava, so she could feel it. Baby, dozing in his mistress's lap, growled in his sleep.

'Did you know that this writing is nearly forty centuries old?' Vrăja asked. 'It came from a Minoan temple. It's one of the few surviving records of Atlantis. It – like Plato's accounts, and those of other ancients – Posidonius, Hellanicus, Philo – tells us that the island sank because of natural causes.' She looked at the mermaids, then said, 'It lies.'

'Why?' Ava asked.

'Because that's what Merrow wanted the world to know about Atlantis – lies. Stories have great power. Stories endure. Merrow knew that, so she had everything that told the true story of Atlantis expunged.'

'But why would she do that?' Neela asked.

'The truth was too dangerous,' Vrăja said. 'Merrow had seen her people – men and women, little children – swallowed by fire and water. You see, it wasn't an earthquake or a volcano that doomed Atlantis, as you undoubtedly have been taught. Those were only the mechanisms of its ruin. It was one of the island's own who destroyed it.'

'Baba Vrăja, how do you know this?' Serafina asked. She was mesmerized by the witch's words. Ancient Atlantean history was her passion. All her life, she had hungered to know more about the lost island, but there were so few conches from the period, so little information to be had.

'We know from Merrow herself. She gave the truth to the first obârşie in a bloodsong. The obârşie kept it in her heart. On her deathbed, she passed it to her successor, and so on. We are forbidden to speak of it unless the monster rises. For four thousand years, we have been silent.'

'Until now,' Ling said.

'Yes,' Vrăja said. 'Until now. But I have begun at the end, and beginnings are much better places to start. *Whatever you do or dream you can do – begin it. Boldness has genius and power and magic in it*. A terragogg wrote that. Some say it was the poet Goethe. He could have been writing about Atlantis, for that was Atlantis: a *boldness*. A place made of genius and magic. Ah, such magic!' she said, smiling. 'Nothing could compare to it. Athens? A backwater. Rome? A dusty hill town. Thebes? A watering hole. Mines of copper, tin, silver, and gold made Atlantis wealthy. Fertile soil made it fruitful.

Bountiful waters fed its people. This island paradise was governed by mages—'

'The Six Who Ruled,' Becca said.

'Yes. Orfeo, Merrow, Sycorax, Navi, Pyrrha, and Nyx. Their great magic came from the gods, who had given each of them a powerful talisman. They were very close, the greatest of friends, and their powers were never stronger than when they were together. They ruled Atlantis wisely and well, and were revered for it. No decision involving the welfare of the people was made without the agreement of all six. No judgment or sentence was passed. There was a prison on the island – the Carceron. It was built of huge, interlocking stone blocks and had heavy bronze gates fitted with an ingenious lock. The gates could not be opened to admit a prisoner, or free one, unless the talismans of all six mages had been fitted into the lock's six keyholes.'

Vrăja paused to take a sip of her tea. 'No society is perfect,' she continued, setting the cup back into its saucer, 'but Atlantis was just and peaceful. At the time, it was thought that this island civilization would last forever.'

'What happened? Why didn't it?' Serafina asked, listening raptly to Vrăja's every word.

'We do not know entirely. Merrow would not tell the first obârşie. All she would say is that Orfeo had been lost to them, that he'd turned his back on his duties and his people to create Abbadon, a monster whose powers rivalled the gods'. How he made it and of what, she would not say. The other five mages tried to stop him and a battle ensued. Orfeo unleashed his monster and Atlantis was destroyed. Abbadon shook the earth until it cracked open. Lava poured forth, the seas churned, and the dying island sank beneath the waves.'

Serafina sat back in her chair, silently shaking her head.

'You don't believe me, child?' Vrăja asked.

'I don't know what to believe,' she replied. 'How could Abbadon shake the earth? How could it churn the seas? How could anything be that powerful?'

Vrăja took a deep breath. She touched her fingers to her chest and drew a bloodsong, groaning in pain as she did, for it wasn't a skein of blood that came from her heart, but a torrent. It whirled through the room with malevolent force, tearing conches off the shelves, smashing stone jars, turning the waters as dark as night.

Sound and colour spun together violently and then the mermaids saw it – the ruin of Atlantis. People ran shrieking through the streets of Elysia, the capital, as the ground trembled and buildings fell all around them. Bodies were everywhere. Smoke and ash filled the air. Lava flowed down a flight of stone steps. A child, too small to walk, sat at the bottom of them, screaming in terror, her mother dead beside her. A man ran to the girl and snatched her up. Seconds later, the cobblestones upon which she'd sat were submerged by molten rock.

'Run!' a woman's voice shouted. 'Get into the water! Hurry! It's coming this way.' Scores of people ran towards the sea. 'Help them, please . . . oh, great Neria, stop this bloodshed!'

Serafina couldn't see the woman who'd shouted, but she knew who she was – Merrow, her ancestor. This was Merrow's memory.

Serafina heard the monster first. Its voice was that of a thousand voices, all shrieking at once. The sound was so harrowing, it flattened her against her chair. Then she saw the creature.

It was a living darkness, glazed in dusky red. Shaped like a man, it had two legs, and many arms. Powerful muscles gave it strength and speed. Its sightless horned head whipped around, drawn by the sound of running feet, of cries and screams. Hideous hands with eyes sunk into their palms guided the creature. It slashed at the helpless people trying to escape. When it killed, it threw its head back, opened its lipless pit of a mouth, and roared.

'Merrow!' a voice called out.

A man appeared, stumbling through the devastated streets. He was slender and dark-skinned, with blind eyes. He wore a linen tunic, sandals, and a large ruby ring. He had Ava's high cheekbones and her long black braids.

'Nyx!' Merrow said, rushing to him. 'Thank gods you're all right! Where is he?'

'He's barricaded himself inside the Temple of Morsa.'

'We have to get his talisman. And everyone else's. If we can get them all, we can open the Carceron and force the monster inside.'

'He'll never surrender it. We'd have to kill him to get it.'

'Then we will.'

'Merrow, *no*. This is *Orfeo*.'

'There's no other way, Nyx! He'll kill *us*. Find Navi. I'll get Sycorax and Pyrrha. Meet us at the temple.'

And then the bloodsong faded and the waters cleared and the six mermaids sat in their chairs, shaken and silent.

Vrăja was the first to speak. 'Nyx was killed by Abbadon before he could get to the temple, but he'd found Navi. She was badly injured, but she made it to the temple with Nyx's talisman and her own. Merrow managed to corner Orfeo, kill him, and take his talisman. The surviving mages succeeded in driving Abbadon into the Carceron, but Navi and Pyrrha were killed in the struggle. As soon as the monster was locked away, Merrow took the talismans out of the lock, then led her people into the water. Sycorax, with the help of a thousand whales, dragged the Carceron to the Southern Sea and sank it under the ice. She died there. The whales sang her to her grave. And ever since, Abbadon has slept buried under the ice. Forgotten. Lost to time. But now it stirs. Now someone is trying to free it. And already it makes its evil presence felt. Realms wage war. Mer die. The waters turn red with blood. And now you must destroy it. You must gather the six talismans, use them to open the Carceron, then go inside and kill it.'

'Baba Vrăja, why us?' Serafina asked. 'Why have you summoned *us*, six teenage merls, to kill Abbadon? Why not emperors or admirals or commanders with their soldiers? Why not the waters' most powerful mages?'

Vrăja looked at them each in turn, then said, 'You *are* the most powerful mages. There have been none as powerful in four thousand years. Not since the Six Who Ruled.'

'Oooooo-*kay*. I thought you were nuts. Now I know you are,' Astrid said.

'One of you knows this to be true. One of you sees it,' said Vrăja.

The mermaids looked at each other. They all wore confused expressions except for Ava, who was nodding.

'Do you see something, Ava?' Serafina asked. 'What is it?'

'I don't know why I didn't see it before,' Ava said.

'See *what*?' Astrid said. 'No one here's a canta magus. This is *crazy*!'

'No, it's not,' Ava said. 'It makes perfect sense. There *were* six. There *are* six. Six of them, six of us.'

Becca's eyebrows shot up. 'Wait, you're saying . . . no *way*, Ava. It *can't* be.'

'But it is,' Vrăja said. 'You six are the direct descendants of the six greatest mages who ever lived. Heiresses to their powers. Merrow, Orfeo, Sycorax, Navi, Pyrrha, Nyx . . . The Six Who Ruled live on inside each of *you*.'

# FORTY-THREE

ASTRID BLINKED.

Ava's jaw dropped.

Becca and Ling shook their heads.

Neela turned bright blue.

Serafina spoke.

'Baba Vrăja, how can we be heiresses to the powers of the greatest mages who ever lived? It doesn't make sense. Astrid's right – we'd all be canta magi with perfect voices.'

Vrăja smiled. 'You forget the canta magi are mer, and merpeople's powers are in their voices. The goddess Neria made it so when she transformed the Atlanteans. She strengthened our voices so they would carry in water. But Merrow and her fellow mages – your ancestors – were born human. Human magic takes different forms. Some of your powers may, too. The abilities you demonstrated while fighting Abbadon certainly suggest they do. Neela and Becca cast songspells against Abbadon. Ling chanted. But you didn't sing, Serafina. Neither did Astrid or Ava. Your powers may be a mix of your mage ancestors' human magic and your own sea magic.'

'Who's descended from whom?' Ava asked. 'Serafina's descended from Merrow, of course, but what about the rest of us?'

'A very good question,' Vrăja said. 'Never before have six direct descendants been of the same age at the same time – just as the original six were.' She walked towards Serafina and put her hands on her shoulders. 'As you said, Ava, Serafina is the daughter of Merrow. She was a great leader – brave and just. And a very powerful mage. Her greatest power, however, was love.'

'Love?' Astrid scoffed. 'How is *that* a power?'

'Nothing is more powerful than love,' Vrăja said.

'Oh, no? How about a JK-67 lava-bomb launcher?'

'You have much to learn,' Vrăja said to Astrid. 'Even your lava-bomb launcher could not have saved us today. Only Serafina's quick thinking could. She would have sacrificed herself for all of you. A willingness to lay down one's life for others is born of love.'

'Or stupidity,' Astrid said.

It was Neela's turn next.

'*One who holds the light*,' Vrăja said to her. 'You are the daughter of Navi. She was a wealthy woman who had come to Atlantis from the land we now call India. Kind and goodhearted, she used her riches to build hospitals, orphanages, and homes for the poor. It was said she could hold light in her hands, as well as her heart. She could pull down light from the moon and stars, and like them, she gave her people hope in their darkest hours.'

Neela looked doubtful. 'Baba Vrăja, I don't know how much of Navi's power I've inherited. I mean, sometimes I can cast a decent frag, other times I can barely get a bunch of moon jellies to light up.'

'There's an explanation for that. I believe that your powers – and those of your friends – strengthen when you're in proximity to one another,' Vrăja said. 'How do you think you and Serafina managed to flee into the looking glass at the duca's palazzo? There are canta magi who can't do that.'

'You may be right,' Neela said. 'My songspells are always better when I'm around Sera.'

Vrăja raised an eyebrow. 'I *may* be right?' she said. 'Try to do again what you did in the Incantarium.'

Neela looked around self-consciously. She took a deep breath and sang a fragor lux spell. This time, the light bomb she whirled across the room took a chunk out of the wall.

'Whoa,' she whispered, wide-eyed. 'How did that . . . how did I . . .'

'Magic begets magic,' Vrăja said.

Becca was next.

'*One with spirit sure and strong*. Just like your ancestor Pyrrha,' Vrăja said to her. 'She was a brilliant military commander – one of the greatest. She came from the shores of Atlantica. You are like her.'

'That can't be right,' Becca said. 'I'm just a student. With an after-school job at Baudel's. I plan to major in business when I go to college so I can open my own shop one day. I have a lot of ideas for songpearls, but I don't know a thing about soldiering.'

'Pyrrha started out as an artisan, too – a blacksmith. She could bid fire. She had a forge on Atlantis, as you have at Baudel's,' Vrăja explained. 'One day, she saw enemy ships coming and sent a boy on horseback to the capital, to alert them. Calling up the fire in her forge, she quickly transformed farm tools into weapons and armed everyone in her village. As the invaders marched through it, the villagers ambushed them and held them until troops from Elysia arrived. Pyrrha helped save Atlantis with her quick thinking. As you helped save us today, with your ability to call waterfire.'

'I never knew I had that ability,' said Becca. 'Not until today.'

Vrăja then swam to Ava. 'You are a daughter of Nyx. He came from the shores of a great river now known as the Mississippi. Like you, he was blind. And like you, he felt the things he could not see. Just as a bat does on land, or a shark in the water. Magic strengthened his gift, so that he could not only see what it is, but what will be. It will do the same for you.'

After Vrăja finished with Ava, there were two mermaids left – Ling and Astrid.

'Now for the big fat question: Who is Orfeo's descendant?' Astrid said. 'Let me guess . . . it's *not* Ling.'

'Sycorax is Ling's ancestor,' Vrăja said. 'She came from eastern China, on the shores of Qin. She was born an omnivoxa, and her magical powers strengthened her gift. She could speak not just many languages, but *every* language. And not only human tongues, but those of animals, birds, creatures of the sea, trees, and flowers. She was Atlantis's supreme justice. She solved disputes between citizens and negotiated treaties between realms. She was very wise.'

Ling smiled, but it was tinged with bitterness. 'When I was little, people said I was a liar because I told them I could hear anemones talking. Plankton. Even kelp. I don't have to study a language to know it. I only have to hear it. I've never known why. Now I do,' she said.

Astrid sat glaring the whole time Ling was speaking. 'So *I'm* Orfeo's descendant. That's just perfect. So, like, *I'm* the bad guy, right?' she asked angrily, after Ling had finished.

'Orfeo was a healer. His people loved him. He was a musician, too, and played the lyre to soothe the sick and suffering. He came from Greenland. Of the six mages who ruled Atlantis, Orfeo was the greatest. His powers were unsurpassed. As yours may be, child.'

Astrid laughed harshly. 'You're wrong, Vrăja. *So* wrong. It's not true. Orfeo's *not* my ancestor. The whole idea is totally ridiculous. I mean, if you only *knew* . . .'

'Knew what?' Vrăja asked.

'Never mind. Just forget it,' Astrid said. 'I can't be part of this nutty little playdate any longer. The realms are on the verge of war, in case you haven't noticed. I'm going home to make myself useful.'

'You *can't* leave,' Serafina said, in spite of the distrust she felt for Astrid. 'We're supposed to be six, just like the Six Who Ruled – not five. Vrăja said our powers *put together* would be extraordinary. There's no hope of defeating the monster without *all* of us.'

'I have news for you. There's no hope of defeating it *with* all of us. We're six kids! The only ones dreaming are *them*.' She hooked her thumb in Vrăja's direction. 'They need to stop their bogus chanting, raise an army, and go after this thing.'

'*One who does not yet believe*,' Vrăja said.

'You're right about that,' Astrid said. 'I *don't* believe. I don't believe I came here. I don't believe I wasted my time on this. I don't believe I'm listening to this nonsense—'

'Excuse me.' It was Becca. Her voice, unlike Sera's and Astrid's, was calm and unruffled. 'This isn't helping us make any progress. Where, exactly, *is* the Carceron?' she asked, taking a piece of kelp parchment and a squid ink pen out of her travelling case.

'All we know is that it's somewhere in the Southern Sea,' Vrăja replied.

'Well, *that* narrows it down,' Astrid said.

Becca jotted down a few notes, then asked, 'What are the talismans?'

'We don't know,' Vrăja said. 'Merrow did not reveal them to us. We believe she hid them so no one could ever use them to free Abbadon.'

'If she was so worried about the possibility, why didn't she destroy them?'

'Because they are indestructible. They were given by the gods.'

'Any ideas where she hid them?'

'No,' Vrăja said.

'Of course not!' Astrid said. 'Why do you keep asking questions, Becca? You're not getting any answers! Don't you ever give up?'

Becca's glasses had slipped down her nose. She pushed them back up. 'No, Astrid, I don't.' She turned back to Vrăja. 'And Abbadon – any ideas what it might be made of?' Becca asked.

'It looked like it was made of darkness, but how could that be?' Ling asked.

'Only Orfeo has the answer to your questions, and he's been dead for four thousand years. Not even the five mages who fought Abbadon knew. That's why they couldn't kill him,' Vrăja replied.

'The most powerful magi of all time couldn't kill Abbadon, but *we're* supposed to?' Astrid said.

'Ever hear of positive thinking, *mina*?' Ava asked testily.

'Ever hear of *rational* thinking? How are we supposed to kill it? Sneak up on it? It has like, a dozen hands! With eyes in them! We'll never even get close to it,' Astrid said.

'So what should we do? Just go home? Go shoaling, go shopping? Pretend none of this ever happened?' Ling asked heatedly.

'*Yes!*' Astrid shouted.

'Wait, calm down, everyone. Let's take a deep breath

and look at what we know,' Becca said.

'Which is, umm, hold on, let me see . . . *nothing*!' Astrid said. 'We don't know what the talismans are. Or where they are. We don't know exactly where the monster is or what it is.'

'We do know—' Becca began.

'That we're going to get our wrasses kicked!' Astrid said. 'Abbadon killed thousands of people! He sank an entire island!'

'I would appreciate it if you would stop interrupting me,' Becca said.

'And I would appreciate it if you would stop being mental.'

'You're unbelievably rude.'

'You're clueless.'

'Stop arguing, *please*,' Serafina said, trying to hold the group together. 'It's not helping.'

'You're right, it's not,' Astrid said. 'So, hey, let's just poison everybody. Problem solved. Isn't that how they do things in your neck of the water?'

'*Whoa!*' Ling said. 'Time *out*!'

'Astrid, you are *totally* out of line!' Ava said.

But Astrid didn't listen. And Serafina, infuriated, started tossing insults back at her. And everyone else just talked louder. A few minutes later, they were all arguing, shouting, and flipping their tail fins at one another.

'I grow tired. I shall leave you now,' Vrăja suddenly said, the sound of defeat in her voice. 'The novices have prepared food for you, and beds.' She turned to go.

'Thank you, Baba Vrăja, but I won't need a bed. I'm heading out,' Astrid said.

Vrăja spun around. Her eyes bored into Astrid. 'Orfeo had great powers, child. The greatest the world has ever seen. He had to choose how to use them. He chose evil. Magic is what you make it.'

Astrid's angry expression cracked. It fell from her face like ice off a glacier, revealing raw fear. 'But Baba Vrăja, you don't understand! I *can't* choose!' she said.

It was too late. Vrăja was gone. The doors closed behind her.

The six mermaids were by themselves.

# FORTY-FOUR

SERAFINA LOOKED AT ASTRID. 'What was *that* about?' she asked.

'Nothing,' Astrid said brusquely. 'It's been real, merls. Good luck with it all.'

She tried to swim out of Vrăja's study, but two armed frogs blocked her. They waited until she stopped shouting, then one of them spoke.

'Can you tell me what he said?' Astrid asked Ling.

'So sorry. I don't speak Tĭngjŭ.'

'Tĭngjŭ? What does that mean? The guards don't speak Tĭngjŭ. They speak Amphobos.'

Ling smiled tightly. 'Tĭngjŭ means *jerk*. And I wasn't talking about the guards.'

'Sorry,' Astrid said stiffly. 'Can you *please* tell me what he said?'

'He said, "You will stay, as Baba Vrăja instructed. There is danger in the darkness. You will be safe here."'

'Safe . . . yeah, sure,' Astrid muttered, looking pointedly at Serafina. 'As long as I don't eat anything.'

Serafina said nothing, but her fins flared.

A young river witch appeared and led the mermaids to a suite of rooms. One contained a round stone dining table and chairs, another beds. Two more witches brought food and the six mermaids sat down to eat a late supper. The food was simple, but fresh and delicious – salted frogs' eggs, pickled water spiders, plump leeches in algae sauce, and a salad of marsh grass topped with crunchy water beetles.

Sera was quiet during the meal, overwhelmed by the enormity of what she'd learned in Vrăja's study, and what she'd witnessed in the Incantarium.

As she ate, she realized that everything she'd been taught about the origins of her people was a lie. Merrow had sought to protect the mer by wiping out all traces of the truth of their beginnings, but instead she'd left them dangerously vulnerable to the very evil she'd tried to defeat.

Merrow, the first regina, a mermaid so revered that in the minds of the mer she was seen as infallible, had made a mistake. A big one. And now it was up to herself and five other teenagers to put it right.

Sera remembered the towering statue of her ancestor that had stood in the grounds of the palace. She saw herself, as she had been only weeks ago, looking up at Merrow. Looking up to Merrow. That merl, dressed in a beautiful silk gown, surrounded by Janiçari, protected from the cruelties of the world by her powerful mother, seemed so innocent and naive to her now, a child – one who'd lived in a world made for her, not by her. By decisions made for her. Under Merrow's many decrees.

Part of Sera still felt like that child, and still longed for the strength and wisdom of her mother. But another, braver part realized that childhood was over and that she'd have to find her own way through this, just as she'd been finding her way ever since she'd fled Cerulea.

When everyone had finished eating, Ava fed the scraps to Baby. Serafina, Neela, and Becca cleared the dishes. Ling took out the letter tiles Lena had given her and started making words with them. Astrid pulled a caballabong ball out of her satchel, and started bouncing it against a wall, keeping up a steady *thwak thwak thwak*.

Neela cast a songspell to turn up the light in the dining room. Instead of brightening, though, the lava globes promptly dimmed.

'Oops,' she said, looking embarrassed.

'One who keeps the light!' Ling said, in a spooky voice.

'Descended from the great mage Navi!' Becca chimed in. Serafina restored the light and everyone cracked up, including Neela. But the laughter was short-lived. Neela suddenly lowered her face into her hands, and said, 'Oh, gods. It's *not* funny. It's so *not*. One who keeps the light? *Please*. What if we find the Carceron and instead of unleashing a frag on Abbadon, I dim the lights?'

'I know,' Ling said, rearranging her letter tiles with her good hand. 'I'm worried about the same thing. I mean, how will my great powers of language help defeat the monster? What am I supposed to do? Reason with him?'

'Tell him to use his words,' Neela joked.

Ava, giggling at that, choked on her drink. Her noisy snarf made the others giggle too.

'You could tell him that bullying is totally unacceptable,' Becca suggested.

'Or that he needs to start making good choices,' Sera said.

'Tell Crabby Abby he's going to sit on the naughty chair if he sinks one more island,' Astrid said, catching her ball.

The other five looked at her, astonished, then they all burst into loud, hysterical laughter and couldn't stop. Becca laughed so hard, she snorted like a walrus. Serafina wheezed. Ava held her sides. Ling had tears in her eyes. Neela turned sky blue.

'Astrid, you're funny,' Ling said when the laughter had subsided. 'Who knew?'

'Don't tell anyone,' Astrid said, bouncing her ball again.

'Ah, *gatinhas*,' Ava said. 'How do we do this? Where do we start?'

'Excellent questions,' Becca said.

'How do we find out what the talismans are? And where they are?' Neela asked.

'Before Traho does,' Serafina added.

'Who's Traho?' Becca asked.

Serafina glanced at Astrid, searching her face for some telltale sign – a twitch, a widening of the eyes – that might betray her knowledge of this merman. But Astrid gave none. Either she truly didn't know him or she was an excellent actress.

'Traho and the Ondalinians attacked Miromara,' Sera explained.

'I wouldn't go there if I were you,' Astrid warned.

Sera ignored her. 'They captured Neela and me and held us prisoner. Traho knows about the nightmare, the chant, and the Iele. He wanted the names of the other mermaids who'd been summoned. And he wanted to know if any of us had already found any talismans.'

'What did you tell him?'

'That I didn't know what he was talking about. Which didn't go over well. He threatened to cut my fingers off, so I gave him fake names. Luckily, we escaped before he could check them out.'

'Does Traho know what the talismans are?'

'I think so. If he didn't, he would have asked me. He only asked *where* they are.'

'But how could he know what they are? Not even the Iele know that,' Ling said, still concentrating on her letter tiles.

'Good point,' Sera conceded. 'But he's after them, so he *must* know.'

'Even if we were to find the talismans and get to the Southern Sea before this Traho does, we have no idea how to kill the monster,' Becca said.

'Because it can't be killed. I'll say it again: Merrow and her fellow mages couldn't do it. What makes you think we can?' Astrid asked.

*What's she afraid of?* Serafina wondered. *She fought*

*Abbadon like a tiger shark. How can someone that tough be afraid of anything?*

'It's not question of can we,' Ling said. 'You saw what that thing did to Atlantis. It'll do it again if it gets out. We have to stop asking ourselves "Can we do this?" and "Should we do this?" There's only one question we need to ask . . . *how*.'

Becca nodded. 'Ling's right,' she said. She pulled out the piece of parchment she'd written notes on earlier and looked it over. 'We can't do anything until we find the talismans.'

'True,' Ava said.

'So we have to backtrack. We have to progress logically from the fall of Atlantis, when the talismans were last used . . .'

*Progress*. The word pushed at Serafina's mind. *Why?* She turned the word over and over in her head, sensing that it was important somehow, but unable to grasp how it connected to Abbadon, the Carceron, or the talismans.

'. . . to the rise of Miromara, Merrow's realm. Then we progress to . . .'

*Progress . . . Merrow . . .*

'Becca, that's it!' Serafina shouted. 'Her *progress* – Merrow's Progress! You're a genius!'

'I am?' Becca said, startled.

'Do you know what the talismans are, Sera? Or where Merrow hid them?' Ava asked.

'No, I don't know the *what* or the *where*. I wish I did. But merls, I think I know the *when*.'

# FORTY-FIVE

SERAFINA WAS SO EXCITED, she was talking a million words a minute.

'I'm working on a term conch on Merrow's Progress,' she said. 'I mean I *was* working on it. Before Cerulea was attacked. I've spent hours in the Ostrokon—'

'Wait, Sera, slow down!' Ling said. 'What's a progress?'

Serafina explained. 'Ten years after Atlantis was destroyed, Merrow made a journey throughout the waters of the world. She said she was scouting out safe places for the merfolk to live. Her people were thriving and she knew they would need more space than Miromara could offer. She took a handful of her ministers with her and a few servants. It was the *only time* in her entire reign that she left Miromara.'

'You think she was really hiding the talismans?' said Ava.

'I do.'

'Why wouldn't she hide them in Miromara?' Astrid asked.

'Too risky. There were always courtiers around. Someone would have seen her,' Serafina said. 'As I was saying, Cerulea's Ostrokon has a large collection of conches on Merrow's

Progress. I've listened to about twenty so far, but there are way more than that. Maybe one of them can tell us exactly where she went. And the most dangerous places she visited. That's where she would've hidden the talismans.'

Astrid gave her a sceptical look. 'But Merrow could've hidden the talismans anywhere.'

'I *know* that, Astrid. But it's something. It's a start,' Serafina said.

'Merls! Here's another one!' Ling said, pointing at her letter tiles. 'Look!' She'd spelled out three separate words: *shokoreth*, *apateón*, and *amăgitor*.

'Look at what? It's all nonsense,' Astrid said.

'That's what I thought, too. But they're real words – words that Abbadon said. I thought it was just making monster noises. But it's not. It's talking. The first word is Arabic, the second Greek, the third Romanian. They all mean the same thing – *deceiver*.'

'Why would it say the same word over and over again, and in different languages?' Becca asked.

'I don't know. These words here' – she pointed to another row of tiles – '*Daímonas tis Morsa* – mean *demon of Morsa*.'

'Morsa's an old goddess, right?' Ava said. 'No one really talks about her.'

'She's a seriously dark goddess,' Ling said. 'The old myths say she was the scavenger goddess, and took the form of a jackal. It was the job of Horok, the ancient coelecanth god, to carry the souls of the dead to the underworld, and it was Morsa's job to take away their bodies. But Morsa wanted more power, so she started practising necromancy. She planned to make an army of the dead and overthrow Neria. Neria found out and was furious. She punished Morsa by giving her the face of death and the body of a serpent. Then she placed a crown of scorpions on her head and banished her.'

'Wow. That's *cold*. Moral of the story? Never mess with Neria,' Neela said.

'There was a temple built to Morsa on Atlantis,' Serafina said.

'It might tell us more,' Becca offered. 'If only we could get to it.'

'Fat chance. It's surrounded by Opafago. They'd rip your head off before you got within five leagues of the place,' Astrid said.

'Why is that? I've always wondered. Why is it that a bunch of bloodthirsty cannibals was allowed to take over the ruins of Atlantis?' Neela asked.

'Because Merrow forced them into the Barrens of Thira, the waters around Atlantis,' Serafina explained. 'The Opafago lived in Miromara and hunted mer. Merrow wanted that stopped, so she used her acqua guerrieri to encircle them and herd them into the Barrens.'

'Merrow didn't think that one through, did she?' Neela mused. 'It's the most important archaeological site to the mer, but because of the Opafago, we can't even set fin in it.'

'I thought that, too,' Serafina said. 'I thought it was just another one of her unfathomable decrees. Until Vrăja told us how Atlantis was really destroyed. According to historians, Merrow *said* she put the Opafago in the waters around Atlantis because she needed somewhere to put them and the ruins were . . . well, ruins, and useless. But now I think she settled the Opafago there on purpose. To prevent anyone from ever exploring them.'

'In case they learned the truth,' Ava said.

'Exactly. There are clues we need in those ruins, I'm sure of it. If only we could get to them,' Serafina said.

'The Opafago eat their victims alive, you know,' said Astrid. 'While their heart's still beating and their blood's still pumping. The flesh is juicier that way.'

'What a ray of light you are,' Ling said. She got up from the table. 'We can't get to Atlantis, but we *can* observe Abbadon. And I'm going to do just that. First thing tomorrow. To see if I can find a weakness. I got something out of it today. *Deceiver*. It's not much. It's not a talisman. But like Sera said, it's a start.'

She yawned and told the others she was turning in. Becca, Neela, and Ava were right behind her. Sera didn't join them. She wasn't tired. She was busy thinking.

Astrid had gone back to bouncing her caballabong ball. 'How are you going to do all this, Serafina? How are you going to get into your Ostrokon to listen to conches when Cerulea's occupied? How are you going to get into Atlantis? How are you going to kill Abbadon?'

'I don't know yet, but maybe I can get help. If I can find my uncle, and my brother, they may have ideas. If my mother's still alive—'

Astrid cut her off. 'If, if, if,' she said. 'This *isn't* a start. It's an end. You're going to get yourself killed.' She glanced in the direction of the bedroom. 'And you're going to get *them* killed too. This whole thing's a joke.' She threw her ball harder. 'And here's another one . . . me being a descendant of Orfeo's, the greatest mage who ever lived.'

Astrid said those last words to herself, but Serafina heard them. *Why can't she accept that Orfeo's her ancestor? Is it because of what he did? Or is there more to it?* she wondered.

'Hey, Astrid . . . Baba Vrăja's right, you know. Magic is what you make it. Just because Orfeo was evil doesn't mean you are. Evil isn't inherited. Like eye colour or something.'

Astrid stopped bouncing her ball. She looked at Serafina. 'It's not that. I mean, having Orfeo in your family coral branch *totally* sucks, but . . .'

'But what?'

Astrid shook her head.

'Astrid, what is it?'

'Nothing. Really. Forget it.'

'Okay. Forgotten.'

Serafina, frustrated by Astrid's unwillingness to talk, scooped the tiles Ling had left on the table into their bag. She picked up the stray cups and put them on a tray.

Astrid bounced her ball harder.

'It wasn't us,' she said suddenly. She whirled around to face Serafina. The ball went flying across the room. 'I want you to know that. Ondalina *didn't* invade Miromara. We didn't attack Cerulea. We didn't send an assassin. My father would never do such a thing. He would never hurt Isabella or Bastiaan or the Matalis. He values them, and the peace between our realms, too highly. His own sister lives in Miromara. In Tsarno, as you know. He wouldn't risk her life.'

Serafina weighed Astrid's words, then she said, 'He broke the permutavi, though. It's been honoured by both kingdoms for a hundred years. You were supposed to come to Miromara and Desiderio was supposed to go to Ondalina. Just like your aunt Sigurlin and my uncle Ludovico did at the last permutavi. Why did he break it?'

Astrid sat down across from Serafina. 'There are reasons,' she said. 'If you knew . . . if I could tell you . . .' Her hands, resting on top of the table, knotted into fists. Her long blonde hair, pale as moonlight, swirled around her shoulders. Her ice-blue eyes sought Serafina's. In them, Serafina could see a yearning to talk, to share what was troubling her.

'Astrid, seriously, Abbadon's the enemy, you know? Not me. Not Miromara,' Serafina said, surprised by her own sudden desire to talk to this difficult merl. 'We didn't send any assassins either. The last thing my mother wants is war. Not for her people, not for yours. You said there were reasons why Ondalina broke the permutavi – what are they? Tell me.'

Serafina held Astrid's gaze. For a few seconds, she was certain Astrid would confide in her. But instead of talking, Astrid brusquely pushed back her chair and rose.

'I can't,' she said helplessly. 'I just *can't*.' She swam towards the bedroom. When she got to the door, she turned back to Serafina. 'I'm sorry,' she said. And then she was gone.

Serafina looked at the empty space of the doorway. 'Yeah,' she said softly. 'Me too.'

# FORTY-SIX

'SHE'S GONE,' Serafina said angrily.

She'd just swum into Vrăja's study. It was early the next morning.

'Are you surprised?' Vrăja asked. She was sitting in her chair of bones and antlers, wearing a dress the colour of oxblood. Its high neckline was trimmed with tiny bird skulls, its bodice beaded with hawk talons, wolves' teeth, and polished bits of turtle shell.

'You knew?'

'I heard her leave early this morning.'

'Why didn't you stop her?'

'How? Should I have taken her prisoner? There *was* no stopping her,' Vrăja said. 'She does not wish to be here. Sit down, child.'

Serafina sat in the chair opposite her. 'We're supposed to be the Six,' she said.

'It looks like you are now the Five,' Vrăja said.

'How can we destroy the monster without her?'

'I don't know. But then again, I don't know how you would have done it *with* her.'

'She's scared,' Serafina said.

'You would have to be mad *not* to be scared of Abbadon.'

'I don't think she's scared of Abbadon. I mean, any more than the rest of us are. It's something else that she's swimming from. I don't know what it is.'

'Is it Astrid you speak of, or yourself?' Vrăja asked shrewdly.

Serafina looked at her as if she hadn't heard her correctly. 'Um, *Astrid*,' she said. 'Because *she's* the one who's swimming away.'

'So are you, child.'

'No, I'm not!' Serafina said. 'I *stayed*, Baba Vrăja. Right here with the others. We're making our plans. Trying to figure this all out. Ling's on her way to listen to Abbadon, to try to decipher more of its words. Becca's asking the witch who brought our breakfast how to cast an ochi. Neela's practising her light bombs—'

Vrăja cut her off. 'And you?'

'I'm plotting a route to the Kobolds' waters. To see if the rumours are true and my uncle is there. And to find out whatever I can about my mother and brother. With their help, maybe I can get back to Cerulea. And the Ostrokon. So I can listen to conches on Merrow's Progress. We think she hid the talismans during that journey. The conches might give us clues as to where.'

'Merrow's Progress . . . excellent thinking,' Vrăja said. 'But tell me, why go north first?'

'I *did* tell you. Because my uncle's there.'

'And your people? Are they in the north? Or in Miromara?'

'In Miromara, but—'

Vrăja nodded. 'Precisely. You are fleeing too, child. From that which scares you most.'

'That's not true! Cerulea is occupied. I can't go back to it without my uncle's help.'

Vrăja gave her a long look. 'You treat rumours as certainties. Your mother was badly wounded. Your uncle and brother are missing. Yet you speak of all three as if they are alive and well and just waiting for you to find them at any second. How will you face that which is Abbadon if you cannot first face your own truth?'

Serafina looked at the floor. Vrăja's words angered her. But more than that, they cut her. Deeply. Because they were true.

'You fear you will fail at the very thing you were born for,' Vrăja said. 'And your fear torments you, so you try to swim away from it. Instead of shunning your fear, you must let it speak and listen carefully to what it's trying to tell you. It will give you good counsel.'

Serafina picked her head up. 'But all I do is make mistakes, Baba Vrăja. I couldn't help my father. I couldn't save my mother. I trusted people I shouldn't have. I went shoaling and got Ling caught in a trawler's net. I couldn't even convince Astrid to stay.' Serafina blinked back tears, then said, 'My mother wouldn't have made *any* of those mistakes. She's better than that. I'm not like her. I'm not like you.'

Vrăja laughed. 'Not like me? I should hope not! Let me tell you about me, child. About two hundred years ago, the old obârşie was dying. The elders came to fetch me so she could tell me all the things I needed to know. I was so scared it took the elders an hour to coax me out of my room. One is not born knowing how to lead; one learns.'

'But Baba Vrăja, I don't have time to learn,' Serafina said. 'What's happening in the waters – right now – is life or death. My people, my friends . . . they deserve the best leader they can get. Not me.'

Vrăja threw her hands up. 'If you wish to be the *best* leader, I cannot help you, for there is no such thing. We all make our mistakes and we all must live with them. If you wish to be a *good* leader, perhaps I can. Listen to me, child, Astrid swam away because she does not believe.'

'In Abbadon? How can she not? She saw him. Fought him. We all did.'

'No, in herself. Help the others believe, Serafina. Help Ling believe she can break through the silences. Help Neela believe her greatest power comes from within, not without. Help Becca believe the warmest fire is the one that's shared. Help Ava believe the gods *did* know what they were doing. *That's* what a leader does – she inspires others to believe in themselves.'

'But *how*, Baba Vrăja?' Serafina said helplessly. 'Teach me how.'

'Serafina, can't you see?' Vrăja said. She reached across her desk and took her hand. 'By first believing in *yourself*.'

# FORTY-SEVEN

THE RIVER WITCH Magdalena looked at the spidery crack Neela had just put into the cave's wall and shook her head.

'You're dead. You missed him by a mile,' she said. 'And then it was his turn. And he *didn't* miss.'

Neela wiped a drop of blood from her nose.

'Try again.'

'She's bleeding,' Serafina said. 'She needs a rest.'

Serafina was sitting on the floor of an empty cave the Iele used for spell practice, recovering. Neela, Ava, and Becca were with her. Ling was with Abbadon, where she'd spent most of the last four days.

Before Neela's turn, Magdalena had made Serafina cast an *apă piatră*, an old Romanian protection songspell in which she had to raise a wall of water ten feet high, then make it as hard as stone in order to shield herself from an attack. She'd held it up for a full two minutes, but the effort had left her with a blinding headache.

'Here,' Magdalena said now, handing Neela a cloth for her nose.

'You're pushing her too hard,' Serafina protested, worried about her friend.

'Abbadon will push her even harder,' said Magdalena.

'It's okay, Sera, I'm good. Let's do it,' Neela said, stuffing the bloody cloth in her pocket.

Magdalena swam a few feet to the right of the crack. She picked up a rock and scratched a hulking figure with horns and a big ugly face on the wall, then drew an *X* in the middle of its forehead. 'Right there,' she said, tapping the *X*. 'Focus.'

Neela, looking at the cave floor, nodded.

'Bring it, baby merl!' Ava called out.

'Right between the eyes, Neela,' Becca said.

'Focus, dragă,' Magdalena said.

Neela picked her head up. She fixed her gaze on the *X*, and started to sing.

*I summon to me*
*rays of light*
*And make of them*
*a weapon bright. . . .*

As she did, light leapt towards her from the room's lava globes. She caught it and whirled it into a ball, just as she always did when casting a fragor lux. But this time, she made the ball smaller, tighter, and harder. Just as Magdalena had taught her.

*Magic, help me*
*Fight the dark,*
*Guide this missile*
*To its mark.*

With a loud cry, she launched the frag as hard and fast as she could. It hit the wall with an explosive impact. Everyone ducked as shattered rock flew through the water. When the silt settled, there was nothing but a deep hole where Abbadon's head had been.

'Excellent!' Magdalena shouted. 'Well done!'

'That was *amazing*!' Becca said.

Neela smiled. A bright gush of blood burst from her nose.

'Neela!' Serafina cried. She swam to her friend, pulled the cloth from her pocket, and pressed it to her nose. 'That's it. You're done,' she said. 'The magic is supposed to explode Abbadon's head, not your own. Come and sit down.'

As she watched Neela pinch her nose, Sera thought how right Vrăja had been – they *were* stronger when they were together. But their new powers took a toll. Headaches and nosebleeds were only part of it. The hard training they did together also gave them bruises and cramps. Ava had been sick to her stomach several times. Ling's broken wrist started paining her fiercely. They were all exhausted. Magdalena, who would become the next obârşie, was helping them develop the powers passed down by their mage ancestors, and teaching them some old Romanian spells of the Iele. There was much they had to learn if they were going to fight

Abbadon and too little time in which to learn it. Magdalena didn't give them many breaks.

'Becca, you're up next,' she said now. 'Sing a good strong flăcări spell. Call up some waterfire.'

Becca rose and swam to the other end of the cave. She positioned herself so that she was floating just inches off the cave floor, then began to songcast.

*Whirl around me*
*Like a gyre,*
*This I ask you,*
*Ancient fire.*

Faint, flickering fingers of waterfire snaked up out of the ground in a circle around her, summoned from the earth's molten core.

Magdalena snorted. 'You call that waterfire? Those flames couldn't heat a teapot. You're. Not. *Focusing*. You have to be able to call the fire every time you need it. What happens if Abbadon's advancing on you and you can't make the fire come? You die. Do it again,' she said.

Becca took a deep breath and started over. Her voice was louder now, and more forceful.

*Whirl around me*
*Like a gyre,*
*This I ask you,*
*Ancient fire.*

*Hot blue flames,*
*Throw your heat,*
*Cause my enemy*
*To retreat.*

As the last note left her lips, there was a loud *whoosh*. The waterfire shot up in a roiling orange column all the way to the top of the cave. Becca was lost inside it.

Magdalena cupped her hands around her mouth. 'Becca? Becca, can you hear me? DIAL IT BACK!' she shouted.

All at once, the fire collapsed, its flames sinking back into the earth. Becca was still floating slightly off the ground. She looked dazed. Her curls were singed. Her dress was scorched. She'd burst a small blood vessel near one eye.

'Your powers grow by the hour,' Magdalena said. 'Unfortunately, your mastery of them does not.'

'She needs more time. We all do,' Serafina said.

'You don't have it. And I can't give it to you. What I *can* give you is help channelling your magic, if you want it,' Magdalena said crisply. 'Ava, you're next! I want you to cast an ochi just like you did yesterday. I want you to hold it and then go right into a *convoca*, so you can show it to the others. Do you think you can do it?'

Ava nodded.

Serafina knew the ochi was a hard spell to cast. It was what the Iele used to watch Abbadon. It required that a *gândac*, or bug, be planted near the person or thing the songcaster wished to observe in order to catch the spell and hold it there. Shells, with their ability to capture sound, worked best. They'd all tried casting ochis. Serafina had only been able to see around a corner. Ling had been able to see into Vrăja's study. The obârşie had looked up from her desk, amused, and waved. Neela and Becca had seen the Malacostraca.

Ava had been able to see Abbadon by using the same gândac the Iele used – a shell cast of gold that Sycorax had once worn on a chain around her neck. Generations ago, Abbadon had slashed at Sycorax through the bars of the gate, mortally wounding her. His claws had caught her necklace and ripped it off. As it sank through the water, its chain got tangled in one of the crossbars at the bottom of the gate. It hung there still, glazed with ice, unnoticed by the monster.

Today Ava had only been able to hold her vision of Abbadon for about thirty seconds, but Magdalena was amazed she'd done it at all.

As hard as an ochi was, a convoca, or summoning spell, was even more difficult. It was what Vrăja herself had cast to call them here. Magdalena wanted them all to be able to learn it, because it could be used not only for summoning people, but also for communicating with them.

Ava concentrated. Her eyes could no longer see, but her mind still could. Sera wondered what she was going to try to show them. Not Abbadon, she hoped.

'Do you have it?' Magdalena asked.

Ava nodded. 'I'm going to try to show you Macapá, my

home. I'll use one of the shells on my windowsill as the gândac,' she explained.

'Ambitious. I like it,' Magdalena said approvingly.

Ava began her songspell.

*Gods of darkness,*
*Hear my plight,*
*Give to me*
*the gift of sight.*
*Gods of light*
*From up above,*
*Help me see*
*The place I love.*

Ava was smiling now.

*A river wide,*
*A river fast,*
*I ask you now*
*To help me cast*
*A vision clear*
*To show my friends*
*My home,*
*The place the river ends.*

Serafina closed her eyes, waiting for Ava to shift from ochi to convoca, expecting to see in her mind's eye the Amazon River, where her friend had grown up. Instead, she saw herself. A split second later, she heard a voice inside her head.

'Sera? Is that you?'

'Ava!'

'Wow! I'm in your head, *gatinha*!'

'This is *weird*, Ava.'

'Ava? Sera?'

'Neela?'

'Yes!'

'Hey there!'

'Becca!'

'Yeah, it's me! I can hear you, Ava! I can hear all of you!'

Another voice chimed in – Magdalena's. 'Well, the convoca obviously worked, since Ava is talking to us without talking to us, but the ochi is a total fail. You're supposed to be showing us something far away – the Amazon, right? – but all I'm seeing is Sera and she's right next to me!'

'Wait a minute,' Serafina said as the image came more sharply into focus. 'That's not the practice cave. And what on earth am I wearing?'

The Serafina in the image was clad in armour and riding a huge black hippokamp. She was bellowing at soldiers, moving them into position.

The mermaids soon saw why. On the other end of the field, a fearsome army was amassing.

Ava let out a low whistle. '*Meu deus!* Those are some mad ugly goblins,' she said.

'Feuerkumpel,' Becca said grimly.

'Sera, watch out!' Neela shouted.

A goblin had crept up behind Serafina. His black hair stood high in a topknot. He had a sallow face pocked by lava burns, nostrils but no nose, and a mouthful of sharp teeth, blackened by rot. His small, brutal eyes were as transparent as jellyfish. Serafina could see the network of veins running through them, pulsing with brown blood, and behind them, the dull yellow of his brain. Hard, bony black plates, like the chitin of a crab, covered his body. He was carrying a double-headed axe, its blades curved like crescent moons. As the mermaids watched, he raised it high over his head – then swung it.

'No!' Ava screamed. She scrabbled backwards on the floor, as if trying to get away from the vision. As quickly as it had come, it disappeared. '*Que diabo!*' she said out loud. 'What was *that*?'

'Your gift growing stronger,' Magdalena said.

'No way! It's *not* my gift. My gift is sight. It always has been. I can see the truth. I can see what really is.'

'No, Ava. Not any more. Your ancestor Nyx not only saw what is, he saw what will be. He had the power of prophecy. You do too. You just never felt it until now. It's being near the others that's bringing it out.'

'So I saw something from the future?' Ava asked.

'I think so,' Magdalena replied.

'Great,' Serafina said. 'Looks like we have a battle with axe-wielding goblins to look forward to. I'm so happy about that. Because, you know, Abbadon just isn't enough of a challenge for me.'

'Magdalena!' a voice called from the doorway. It was Tatiana, another one of the Iele.

'Baba Vrăja wants to see you. Right away.' There was panic in her voice.

'What's wrong?' Magdalena asked.

'Captain Traho just entered the mouth of the Olt. The cadavru saw him.'

'So? He's done it before. It's only a search party,' Magdalena said.

'He has five hundred death riders with him. *Five hundred!*' Tatiana said, her voice edging towards hysteria.

'Calm down, Tatiana. He doesn't know where we are,' Magdalena said. 'No one knows where we are.'

'*He does now*.'

It was Ling. She was leaning on the doorjamb, panting. Her face was flushed from swimming fast.

'But how is that possible? Who told him?' Magdalena asked.

'Abbadon.'

# FORTY-EIGHT

'I WAS *SO* WRONG,' Ling said.

She swam into the room. 'All this time, I thought Abbadon was talking to itself,' she said. 'Monster speaks, like, two hundred languages. And a lot of them are very old forms. That's why it took me so long to see the pattern. I mean, ever try to make sense of ancient Abahatta?'

'What pattern, Ling? What are you saying?' Serafina asked, alarmed.

'I'm saying that Abbadon talks. But not to itself. It talks about us. Constantly. I didn't understand at first. It kept changing languages so I couldn't follow what it was saying, but now I can. Here, look . . . I wrote down a lot of its words.' She showed them a piece of parchment. It was covered with lines.

'*Six children the witch sends to defeat Abbadon . . . Scared little children . . . stupid and weak . . . They will not find the talismans . . . They will die . . . Their realms will fall . . . and Abbadon will rise again. . . .*' she read aloud. Then she looked at the others. 'It hears *everything* spoken in these caves. It says our *names*. Where we're from. Who our mage ancestors were.

What our powers are. It talks about everything we've talked about for the past few days. About landmarks – the ones Vrăja gave us to lead us here. It talks about the Malacostraca. Because we talked about them and it heard us,' she said.

'Oh, no,' Becca whispered.

'Look, do you see this word here? *Kýrios*. And these? *Zhŭ . . . stăpân . . . dominus*. They all mean the same thing: *master*. It's talking to Traho, or Kolfinn, or whoever wants to free it. It's telling him *everything*,' Ling said.

'Which means he knows where we are,' Serafina said, fear squeezing her stomach.

'And how to get here,' Becca said.

'If the death riders find the entrance to these caves . . .' Neela said.

'You mean *when* they find it. If Abbadon told Traho about the landmarks – the Maiden's Leap, the bones, the waters of the Malacostraca – then it's only a matter of time.'

'You have to get out of here,' Magdelena said. 'There's a tunnel beneath our caves. It will take you several leagues south of here. Well away from Traho and his soldiers. Get your things and meet me in Vrăja's study.' She left then, swimming rapidly after Tatiana.

Fury rose from deep in Serafina's heart, like waterfire from the depths of the earth. It pushed out the fear. Traho was forcing them to flee again. He'd torn her away from her home, from the safety of the duca's palazzo, and from Blu. Now he was tearing her apart from the other mermaids when they'd only just come together.

'She's right,' Ling said. 'We better not be here when Traho knocks on the door.'

'No. Forget it. I'm not leaving. Not like this,' Serafina said defiantly.

'But we can't stay,' Becca said.

'We'll go, but not yet. First, let's really give Abbadon something to talk about.'

'Such as?'

'A bloodbind.'

'Whoa,' Ling said. '*Really?*'

'Really.'

'It's darksong, Sera,' Ava said. 'It's canta malus.'

'These are dark times,' Serafina replied.

Canta malus was said to have been a poisonous gift to the mer from Morsa, in mockery of Neria's gifts. The invocation of some malus spells could get the caster imprisoned: the clepio spells, used for stealing; a habeo, which took control of another's mind or body; the nocérus, used to cause harm; and the nex songspell, which was used to kill.

'Outlaws use bloodbinds,' Becca said. 'So they can never turn against each other.'

'Traho has made outlaws of us,' Sera countered.

'A bloodbind is forever. You break it, you die,' Ava said.

'I know that,' Sera said. 'I want to show Traho that we mean it. That we're all in. Abbadon called us a lot of things. It's right about one – we're scared. But we're not stupid, we're not weak, we're not children, and we won't quit. I still don't know how we're going to do this. I don't know how to use all my powers. I don't even know how to stop Neela's nosebleed. But I do know this: I will fight to the death with you, and for you. It's time Abbadon and Traho and every single sea scum death rider knew that too.'

'I'm *so* in,' Ling said.

'Me too,' Becca and Neela said.

'And me,' Ava said. 'When do we do it?'

'Now,' Serafina said.

'Where?' Becca asked.

'In the Incantarium. By the waterfire. To make sure Abbadon hears us. Loud and clear.'

# FORTY-NINE

'HEY, can I borrow that? Thanks!'

Ling got the halberd away from the guard with a magnitis spell before he even knew what had happened. As he was blinking at his empty hands, she swam into the Incantarium, ducked under the arms of a circling incanta, and stuck the weapon's axelike blade through the waterfire. Serafina and the others followed her into the room. Baby swam behind them.

'Hey! Hey, blabbermouth! Wake up!' Ling yelled, poking the rippling image of the Carceron.

'Great Neria, what are you doing?' an incanta shouted. 'You'll get yourself killed!'

'It's a strong possibility,' Ling said. She peered at the Carceron's gates. There was only darkness behind them. 'Hey! Are you listening, you sorry sack of silt?' she shouted. 'Then listen to *this*! We're doing a bind. A bloodbind. You hear that? I said, a BLOODBIND, monster man! Tell *that* to your boss!'

She backed away from the waterfire and waited. Serafina felt her heart slamming in her chest. At first there was only silence, but then they could hear a low growl. A few seconds later, something moved in the darkness. An arm shot out from between the bars, and then two more. They pushed through the ochi, through the water, and into the Incantarium. Hands opened like dark, sinister sea flowers; the eyes in the centre of their palms stared.

'You watching, son? Keep watching. We'll see who's weak.'

Ling swam away from the waterfire and threw the halberd down. The others were waiting for her.

'There you are!' It was Magdalena, breathless. 'I'm to lead you out of here and into the tunnel. Baba Vrăja's orders. All of us are to go except the incanti. If we hurry, we can make the Dun rea by nightfall.'

The mermaids ignored her. Serafina pulled her dagger from a pocket.

'Didn't you hear me?' Magdalena said. 'We've got to *go*!'

Serafina held the dagger in her right hand and turned her left palm up. Without flinching, she drew the blade across her flesh. Her blood spiralled through the water. As it did, she sang. Clearly. Loudly. With everything inside her.

*Abbadon, your end has come.*
*This we vow, as chosen ones:*
*Drop by drop, our blood is binding,*
*Forever lives and fates entwining.*

Abbadon growled menacingly. More hands appeared. Sera knew they could have struck at her easily. But they didn't. Abbadon wanted to see what the merls were doing. So it could tell its master. *Good*, Serafina thought.

Neela took the dagger next, and sliced her own palm. Her blood rose in the water. As she covered Serafina's hand with her own, she sang.

*Our spell is strong, and soon our blood*
*Will turn the tide and stem the flood*
*Of Orfeo's evil, dark and dread,*
*That wakes now from its icy bed.*

Becca followed Neela. Abbadon shrieked. It shook the bars of the Carceron.

*Together, we'll find the magic pieces*
*Belonging to the six who ruled,*
*Hidden under treacherous waters*
*After light and darkness duelled.*

Ava was next.

*These talismans won't be united*
*In anger, greed, or deadly rage,*
*But with boldness, trust, and courage*
*As we unlock destruction's cage.*

Ling was last. She winced as she gripped the dagger with her bad hand, then cut the palm of her good one. As her blood rose in the water, and she covered Ava's hand, she sang the end of the bloodbind.

*We've gathered here from sea and river,*
*With a purpose brave and true,*
*We vow to drive an ancient evil*
*From our home, the vast deep blue.*

As the last notes of the songspell rose, the blood of all five mermaids spiralled together into a crimson helix and wrapped itself around their hands. Like the sea pulling the tide back to itself, their flesh summoned the blood's return. It came, flowing back through the water, back through the wounds. The slashed edges of their palms closed and healed. A scar was left on each hand, a livid reminder that each carried the blood of the others now.

Sera felt that blood inside her. She heard it singing in her veins and thundering through her heart, making her stronger and braver than ever before. Neela, Ling, Becca, Ava – they were more than her friends now, they were her sisters, bloodbound forever.

It wasn't over, this quest that Vrăja had given them; it had only just begun. Sera had no idea if any of them would survive the darkness and danger that lay ahead, but she knew they'd give everything they were, and everything they had – even their lives – to defeat the evil in the Southern Sea.

She could see their determination in Ling's challenging gaze, in the defiant tilt of Ava's head, in the way Becca held herself so straight and true, and in the brilliance of Neela's glow.

Ling left the group now and swam to the waterfire. Abbadon moved closer to the bars. 'Did you get a good look, monster man? Did you see the blood bind?' she asked it. 'Go. Call for your master. You have lots to tell him now.'

But Abbadon didn't move.

Becca joined Ling. She sang a powerful flăcări. The waterfire flared high and hot, surging through the bars of the Carceron. Abbadon roared. It flailed madly at the flames, then ran back into the prison's depths. They heard its voice grow fainter and fainter, until they couldn't hear it at all.

'You finished?' Magdalena asked. 'Because you've *got* to get out of here. We're running out of time.'

'They cannot. The tunnels are sealed now. The caves are empty. Everyone is gone except those of us in this room.' It was Vrăja. She had a satchel slung over her back and was bolting the doors to the Incantarium. 'In the gods' names, why are you still here? You were told to leave.'

'We cast a bloodbind. In front of Abbadon. We vowed we would find the talismans, unlock the Carceron, and kill it. The bind can only be broken by death,' Serafina said.

'Which may happen sooner than you think if you don't go *now*,' Vrăja said.

'How? You just locked the doors!' Becca said.

Vrăja swam to the far end of the room. A tall object rested

against one wall, draped in black cloth. Serafina hadn't noticed it before. Vrăja yanked the cloth. It fell away to reveal a looking glass.

'I cast a *baricadă*, a strong blocking spell. It'll hold them off until you escape through the mirror.'

The obârşie had just finished speaking when a massive explosion came from above. Shock waves tore through the water.

'They're here,' Vrăja said.

For the first time, Serafina saw fear in her eyes.

'But they were at the mouth of the Olt only minutes ago,' Becca said, casting a frightened glance at the door. 'It takes longer than a few minutes to get to these caves.'

'I daresay this Traho knows how to cast a velo. Most military mermen know how to speed their troops. Into the mirror with you. Hurry.'

'Let's go in together,' Neela said. 'There's strength in numbers.'

'No, you mustn't travel together. We cannot afford for all five of you to be taken,' Vrăja said.

There was a pounding, sudden and loud. Traho was on the other side of the door.

Serafina knew it was iron, and impervious to magic. He was trying to batter it down.

'Take these,' Vrăja said. She dug in her satchel, pulled out vials of liquid, and handed them around. 'It's Moses potion, from the Moses sole in the Red Sea. Sharks hate it. Maybe death riders do, too. Here are some quartz pebbles charmed with transparensea spells. And some ink bombs. They are crude, but effective. They've got me out of more scrapes than I care to remember.'

Vrăja dug once more, pulled out a handful of dead beetles, and gave some to each mermaid. 'I had hoped to teach you the secrets of mirror travel, but there's no time. As soon as you're in the silver, rattle these beetles. There are silverfish in the mirror – large, fast creatures who love to eat them. One will come to you. Tell it where you need to go and it will take you. Hopefully you'll be out of Rorrim's realm before he knows you were in. Neela, you first.'

'But Baba Vrăja, I'm not ready for this!' she said, pocketing her beetles.

The battering grew louder.

'Go, child!' Vrăja said.

'How will we contact each other?' Neela asked.

'A convoca. The mirror. A pelican, if you must.'

Sera threw her arms around Neela and hugged her goodbye. 'Don't be scared, Neels,' she said. 'Nothing, and no one, is more invincible than you.'

Becca was next, then Ava with Baby, then Ling. Sera felt as if each was taking a piece of her heart with them. The iron door groaned under the pounding of Traho's troops. She could hear their voices coming from the other side. A hinge came loose with a wrenching screech.

'It's your turn, Sera. Go now,' Vrăja said. She held her close and kissed her. 'I may not see you again. Not in this life.'

'No, Baba Vrăja, don't say that, *please*.'

'Godspeed, child. The hopes of all the waters of the world lie with you now. Find the talismans. Kill the monster. Before the dream dies and the nightmare rises.'

Another hinge gave way. The door crashed into the room.

'Go!' Vrăja cried.

Serafina leapt into the mirror and the liquid silver closed around her. She looked back, with tears in her eyes, in time to see death riders flood into the Incantarium. In time to see Traho break the circle.

In time to see Vrăja pick up a rock and smash the mirror.

COMING IN 2015:

Waterfire Saga Book Two:

# ROGUE WAVE

Read on for a sneak peek . . .

# PROLOGUE

Behind the silver glass, the man with no eyes smiled.

She was here. She had come. As he'd known she would. Her heart was strong and true, and it had led her home.

She had come hoping that there was someone left. Her mother, the queen. Thalassa, the powerful canta magus. Her warrior brother or fierce uncle.

The man watched the mermaid as she swam through the ruined stateroom of her mother's palace. He watched with eyes that were fathomless pits of darkness.

She looked different now. Her clothing was that of the currents, hard and edgy. She'd cut her long, copper-brown hair short and dyed it black. Her green eyes were wary and guarded.

Yet, in some ways, she had not changed. Her movements were halting. There was uncertainty in her glance. The man saw that she still did not recognize the source of her power and so did not believe in it. That was good. By the time she did understand, it would be too late. For her. For the seas. For the world.

The mermaid looked at the gaping hole where the stateroom's east wall had once stood. A current, mournful and low, swept through it. Anemones and seaweeds had begun to colonize its jagged edges. The mermaid swam to the broken throne, then bent to touch the floor near it.

Head bowed, she stayed there for quite some time. Then she rose and backed away from the throne, moving closer to the north wall.

Closer to him.

He'd tried to kill her once, before the attack on her realm. He'd come through a mirror in her bedroom, but a servant had appeared, forcing him back into the silver.

It was the long, jagged cracks, covering the mirror like a net, that held him back now. The spaces between the cracks were too small to fit his body through, but large enough for his hands.

Slowly, silently, they came through the glass, hovering only inches from the mermaid. It would so easy to wrap them around her slender neck and end what Iele had started.

But no, the man thought, drawing back. That wouldn't be wise. Her courage and strength were greater than he'd imagined. She might yet succeed where others had failed – she might find the talismans. And if she did, he would take them from her. A merman she'd once loved and trusted would help him.

The man with no eyes had waited so long. He knew he must not lose patience now. He retreated into the glass, blending back into its liquid silver. In the hollows where his eyes once were darkness shone, bright and alive. It was a darkness that watched and waited. A darkness that crouched. A darkness as ancient as the gods.

In her last moments, she would see it. He would turn her face to his and make her look into those bottomless black depths. She would know that she had lost.

And that the darkness had won.

# ONE

'Here, fish! Here, silverfish!'

Serafina, breathless and trembling, called out as loudly as she dared. Liquid silver rippled around her as she moved through the Hall of Sighs in Vadus, the mirror realm. Its walls were hung with thousands of looking glasses. Light from flickering chandeliers danced inside them. Except for a few vitrina, who were gazing vacantly at their reflections, the hall was empty. No one had followed her. Baba Vrăja had seen to that by smashing the mirror Sera had swum through, allowing her to escape Markus Traho and his death riders.

'Come, silverfish!' she called again, her voice barely a whisper.

She had to be quiet. To make as few ripples as possible. She didn't want the mirror lord to know she was here. He was every bit as dangerous as Traho.

She remembered the beetles. Vrăja had given her a handful of them to-summon a silverfish. She pulled them out of her pocket and rattled them in her fist.

'Here, fish, fish, fish!' she called. The quicker she found one, the quicker she'd get home.

*Home.*

Serafina had fled Miromara two weeks ago, after Cerulea – its capital city – had been invaded. The attackers had tried to assassinate her mother. They'd murdered her father. They'd been sent by Admiral Kolfinn of Ondalina, an arctic mer realm, under the leadership of the brutal Captain Traho.

At least, that's what Sera had suspected until she'd met Astrid, Kolfinn's daughter, in the Iele's caves. Astrid had sworn to her that her father had not attacked Ondalina. But Sera didn't trust her.

Like Serafina herself, and four other mermaids – Neela, Becca, Ling, and Ava— Astrid had been summoned by the Iele, a clan of powerful river witches. From Vrăja, the Iele's leader, the mermaids had learned that they were direct descendants of the Six Who Ruled – powerful mages who had once governed the lost island empire of Atlantis.

They'd also learned that Orfeo, the most powerful of the Six, had unleashed a great evil upon the island – the monster Abbadon. The creature had destroyed Atlantis before it was finally defeated by Orfeo's five fellow mages. They had imprisoned it in the Carceron; then one of them – Sycorax – had dragged the prison to the Southern Sea, where she'd sunk it beneath the ice. But now, the monster was stirring again. Someone had woken it. Serafina was convinced it was Kolfinn. She believed he wished to use its power to take over all the mer realms.

Vrăja had told the mermaids that they needed to destroy

Abbadon before whomever had woken it could free it. To do this, they would need to find ancient talismans that had belonged to the Six Who Ruled. With these objects, the mermaids could open the lock to the Carcercon and kill the monster.

Sera knew her best hope of finding out where the talismans were was in Cerulea's ostrokon, among the ancient conch recordings about Merrow's Progress. She believed that Merrow, the merfolk's first leader, had hidden the talismans during a journey she'd taken through the world's waters and that the conches might reveal their locations.

Though she knew it was extremely dangerous – and she was scared of seeing Cerulea in ruins – she *had* to go back home.

But not yet.

There was someplace else she had to go first.

*No, Sera!* a voice said forcefully.

She whirled around, looking for whomever had spoken, but no one was there.

*Don't go, mina. It's too dangerous.*

'Ava?' Sera whispered. 'Is that you? Where are you?'

*In your head.*

'Is this a convoca?' Sera asked, remembering the difficult summoning spell the Iele had taught them.

*Yes . . . trying . . . can't hold it . . . ember . . . Astrid . . .*

'Ava, you're breaking up! I'm losing you!' Sera said.

There was no sound for a few seconds, then Ava's voice came back. *Remember what Astrid said? 'The Opafago eat their victims alive . . . while their heart's still beating and their blood's still pumping.*'

'I know, but I *have* to go,' Sera said.

*The Ostrokon . . . safer . . . please* . . . Ava was fading again.

'I can't, Ava. Not yet. Before we can find out where the talismans are, we have to find out what they are.'

Sera waited for Ava's response, but it didn't come.

'Here, silverfish!' Sera said, more urgently now. Time was passing. She had to make wake. 'Here, fish! I have a tasty treat for you!'

'How fabulous! I *love* treats!' a new voice said. From right behind her.

Serafina's blood froze. *Rorrim Drol.* He'd found her after all. She slowly turned around.

'Principessa! How lovely to see you again!' said the mirror lord. His eyes travelled over her face, taking in its pallor. He noted the deep cuts on her tail, put there by the monster. His oily smile widened. 'I must say, though, you're not looking very well.'

'*You* are. Well-fed, that is,' Serafina said, backing away from him.

His face was as round as a full moon. He wore an acid-green silk robe. Its voluminous folds couldn't conceal his girth.

'Why, thank you, my dear!' he said. 'As a matter of fact, I've just had the most *wonderful* meal. Courtesy of a young human. A girl about your age.' He burped loudly, then covered his mouth. 'Oh, my. Do excuse me. I rather overdid it. There were *so* many delicious danklings to be had.'

Danklings were a person's deepest fears. Rorrim fed on them.

'So that's why you're fat as a walrus,' Serafina said, keeping her distance from him.

'I couldn't resist. That silly girl made it so easy! She reads these things called *magazines*, you see. They have pictures in them of other girls, only the pictures have been enchanted somehow to make those girls look flawless. But *she* can't see that. All she sees is that they're perfect and she's not. She spends *hours* fretting in her mirror, and I stand on the other side whispering to her that that she'll *never* be thin enough, pretty enough, or smart enough. And when she's utterly scared and miserable, I feast!'

*Poor thing*, Sera thought, remembering how bad it felt to fall short of others' expectations. How bad it *still* felt sometimes.

'Isn't it *brilliant*, Principessa? Ah, the goggs! I simply *adore* them. They do *so* much of my work for me. But enough about them. The things I hear about *you* these days!' Rorrim said, wagging a finger. 'You've got Captain Traho tearing up entire rivers looking for you. What are you doing in Vadus? Where are you going?'

'Home.'

Rorrim narrowed his eyes. He licked his lips. 'Surely you don't have to leave so soon?' He was behind Serafina before she even realized he'd moved. She gasped as she felt a liquid chill run up her spine.

'Still so strong!' he said unhappily.

'Get your hands off me!' Sera cried, swimming away from him.

But he caught up to her. 'Why were you calling my silverfish? Where are you *really* going?' he asked her.

'I told you, *home*,' she said.

Sera knew she had to hide her fears from him. He would use them to keep her here forever, like a vitrina. But it was too late; she suddenly felt a sharp pain.

'Ah! *There* it is!' Rorrim whispered, his breath cold upon her neck. 'Little principessa, you think you're so clever and brave, but you're not. I know it. And so does your mother. You disappointed her time and time again. You let her down. And then you left her to die.'

'No!' Serafina cried.

Rorrim's quicksilver fingers probed her backbone cruelly, rooting out her deepest fears. 'But wait, there's more! Just *look* at what you've been up to!' He fell silent for a moment, then said, 'My *word*, what a task Vrăja's given you. And you honestly think you can do it? *You?* What will she do when you fail? I imagine she'll find someone else. Someone better. Just like Mahdi did.'

His venomous words struck at Serafina's heart like a stingray's barb. Mahdi, the crown prince of Matali, a merman she'd loved, had betrayed her for another and the wound was still raw. She looked down at the ground, paralyzed by pain. She forgot why she was here. And where she was going. Her will was ebbing away. A suffocating greyness descended on her like a sea fog.

With a purr of pleasure, Rorrim plucked a small, dark thing hiding between two vertebrae. The dankling screeched and flailed as he popped it into his mouth.

'*So* delicious!' he said, swallowing. 'I shouldn't have any more, but I can't help myself!' He ate another, then said, 'You'll *never* defeat Traho. He'll find you sooner or later.'

The brightness in Serafina's eyes dimmed. Her head dipped. Rorrim plucked more danklings, cramming them into his mouth with the heel of his hand.

'Mmm! Divine!' he said, gulping them down. A rumbling burp escaped him.

The rude noise broke through Serafina's lethargy. For a few seconds, the grey lifted and her mind was clear again. *He's taking me apart. I can't let him*, she thought desperately. *But how can I fight him? He's so strong . . .*

With great effort, she lifted her head – and gasped.

# ACKNOWLEDGEMENTS

MY HEARTFELT THANKS to Stephanie Lurie, Suzanne Murphy, Jeanne Mosure, and the whole Disney team for introducing me to Sera and the gang; to Steve Malk for being the most wonderful agent an author could ask for; and to my mother, Wilfriede; my husband, Doug; and my daughter, Daisy, for their love and encouragement, and for always, always being there for me.

# GLOSSARY

**Abbadon** an immense monster, created by Orfeo, then defeated and caged in the Antarctic waters

**Acqua Bella** a village off the coast of Sardinia

**Acqua guerrieri** Miromaran soldiers

**Ahadi, Empress** the female ruler of Matali; Madhi's mother

**Alítheia** a twelve-foot, venomous sea spider made out of bronze, combined with drops of Merrow's blood. Bellogrim, the blacksmith god, forged her, and the sea goddess Neria breathed life into her to protect the throne of Miromara from any pretenders.

**Amăgitor** Romanian word for *deceiver*

**Amphobos** the language spoken by amphibians

**Apă piatră** an old Romanian protection songspell that raises water ten feet high and then hardens it into a shield

**Āparădhika** Matali word for *criminals*

**Apateón** Greek word for *deceiver*

**Aquaba** a mer village near the mouth of the Dunărea river

**Anarachna** Miromaran word for *spider*

**Arata** a spell that allows its caster to manifest in a chosen location

**Armando Contorini** duca di Venezia, leader of the Praedatori (a.k.a. Karkharias, the Shark)

**Astrid** teenage daughter of Kolfinn, ruler of Ondalina

**Atlantica** the mer domain in the Atlantic Ocean

**Atlantis** an ancient island paradise in the Mediterranean peopled with the ancestors of the mer. Six mages ruled the island wisely and well: Orfeo, Merrow, Sycorax, Navi, Pyrra, and Nyx. When the island was destroyed, Merrow saved the Atlanteans by calling on Neria to give them fins and tails.

**Ava** teenage mermaid from the Amazon River; she is blind but able to sense things

**Avarus** Lucia Volerno's pet scorpion fish

**Baba Vrăja** the elder leader – or obârşie – of the Iele, river witches

**Baby** Ava's guide piranha

**Baco Goga** captor of Serafina and Neela, in league with Traho

**Baricadă** a strong blocking spell

**Barrens of Thira** the waters around Atlantis, where the Opafago live

**Bartolomeo, Conte** the oldest and wisest of Regina Isabella's ministers

**Bastiaan, Principe Consorte** Regina Isabella's husband and Serafina's father; a son of the noble House of Kaden from the Sea of Marmara

**Baudel's** the songpearl shop where Becca works as a spellbinder

**Becca** a teenage mermaid from Atlantica

***Bedrieër*** one of three trawlers that Rafe Mfeme owns

**Bianca di Remora** one of Serafina's ladies-in-waiting

**Bibic** Romanian word for *darling*

**Bilaal, Emperor** the male ruler of Matali; Mahdi's father

**Bioluminescent** a sea creature that emits its own glow

**Bloodbind** a spell in which blood from different mages is combined to form an unbreakable bond and allow them to share abilities

**Bloodsong** blood drawn from one's heart that contains memories and allows them to become visible to others

**Blu, Grigrio, and Verde** three Praedatori who help Neela and Serafina escape Traho

**Boru** long, thin herald trumpets

**Caballabong** a game involving hippokamps, similar to the human game polo

**Cadavru** living human corpses, devoid of a soul (see also Rotters). The Iele use them as sentries.

**Canta magus** one of the Miromaran magi, the keeper of magic (magi, pl.)

**Canta malus** darksong, a poisonous gift to the mer from Morsa, in mockery of Neria's gifts

**Canta mirus** special song

**Canta prax** a plainsong spell

**Carceron** the prison on Atlantis. The lock could only be opened by all six talismans. It is now located somewhere in the Southern Sea.

**Cassio** god of the skies

**Cerulea** the royal city in Miromara, where Serafina lives

**Circe** a witch who lived in ancient Greece

**Clepio** a malus spell used for stealing

**Clio** Serafina's hippokamp

**Conch** a shell in which recorded information is stored

**Confuto** a canta prax spell that makes humans sound insane when they talk about seeing merpeople

**Conte Orsino** Miromara's minister of defence

**Convoca** a songspell that can be used for summoning and communicating with people

**Currensea** mer money; gold trocii (trocus, sing.), silver drupe, copper cowries; gold doubloons are black market currensea

**Daímonas tis Morsa** demon of Morsa

**Davul** bass drums made out of giant clamshells, played with whalebone sticks

**Death riders** Traho's soldiers, who ride on black water horses

**Deflecto** a songspell that casts a protective shield

***Demeter*** the ship that Maria Theresa, an infanta of Spain, was sailing on when it was lost in 1582 en route to France

**Depulsio** a songspell that moves objects

**Desiderio** Serafina's older brother

**Devil's Tail** a protective thorn thicket that floats above Cerulea

**Dokimí** Greek word for *trial*; a ceremony in which the heir to the Miromaran throne has to prove that she is a true descendant of Merrow by spilling blood for Alítheia, the sea spider. She must then songcast, make her betrothal vows, and swear to one day give the realm a daughter.

**Dolpheen** the language spoken by dolphins

**Dracdemara** the language spoken by catfish

**Duchi of Venezia** created by Merrow to protect the seas and its creatures from terragoggs

**Ejderha** Turkish for *dragon*

**Feuerkumpel** goblin miners, one of the Kobold tribes, who channel magma from deep seams under the North Sea in order to obtain lava for lighting and heating

**Filomena** Duca Armando's cook

**Flăcări** a songspell to summon waterfire

**Fossegrim** one of the Miromaran magi, the liber magus, the keeper of knowledge

**Fragor** the storm god

**Fragor lux** a songspell to cast a light bomb

**Freshwaters** the mer domain in rivers, lakes, and ponds

**Gândac** a bug that is planted near a person or thing that a songcaster wants to observe; it catches and holds the ochi spell

**Habeo** a malus spell used to take control of another's mind or body

**Hippokamps** creatures that are half horse, half serpent, with snake-like eyes

**Höllebläser** goblin glassblowers, one of the Kobold tribes

**Iele** river witches

**Illuminata** a songspell to create light

**Illusio** a spell to create a disguise

**Incanta (incanti, pl.)** river witch

**Incantarium** the room where the incanta – river witches – keep Abbadon at bay through chanting and waterfire

**Iron** repels magic

**Isabella, La Serenissima Regina** Miromara's ruler; Serafina's mother

**Janiçari Regina** Isabella's personal guard

**Kalumnus** a member of the Volnero family who tried to assassinate Merrow

**Karkharias** 'the Shark', or leader of the Praedatori

**Kobold** North Sea goblin tribes

**Kolegio** the mer equivalent of college

**Kolfinn** Admiral of the artic region, Ondalina

**Kolisseo** a huge open-water stone theatre in Miromara that dates back to Merrow's time

**Lagoon** the waters off the human city of Venice, forbidden to merfolk

**Lava globe** a light source, lit by magma mined and refined into white lava by the Feuerkumpel

**Lena** a freshwater mermaid – and the owner of several catfish – who hides Serafina, Neela, and Ling from Traho

**Liber magus** one of the Miromaran magi; the keeper of knowledge

**Ling** a teenage mermaid from the realm of Qin; she is an omnivoxa

**Liquesco** a songspell that liquefies objects

**Loquoro** a songspell that enables a mer to temporarily understand another creature's language

**Lucia Volnero** one of Serafina's ladies-in-waiting; a member of the Volnero, a noble family as old – and nearly as powerful – as the Merrovingia

**Magdalena** one of the Iele, or river witches, who helps the mermaids master their magic

**Magnitis** a songspell that allows the caster to attract something like a magnet

**Mahdi** crown prince of Matali; Serafina's betrothed; cousin of Yazeed and Neela

**Malacostraca** huge crayfish that guard the entrance to the Iele's caves

**Markus Traho, Captain** leader of the Death Riders

**Matali** the mer realm in the Indian Ocean. It started as a small outpost off the Seychelle Islands and grew into an empire that stretches west to the African waters, north to the Arabian Sea and the Bay of Bengal, and east to the shores of Malaysia and Australia.

**Matalin** from Matali

**Mehterbaşi** leader of the Janiçari

**Merl** Mermish equivalent of *girl*

**Mermish** the common language of the sea people

**Merrow** a great mage, one of the six rulers of Atlantis, and Serafina's ancestor. First ruler of the merpeople; songspell originated with her, and she decreed the Dokimí.

**Merrovingia** descendents of Merrow

**Merrow's Progress** Ten years after the destruction of Atlantis, Merrow made a journey to all of the waters of the world, scouting out safe places for the merfolk to colonize.

**Meu Deus** Portuguese for *my God*

**Mia amica** Italian for *my friend*

**Mina** Brazilian slang for *a female friend*

**Miromara** the realm where Serafina comes from; an empire that spans the Mediterranean Sea, the Adriatic, Aegean, Baltic, Black, Ionian, Ligurian, and Tyrrhenean Seas, the Seas of Azov and Marmara, the Straits of Gibraltar, the Dardanelles, and the Bosphorus

**Moarte** piloti death riders

**Morsa** an ancient scavenger goddess, whose job it was to take away the bodies of the dead. She planned to overthrow Neria with an army of the dead. Neria punished her by giving her the face of death and the body of a serpent and banishing her.

**Navi** one of the six mages who ruled Atlantis; Neela's ancestor

**Neela** a Matalin princess; Serafina's best friend; Yazeed's sister; Mahdi's cousin. She is a bioluminescent.

**Neria** the sea goddess

**Nex** a darksong spell used to kill

**Nocérus** a darksong spell used to cause harm

**Nyx** one of the six mages who ruled Atlantis; Ava's ancestor

**Obârşie** the leader of the Iele

**Ochi** a powerful spying spell in which the songcaster plants a gândac, or bug, near the person or thing being observed

**Olt** the river in Romania where the Iele are located

**Omnivoxa (omni)** mer who have the natural ability to

speak every dialect of Mermish and communicate with sea creatures

**Ondalina** the mer realm in the Arctic waters

**Opafago** cannibalistic sea creatures that lived in Miromara and hunted mer until Merrow forced them into the Barrens of Thira, which surround the ruins of Atlantis

**Orfeo** one of the six mages who ruled Atlantis; Astrid's ancestor

**Ostrokon** the mer version of a library

**Palazzo** Italian for *palace*

**Permutavi** a pact between Miromara and Ondalina, enacted after the War of Reykjanes Ridge, that decreed the exchange of the rulers' children

**Pesca** the language spoken by some species of fish

**Porpoisha** the language spoken by porpoises

**Portia Volnero** mother of Lucia, one of Serafina's ladies-in waiting; wanted to marry Vallerio, Serafina's uncle

**Praedatori** soldiers who defend the sea and its creatures against terragoggs; known as Wave Warriors on land

**Praesidio** Duca Contorini's home in Venice

**Prax** practical magic that helps the mer survive, such as camouflage spells, echolocation spells, spells to improve speed or darken an ink cloud. Even those with little magical ability can cast them.

**Principessa** Italian for *princess*

**Pyrra** one of the six rulers of Atlantis; Becca's ancestor

**Qin** the mer realm in the Pacific Ocean; Ling's home

**Que diabo** Portuguese for *what the hell*

**Querida** Portuguese for *darling*

**Qui vadit ibi?** Latin for *Who goes there?*

**Quia Merrow decrevit** Latin for *Because Merrow decreed it*

**Rafe Iaoro Mfeme** worst of the terragoggs; he runs a fleet of dredgers and super trawlers that threaten to pull every last fish out of the sea

**RaySay** the language spoken by manta rays

**Reggia** Merrow's ancient palace

**Regina** Italian for *queen*

**Rorrim Drol** lord of Vadus, the mirror realm

**Rotter** an animated human corpse, devoid of a soul

**Rursus** the language of Vadus, the mirror realm

**Rusalka** ghosts of human girls who jumped into a river and drowned themselves because of a broken heart

***Sagi-shi*** one of three trawlers that Rafe Mfeme owns

**Sejanus Adaro** Portia Volerno's husband, who died a year after Lucia's birth

**Serafina** principessa di Miromara

**Sculpin** venomous arctic fish

**Shoaling** swimming with schools of fish near the surface of the water, a risky sport for merpeople

**Shokoreth** Arabic word for *deceiver*

**Stilo** a songspell that makes spikes sprout out of a water ball

**Suma** Neela's ayah, or nurse

***Svikari*** one of three trawlers that Rafe Mfeme owns

**Swash** Mermish slang; a shortened version of *swashbuckler*, suggesting a flamboyant adventurer

**Sycorax** one of the six rulers of Atlantis; Ling's ancestor

**Sylvestre** Serafina's pet octopus

**Talisman** object with magical properties

**Tajdar** Foreign Secretary of Matali

**Tavia** Serafina's nurse

**Terragoggs (goggs)** humans. Before now they haven't been able to get past the merpeople's spells.

**Thalassa** the canta magus, or keeper of magic, of Miromara; addressed as Magistra

**Tĭngjŭ** Qin word for *jerk*

**Tortoisha** the language spoken by sea turtles

**Transparensea** pearl a pearl that contains a songspell of invisibility

**Trezi** the songspell used to turn a corpse into a cadavru

**Trykel and Spume** twin brother gods of the tides

**Tsarno** a fortress town in the western Mediterranean

**Tubarão** Portuguese for *shark*

**Tudo bem, gatinhas?** Portuguese for *Everything well with you, girls?*

**Vadus** the mirror realm

**Vallerio, Principe del Sangue** Regina Isabella's brother; Miromara's high commander; Serafina's uncle

**Velo** a songspell to increase one's speed

**Vitrina** souls of beautiful, vain humans who spent so much time admiring themselves in mirrors that they are now trapped inside

**Waterfire** magical fire used to enclose or contain

**Wave Warriors** humans who fight for the sea and its creatures

**Yazeed** Neela's brother; Madhi's cousin

**Zeno Piscor** traitor to Serafina and Neela, in league with Traho